THE VENDING MACHINE OF JUSTICE

By the same author and available from Quartet Books

As Good As It Gets

SIMON NOLAN
THE VENDING MACHINE OF JUSTICE

Q QUARTET BOOKS

First published by Quartet Books Limited in 2000
A member of the Namara Group
27 Goodge Street
London W1P 2LD

A catalogue record for this book is available from the British Library

ISBN 0 7043 8106 0

Printed and bound in Finland by WSOY

'Does Magna Carta mean nothing to you?
Did she die in vain?'

Tony Hancock, '12 Angry Men'
(R. Galton & S. Simpson)

ACKNOWLEDGEMENTS

Thanks to John and Llewellyn for letting me watch. Thanks to Sarah, Audra and Moira for explaining about 'tops'. Thanks to my agent, Caroline Davidson, and my editor, Piers Blofeld, for their patience and enthusiasm. Thanks to Hugh for putting up with it all.

BOOK ONE
...THE ASSEMBLING

Interview conducted by: Detective Inspector T.M. Waalgren and Detective Sergeant P.J. Denning.

With: Mr Harold E. Hook, *DOB*: 18–8–1945.

Also present: Mr G.T. Bland, of Cramp and Pergamon, Solicitors, representing Mr H.E. Hook.

Interview number: 96–005181/ESPC/20–7–96; *Crime number*: 96–00518.

Interview held at: Interview room 3, Hove Police Station.

Date/time: Monday 22 July 1996, 4.11 p.m.

Pages 4–7 *of* 17.

DI **Waalgren**: *And which end of the wooden pineapple was inserted into your, er...*

(Long pause)

DI **Waalgren**: *Mr Hook? I have to ask you these things, since they will certainly come up. You are making allegations and you will be asked about them. There's nothing I can do about that. Now. Just to be absolutely clear. Do I understand you right, that an attempt was made to insert a carved wooden pineapple up your –*

H.E.H: *Yes.*

DI **Waalgren**: *Which end of the pineapple?*

H.E.H: *Which end? Well, I suppose you'd call it the blunt end. Without foliage.*

DI **Waalgren**: *And this pineapple, this was a part of a four-poster bed you said?*

H.E.H: *It was a component of the pelmet assembly, yes, or rather I should say it was partially attached to the pelmet. Late eighteenth century, very fine piece of work. Somewhat more elongated, less fat than a pineapple of today, of course.*

DI **Waalgren**: *Sorry, I don't...*

H.E.H: *Well, pineapples today are considerably bigger, fatter than they were then. Selective breeding and all that. An eighteenth-century pineapple was a longer, leaner affair, more missile-shaped.*

DI **Waalgren**: *Yes. Yes... ...And so it was this, this pineapple that was inserted –*

H.E.H: *No, it was never inserted, I never said it was inserted.*

3

DI Waalgren: *Oh! But I thought your statement was, let's see now. Ah. Hm. Da de dum. Yes...Are you intending to change your statement, Mr Hook, with regard to the pineapple?*

H.E.H: *I said an attempt was made to insert it. The attempt proved fruitless. So to speak.*

DI Waalgren: *Um...I'm just...*

H.E.H: *The object was simply the wrong shape. It wouldn't go in. Or up.*

DI Waalgren: *...(coughing)...I see. I see. Yes. I'm getting the picture...(coughing)...And this took place as part of a prolonged assault of a sexual character which you say was committed on you by this...wait a moment...Bryn Sweetman.*

H.E.H: *Yes.*

DI Waalgren: *And you have no explanation as to why this attack may have occurred?*

H.E.H: *None whatsoever. You tell me.*

DI Waalgren: *Yes, yes. Uhuh.*

(Long pause)

H.E.H: *(unintelligible)...*

DI Waalgren: *Sorry. I didn't quite –*

G.T.B: *Might it be an idea at this point...*

H.E.H: *Would you like to, er...(unintelligible) which is to say...I (unintelligible) I would like to, or shall I say, I prefer, or I would, er, prefer not to press charges in the matter of the pineapple...*

DI Waalgren: *You do not wish...*

H.E.H: *Yes, that it is my wish to, er...*

DI Waalgren: *Can I make sure I understand you aright here, that it is your wish not to proceed with the allegations as they relate to the unauthorized use of a carved wooden pineapple on your, er, person...*

H.E.H: *Uh.*

DI Waalgren: *So, in effect, you want me to withdraw the pineapple –*

H.E.H: *I wish the pineapple to be withdrawn, that is correct.*

DI Waalgren: (coughing)...
DS Denning: (coughing)...
G.T.B: ...*I think it might* –
H.E.H: *Is that fucking thing still on?*
DI Waalgren: *Please leave the tape recorder alone, Mr Hook. Mr Hook* –

Interview interrupted at 4.38 p.m.

DRUNK

Elsa progressed across the room, plastic cup of wine in hand, spilling hardly any.

She headed for the front room, where the dancing was, where an eighties revival was in full cry. Amazingly, everyone knew all the words to 'Rio' and 'Karma Chameleon'. Elsa caught sight of Liam, the boyfriend, who was sat by the stereo reading a CD sleeve. She quickly ducked away again, back downstairs to the kitchen, where the seemingly limitless supplies of wine were. No one was dancing in the kitchen. What people were doing in the kitchen was drinking, and Elsa was with them.

She found herself leaning slightly. The man beside her was at something of an angle as well, adjusting his attitude every minute or so, leading from the head, but apparently unable to calculate the vectors quite right.

'You're over-correcting,' Elsa said to him, out of a long amiable silence. 'That's why you keep tilting over like that.'

She considered the comment, and wondered exactly how drunk she must be to have made it.

'Listen, have you ever done jury service?' she asked, out of the thick leaning silence between them. She had been asking everyone she met lately, since she'd received her summons.

The leaning man thought deeply.

'No,' he said after a minute. 'No. But I saw *Twelve Angry Men*. You know, Henry Fonda, all that.'

'You know what I always wondered,' Elsa said, 'is why twelve? Why's it twelve?'

The man swayed and pondered, gripping the edge of the draining board as he did so.

'Well, twelve,' he pronounced finally, 'is the traditional number of completeness.'

'No kidding.'

'You know, twelve disciples, twelve months of the year.'

'Yeah...'

'Twelve star signs. Twelve dwarfs.'

'Twelve? Seven surely. Seven dwarfs.'

'Twelve days of Christmas...'

'Yeah, and what exactly has that got to do with juries?'

'It's like seven...'

'No, it isn't.'

'Yeah, because it's made up of a three, which is spirit, and four which is matter. Three times four is twelve, three plus four is seven. You see? They're both kind of a numerological marriage. Of course, for Cornelius Agrippa – '

'So you've never actually done it then?'

Another long pause.

'Well, not as such, no. But I've read *Crime and Punishment*, so you know...'

Elsa sighed. She was rapidly wearying of tilting man, but became aware of Liam at the turn of the stairs down to this intimate basement kitchen, his head leaning down, scanning. Looking for her. He'd be thinking of pushing off, no doubt. He usually was. If she could just get herself a fraction to the right, so he couldn't see her...

Elsa was long and gorgeous and slightly frosty. Well, *gorgeous*...that would depend on the angle of the light, the time of day, the mood, the alcohol intake. Sometimes she was gorgeous. Sometimes for whole minutes at a time. Long straight black hair, nothing as definite as a bosom though she lived in hope, and a something about the eyes, which had been characterized by a long-gone boyfriend as 'snaky'. The boyfriend had departed (ignominiously: money was involved) before he'd been able to define exactly what this snakiness involved. She was prepared to take it as a compliment though. In fact she was determined to.

The frostiness was a different matter. It related to the snakiness, in that Elsa often found herself looking at people as if from a great distance, eyes somewhat narrowed and head held slightly back. Although she meant nothing at all by this, it was often interpreted as indicating disapproval. There was also the mouth. She had been told more than once that she had a smart mouth on her, but she couldn't help it, things just came out.

Claire from work was usually around to smooth things over though. Claire could stop a fight at two hundred paces just by going like *that* with her bottom lip. She was what people called 'formidable'. Long legs, long neck and a look you just didn't mess with. Strong too: Elsa had once taken a punch from her, intended for someone else, and was now careful to keep at arm's length when Claire was feeling fisty. Claire liked drinking and arguing, preferably both at the same time.

Elsa went in search of her, but instead found Liam. Head on. Half-way up the stairs to the first floor.

'Li.'

'I was thinking of...'

'Pushing off?'

She regarded him, hair longish and lank, and terrible glittery eyes. He could seem utterly ferocious without ever intending to. It had been at a party very much like this one, six months ago, that she'd first met him. In the kitchen, as it happened. He had seemed sardonic and deep. It had taken her about three months to realize that he wasn't deep – he was stagnant. He was a t'ai chi devotee. And she had never really got over the disappointment of seeing him naked for the first time. Sorry and all that, but. There are things that matter and things that don't, and Liam had plenty of the first kind. What

Elsa was beginning to realize, as she regarded him swaying above her on the stairs, was that basically he wouldn't do at all.

They assessed each other, quick indices of drunkenness, tractability etc. Nothing looking too good, just at the moment. Everything jammed.

'OK, Li, look, why don't I give you a call tomorrow?'

'Right.'

She knew what he wanted; he wanted her to come back to his place which was sort of infested and dank and had people coming in and out of it at strange times.

'OK. Bye, Li,' she said decisively and gave him a quick peck. He stood swaying and smiling, one hand on the banister. She squeezed past him. Looking for Claire. She'd deal with him tomorrow.

'Yes, but my question is, have you ever *done* jury service? I mean actually?'

She was talking now to a slight, plump, gingerish man she'd taken a fancy to, who was sitting in a corner of the dancing room, where by now there was much less dancing. No sign of Claire anywhere. This man was called Gray. Short for Graham.

'Not allowed.'

'Why? What's wrong with you?'

'I'm a clerk. Magistrates' clerk. Not allowed.'

'Really?'

'No legal professionals of any kind allowed.'

'That's a bit odd, isn't it?'

'Well, I think the idea is that people with legal knowledge would have too much influence on everyone else on the jury.'

'Yeah, but what do I know about any of it? Huh?'

'That's really the point, you see...'

'Is it?'

'Of course. Jurors need to be legal virgins so they'll have a fresh eye. Independent. Unjaundiced. All that. Not what judges call "case-hardened".'

'Yes, but isn't it all terribly complicated? The law and

everything?' She tried to think of an example and came up with a comedy courtroom, a judge wearing flippers and a gas mask and the defendant getting buckets of water thrown at him.

The gingery man gave her a good hard look.

'You doubt your ability to be a good juror?'

'Well, I'm just not remotely qualified for anything like that...'

'There's a little test you can do,' he said, 'to see if you are or not. I could administer it now. If you like. Do you want me to do it?'

He took her hand, and his thumb moved to her wrist, just above her watch strap. He held it still for a few seconds, his lips moving slightly.

'Yup,' he said. 'You've got a pulse. You're qualified.'

He let her hand go again. He was making a great deal of eye contact, Elsa thought, the little whippersnapper. She ponced a fag off him. She only ever smoked at parties.

'Of course, up until '74 there was still the property requirement. You had to own a house basically.'

'1874?'

'19. 1974. And there are still exclusions, of course. No priests. No insane. No Irish. Only joking...' He sipped from his can. 'About the insane. Are you, for instance, one of the Active Elder Brethren of the Corporation of Trinity House of Deptford Strond?'

She gave him a long look.

'Well, that would depend on what exactly you mean – '

'Yes or no will suffice.'

'Would I know if I was one?'

'OK. We'll pass on that. There's one other question, which is: are you infamous?'

'Am I...'

'Infamous. *Propter delictu*. Are you infamous?'

She folded her arms and leaned against the edge of the chair. He wasn't quite so little or gingerish as she'd thought at first.

'Infamous?' She blew smoke slowly out of the corner of her

mouth, something else she only ever did at parties. 'I've been round the block.'

'No, infamous is a bit more complicated than that. Particularly for women. It refers specifically to sodomites, who are a male species legally.' She waited for him to say he was kidding again.

'Look, can't I get out of it somehow?'

'Why should you? Be a citizen. Subject, I mean. Your country needs you,' he said. 'Justice herself has jabbed her warty finger at you. You'll enjoy it. People do.'

'*Elsa!*'

'Claire.' She'd turned up sitting on the steps outside the house.

'*Elsa!*'

'Claire.'

'Elsa They made me get *drunk* ...'

'Bastards. Who did?'

Claire pointed vaguely at the house, the party. Elsa sighed. Claire, just because of her length and general limbiness, could be a nightmare to get into a taxi. Out again was also tricky. If she fell it was like righting a lipsticked camel.

'Claire. OK. You and me are going in a little taxi now. All right?'

'Where is it?' Claire demanded.

'We're going to go and find it, sweet.'

'Are we?'

'Yes, love. A nice lovely taxi.'

Elsa led the way. They found a taxi on St James Street and Elsa managed all the difficult stuff, the doors and everything.

THE HELEN MIRREN METHOD

The night before her jury service began, Elsa got so drunk she spilled Malibu-and-milk into the CD player. She also got some on her cream linen jacket, the one she was intending to wear to court. Sadly she was too pissed to take any proper remedial action and was reduced to just dabbing at it with a tea-towel. Apart from the jacket, she was intending to wear her work clothes, her lattice-front tops in shades of oyster, champagne, buttermilk, three-quarter-length skirts, cream-coloured courts. Otherwise she'd be getting into wedding clothes territory, strappy dresses and so on. She wanted to look efficient, dependable, professional. Gorgeous, also, of course. Oh, and wise as well, preferably.

Claire was there too, both of them packed into Elsa's undersized front room, dangerously tripping over piles of laundry and Land's End catalogues and plastic bags stuffed with old newspapers. You had to negotiate an ironing board to get into the kitchen, and Claire was failing to improve her fine motor control. She claimed an inner ear problem, but Elsa wasn't having any of it.

'I didn't think you were pouring it into your inner ear,' she said. Claire disdained Malibu and had brought her own supplies, a squat bottle of Jack Daniel's. She and Claire were at the window, a warm wind rocking the trees in Norfolk Square below them.

'What if it all gets really complicated?' Elsa said. 'What if it's some kind of international conspiracy fraud business?'

'What, at Hove Crown Court? Nah. It'll just be shoplifting and that. Anyway if it gets complicated you must just do what Helen Mirren would do.' They had both seen the original *Prime Suspect* at least three times. Elsa even had bits of it on video.

'What, look like an old dog and get on everyone's tit?'

'No, you have to do that thing she does, she goes out on a balcony after they've interviewed some lowlife, her and the good-looking one from Newcastle.'

'Call him Geordie.'

'Of course. So she's there and Geordie's there, and they both just *know* that that slag they just interviewed – '

'Call her... call her...' Elsa waved her glass around expansively.

'Low life Scrubber.'

'Yeah, she's got these really lowlife teeth...'

'...and she's protecting the suspect, she's his alibi, she's the whole thing. Anyway they're on the balcony – '

'Twelfth floor...'

'Yeah, it's a long way down and it's raining. And Geordie lights up a ciggie...'

'He's got this really sexy way of screwing his face up when he does it...'

'Well, of course he has, that's all part of his repressed Northern potency shag thing...'

'Repressed Northern potency shag thing,' Elsa stated meditatively. 'God, I could do with some of that actually...'

'...and Helen Mirren, she pulls this face and she goes...'

'"Give us a drag, Geordie."'

'And then he says, "Thought you gave up, Madam"...'

'And she goes, "Just give it here"...'

'Right. So if I get a *really* complicated case...' Elsa said.

'You know what to do.'

She and Claire were supposed to be organizing how Claire was going to take over at work while Elsa did her jury service. They worked together in a tranquil corner of Hove Town Hall. If anyone asked, Elsa would loftily say she worked in local government, which was putting it a bit high really. It was essentially admin work. There wasn't a great deal to discuss; all Claire could really do was take messages and wait for her to get back. Elsa alone understood the mysteries of the procedure. It was Elsa who knew where each case was up to, how far it had got, what exactly had gone wrong with it this time. Or at least where the file was. Usually.

'So look, I don't care what you do but I don't want you fingering my mouse mat. OK?' The mouse mat in question was a cutout of a muscle boy with chocolate-brown nipples and lewdly distended Speedos.

'I don't *finger* things – '

'I've seen you looking. Oh, and don't let Ted Slaughter start messing round with my computer. He doesn't understand it.'

'I won't tell him your password.'

'Say you don't know it. I just don't want him poking about in there. There's things in there he doesn't need to know about.'

The phone rang and Elsa eyed it malevolently. It would be Liam. He'd be ironic and disapproving because she was drunk. She let the machine take it and allowed herself a long slow mouthful of iced Malibu-and-milk.

'I didn't mean she really looks like an old dog,' Elsa said. 'I just mean they make her look that way.'

'That'd be a good job, wouldn't it? Hello, what do you do? Well, actually I'm the person who makes Helen Mirren look like an old dog.'

''Cos really she's gorgeous.'

'I love Helen Mirren.'

'If she was here now, do you know what I'd do?'

'What?'

'I'd give her a fag. I'd say, "Go on, love. You have it. You deserve it."' Elsa clinked her ice. 'And do you know what I'd do if Geordie was here?'

'Yes, Elsa, I think I do.'

'Listen, if I come back and find you've made my mouse mat sticky – '

'Yeah, and how exactly am I going to make it sticky? Hm?'

'I don't know. You might secrete things on it – '

'I don't secrete thing...'

'Everyone secretes things,' Elsa said, and sighed, as if pronouncing some great truth. 'Everyone secretes something.'

DISGUSTING JOKES

Elsa arrived at Hove courthouse ten minutes late, hung over, flushed, clutching the envelope with the details and the map and everything in it. She was overheating because at the last minute she had decided on her cream linen jacket after all, despite the stain, just for the look really, but it was far too hot.

The building, set back among quiet residential streets, was low and dull and was giving absolutely nothing away. In fact, it seemed to be trying to draw attention away from itself. Not here, it said, not me. She didn't know quite where she was supposed to report to, it was a confusion of disabled access ramps and low concrete trenches at peculiar angles and ugly dying shrubs.

There were a few people loitering about on the steps, including a man in a grey wig and black gown talking urgently to a young man in a suit with a shaved head. Elsa started towards the man in the wig, since he seemed official, but he ducked away before she could reach him and she was left with the shaved young man, who didn't look very official at all, not close up.

'Excuse me, are you a juror?' she said.

'You what?' He scrutinized her with eyes that appeared bruised and deep set, and for the brief moment that she held his eye she felt abruptly, and quite startlingly, swamped by a great thick wallop of something, some internal shock, low down. Jesus Christ, she thought, what was that? It was as if he'd punched her in the stomach. Then his lips parted and a quarter of an inch of tongue came into view, and she was able to name the feeling: full-on sex, right here on the steps of Hove Crown Court, bright and early on a Monday morning. That was what he was doing with his eyes and tongue; he was promising limitless sensual possibilities, long languid sessions, and he was sending out coded but unmistakable messages about readiness, willingness and availability. The cocky little bugger! Elsa had been prepared for anything, she thought, but not, somehow, this, this sex thing. On top of her nerves and hangover, it was making her feel sick. And anyway it was surely the wrong thing to be feeling, wasn't it? She should be thinking about justice. She narrowed her eyes.

'Say again? Am I a what?' he said. Traces of a North-west accent, a bit like her dad. Warrington, Widnes, somewhere like that. 'I mean, I've been called a lot of things lately,' he continued, 'but not that.'

'Is this the main door? I don't know what door I'm supposed to go in...' she said, gesturing at the steps and the maze of concrete ramps and gulleys and canyons. There was a door at the top of the steps but it didn't look like a main door particularly. Might be, might not be, it seemed to say. Who's asking?

'Show us that a minute,' he said and she handed over the envelope. He pulled out the contents, including the woefully inadequate photocopied map, and turned a few sheets over. His finger ran down the page, then he indicated a line and passed it back to her.

Elsa read, '7: Jurors are warned that they must not speak to or in any way communicate with anyone in or around the courthouse or in any of the precincts. Failure to observe this notice could result in a prosecution under section 8 of the Contempt of Court Act 1981 resulting in a fine not exceeding...'

'There's only one trial starting today,' he said, leaning in close so she could smell him – Shreddies, Colgate, Lynx – 'which is mine, and if you're a juror then you're going exactly the right way to get it stopped...'

Elsa, completely unnerved, stuffed the papers back into the envelope and made for the door at the top of the steps.

'Oi!'

Oh, God, now he was yelling at her. She found herself breaking into a sweat, felt it trickling under arms and behind knees. What was she getting into here? She tried to ignore him.

'Oi, no, listen, I want to ask you something...'

Reluctantly, fear of embarrassment overcoming fear of wrongdoing and the threat of a fine not exceeding, she turned and raised her eyebrows: yes?

'No, listen, come down here again a minute...' He was smiling, wheedling, beckoning. If she didn't do as he said he might start shouting and there would be a scene. The idea of getting involved in some kind of undignified fracas sent her back down the steps to him. She tried to look busy and properly impersonal. Brisk. Judicious.

'Yes?'

He ducked in close again, confiding.

'Listen, right. What did the leper say to the prostitute?'

She couldn't help taking a clumsy half-step away from him, in simple horror. What kind of creature was this? He seemed to be all over her somehow, drooling like some big dog. She backed away. She tilted her head back.

'Sorry, sorry...' Smiling an idiotically inappropriate smile, half apology and half professional good humour, she gained the top of the steps again.

Safe now, her heart pumping, she glanced back. The man in wig and gown, who had returned with a plastic cup of coffee, was speaking to the shaved man, urging him to do something. But the young man's face had taken on an expression of such concentrated innocence that he looked almost saintly He shook his head: he was having none of it. Whatever the urging was about, it was just not damn saintly enough. He caught Elsa's eye again and, giving his crotch a quick tug, winked.

Elsa entered the building and found a proper official to show her smudgy papers to. Her hands were trembling and clammy.

Fourteen people had assembled in the lobby by the main door. They had been gathered into a little flock and taken charge of by a tall woman in a black cloak and a name tag who introduced herself as an usher.

'Everybody? I'm going to be your usher for today, so anything you need to know just ask me. We're going down to the jury assembly room now, so please bring everything with you and we'll sort out your loss of earnings forms and everything.' She tossed her head and led them at a brisk trot through the featureless recesses of the building, through fire doors and sudden staircases and a gallery full of penitential-looking people, whispering. They descended again on the other side and reached the jury assembly room.

'Exciting all this, isn't it?' Elsa said to the girl beside her, quietly, as if they were in church, and the girl shrugged. It was exciting though, Elsa thought. A courtroom. A trial. Human drama. And her, a key player suddenly in someone's life. Here in this dull little building she was about to become powerful. She breathed deeply in, and her lungs filled with power.

'OK. Everyone? I'm just going to park you here for a few minutes. What's going to happen now, you're going to watch a video, about ten minutes, which should answer most of your questions about how it all goes, then I'll be back and hopefully we'll get you into court no later than 10.30. OK?'

She found the remote control and fiddled with the sound, then left, schoolmistressy in her black cloak.

Elsa looked around her. It was a ground-floor room with vertical cloth-louvred blinds, the kind with little chains at top and bottom, resolutely beige. The furniture was standard conference room issue, the ceiling was low and looked fireproof, tediously so, Elsa considered, since a fire was just about the only thing that would liven the room up.

The video came on, presented by a TV face, the kind you knew intimately, had known all your life, but could never put a name to. The music was so calculatedly palatable that Elsa almost found herself wondering what it was called. 'Judicial Moods' maybe? Could you get it on CD?

The nice presenter lady turned to the camera and started talking. She was sitting in a kind of ideal television courtroom, all pale shiny wood and minimally cushioned seating. Impeccable suburban justice, Elsa felt, would be administered in such an irreproachable courtroom. They went through the whole routine, the swearing-in, the selection, prosecution and defence, cross-examination and summing-up. It all seemed simple enough. Then the presenter said it all again, in slightly shorter sentences, for the benefit, presumably, of the benighted and the inattentive and the just plain-not-bothered, and captions appeared on the screen with keywords: 'Swear or Affirm', 'Direct Examination', 'Defence Counsel' and so on. Then the swooshy music came on again and it was over in a swirl of state-of-the-year-before-last's corporate PR video graphics.

The usher came back in and asked for questions. People surprisingly did have questions. They wanted to know things they'd just been told twice by a well-known, if unnameable, television presenter and then had flashed at them again, in writing. They wanted it all again, like children with a story. Elsa caught the eye of a young man in a brightly striped pullover and tight caramel-coloured trousers which were perhaps half an inch on the short side. His hair was strange and puzzling at the back, parted horizontally in some obscure and frankly perplexing manner and he had thick glasses. She smiled at him and he rolled his eyes. Elsa tried to concentrate on the Q and A session.

'The woman in the video,' someone said, 'didn't she use to be on *Animal Hospital*?'

'That wasn't her, that was that other one, what's her name.'

'I thought she was on that programme. You know, the one where they decorate each other's houses and then they have to pretend they like it. Oh, what's it called? On Fridays. You know.'

'Did you see the one where the woman cried?'

'No, I *missed* that one...'

The usher went away again, promising to let them know what would be going on in a few minutes' time, and they all sat in silence and looked at the intimidating immensity of the drinks machine, a great gloomy totem at the front of the room. It looked to Elsa as if it had been assembled in some grim corner of Eastern Europe during a particularly bitter period of austerity. The soup and hot chocolate were simply not available, perhaps deemed too frivolous for such a stern, terrible machine. And as for orange. *Fizzy* orange? If it had been equipped to emit a hollow, humourless laugh then it would certainly have done so.

Someone stood up and approached the machine, and it hissed, violently, and shook itself. He started backwards, then stood beside it and looked at the instructions. The opportunities for embarrassment were almost unlimited. He jingled the change in his pockets for a minute and sat down again. No one else went near it all day.

Lunch-time. They'd been warned not to leave anything in the assembly room when they were let out. The usher was apologetic, but apparently security was less than perfect, there'd been a spate of pilferings, and someone made the obligatory joke about there being a lot of criminals round here.

Elsa headed straight for a bookshop. If the afternoon was going to be like the morning, she was going to have something better to do than look at a drinks machine. She found herself walking beside someone, mid-thirties, a suit that could have been a Paul Smith, a fellow juror.

'Hi. I'm Patrick. Thrilling stuff so far, isn't it?'

She took a look at him. He was as tall as she was, hair just starting to recede into quite a pronounced widow's peak, more grey hairs than you could easily count behind the left ear, and a nice hint of something round the mouth, good mouth altogether actually, she thought. Bet his teeth are bad though. He looked like someone who made a lot of money selling something new and hard to understand and troublesome.

'I was worried it was going to be complicated,' Elsa said, smiling at him sideways, grateful for the opportunity to speak.

'I imagined being flung into some cauldron of abstruse legal argument,' Patrick said. 'And to be honest I was expecting more panelling.'

'Human drama,' Elsa said. 'I was thinking more in terms of witnesses breaking down and being offered glasses of water and that.'

'I also thought we'd be treated a bit better. It's all a bit low rent, isn't it?'

'Yeah. They could at least tell us what's going on.'

'Juries are cattle,' he said. 'I've got this friend, he's appeared as a witness a few times, and he says courts just treat juries as cattle. The only thing anyone cares about is the judge's time, because he's so expensive to run. Juries just get wheeled on and off.'

'But it is exciting though, isn't it?' Elsa demanded. 'Or I mean it will be, once we get going.'

'It's power without responsibility,' Patrick said. 'Which has got to be the best kind.'

'Well, I'm excited anyway. I can't wait to get into court. I'm going to be the one who notices that the witness has got little marks on her nose, which can only mean that she wears glasses, so she couldn't possibly have seen what she says she saw.'

'How do you know she's not a synchronized swimmer? They wear those little nose pieces.'

'Patrick. She's sixty-seven years old. Anyway, how can one person be a synchronized swimmer?'

'Listen, mind if I walk with you? I was getting cabin fever back there. I kept fantasizing about standing up and shouting, "It was me! I did it, and you all know it! Why are you torturing me?"'

'Really?' Elsa looked sideways at him.

'Well, no, not really. That was just something to say, actually. Did you tell me your name? Did I forget already?'

'Elsa.'

'Like the – '

'Don't say it. Yes, like the lion.'

Patrick followed her into the bookshop.

Brilliant forensic pathologist Jody Bartok is being stalked...
by someone she autopsied eleven years ago. Can she
dismember him again in time... 'Compulsively readable,'
Daily Mail.

Elsa fingered the titles uneasily. She didn't read much,
except on holiday. The last book she'd actually gone out and
paid full price for had been *The God of Small Things*, which
had, inexplicably, got Malibu all over it and was now
languishing under the VCR instruction manual by the phone.

There seemed to be only three kinds of book on offer here:
SAS books, cookery books and absolutely deplorable ones.
She glanced at her watch. She really didn't have long to
choose. Apparently the court could electrocute you or
something if you were late. Even though they could keep *you*
waiting indefinitely, seemingly.

Patrick wandered back over to her. He had a biography of
Damon Hill, the racing driver.

'I don't read much,' he said and shrugged. 'What've you
got?'

Elsa showed him the book in her hand.

Gifted Latvian forensic ethnomusicologist Felice
Brsznwskyawjh has got a problem... she can't spell her own
name right! Can she rearrange the letters in time...
'Complex, expert and consistently correctly spelled...' *Daily*
Nail.

'I'm not sure it's quite what I'm after,' she said. She
narrowed the choice down to two: *Due Process*
('extraordinary, unputdownable, a real roller-coaster ride...'
Daily Mail) and a big doorstop of a thing, *Body Parts*
Everywhere! about which the *Daily Mail* was strangely silent.
Elsa read the blurb:

Top genetic scientist Anya Blick discovers accidentally
that her boyfriend, an undercover FBI operative, has

24

identical DNA to a notorious serial rapist and spree killer called Bible Bill, who leaves quotes from the Bible written in semen on the bodies... The samples are all in her freezer, but can she defrost them in time...

'Is she a top *forensic* genetic scientist though?' Patrick wanted to know, 'and is she *troubled*?'

'Well, it doesn't say. She sounds a bit troubled, all those body parts everywhere and everything. I mean *I*'d be troubled. Who wouldn't be?'

'How does she get the sample from the boyfriend anyway? Something a bit creepy about that surely?'

'Hair clippings? No. She could keep a used condom,' Elsa said.

'In the screen? I don't think you should have that book,' he said, taking it from her. 'It doesn't sound very sanitary.' She took it anyway. It was nice and thick. Good value for money. Perfect holiday reading.

Back in the room with the drinks machine, Elsa settled down with *Body Parts Everywhere!* and quickly found herself loving every word of it. Anya Blick, expert witness, was giving an ill-prepared deputy DA hell on the witness stand. She was flame-haired, voluptuous, passionate and clever, was Anya. She said things like, 'Didn't your mama tell you it was rude to contradict a lady, Counselor?' and 'Where'd you take your medical training, mister, vet school?' The judges kept telling her off, but Anya didn't care, she was too sassy for that. She had Polish blood in her. She played Chopin and Szymanowski brilliantly, and if she sometimes drank a little too much schnapps, well, she was entitled to, wasn't she, given her lousy childhood and abusive father? Oh, and she also had a limp...Everyone loved her. Except, oddly, her boyfriend, who was a complete pain in the arse, if not something a good deal more sinister than that. She should just dump him, Elsa thought. It's that simple. Keep moving, pal, you're history. Easy.

Among her fellow jurors she counted two Patricia Cornwells, two John Grishams, one *The Juror* and a *Presumed Innocent* by

Scott Turow. Policiers. Procedurals. Always procedurals. Everyone ravenous for the little details, the ins and outs of another country's legal system. They probably knew more about American law than they did about their own. They probably cared more. Motion for dismissal! You're out of line, Counselor! Sidebars. Assistant DAs. State Prosecutors. The technicalities of hearsay evidence and disclosure. Ambulance-chasing shyster lawyers and Grand Jury subpoenas. Someone else's laws. Why not their own, Elsa wondered?

There was also a rather grim-looking true-crime book called *Inside the Mind of the M4 Rapist*, which belonged to a mild-seeming woman who wore a neat blue two-piece suit and an expression of benign good humour.

Otherwise it was *What PC* and *TV Quick* and even *Inside Soap*, plus a limp self-righteous *Daily Telegraph*. One woman seemed to think it profitable to spend her downtime completing word-search puzzles. A rather vague-looking young man had nothing at all and just fidgeted, biting his nails and sighing, with a kind of kick-me-I'm-thick-as-shit look on his face.

She found her mind wandering. What would she normally be doing on Tuesday morning? She would be sitting at her terminal, fluorescent pens lined up in spectrum order, red to violet, and muscle-boy mouse mat nice and square on, inputting details about a lease or a surveyor's report, with Bob Betjeman and Ted Slaughter breathing down her neck, while Claire wore her usual look of disbelief and mild contempt for it all.

Why not a thriller about the home-improvement-grant application procedure, she thought idly? She imagined the book, a heavy glossy brick of a thing, called *Schedule of Works*, with 'works' written in huge blocky letters and a trail of blood trickling from the 'k'.

'You're full of shit, Slaughter, and you know it.'

'Oh yeah?'

Slaughter leaned back in the gas-damped swivelling office chair and grinned up at Betjeman. Prove it, his smile said. Motherfucker.

Betjeman slammed the file down on the desk, which was beige with a darker brown rim and modular plastic legs. The fluorescent pens in the desk tidy were lined up in spectrum order, as usual. Same old Slaughter, Betjeman thought. What good was victory over such a nonentity? Slaughter would never get to the top of the heap in building regulations now, and Betjeman knew it. Not after this. He had won. So why did it feel so much like defeat? For a moment all the bitterness in his life, his whole shitty life, seemed to well up inside him. He choked it back and when he spoke it was with the knowledge of the futility of all human action.

'Take a look at the date of this lease,' he said, and directed Slaughter's gaze to the relevant page.

'So?'

'So it's June '72.'

Slaughter didn't blink.

'So?'

'So Reg. 17/224/HBC applies to leases signed from 1 January '73.'

Slaughter said nothing. The giant plastic paper clip he always played with, some kind of gift from a Christmas cracker, flicked through his fingers as always. Same old Slaughter. Suddenly Betjeman understood. Everything. The whole shitty deal.

'But then you knew that all along, didn't you? This was all just a front. And I fell for it.'

Slaughter regarded him, almost sadly.

'You always were the last to know anything around here. It's just building regs, Betjeman, that's all. Just building regs. Don't take it so hard . . .

Three o'clock came and went. Finally an usher arrived, shrugged apologetically and asked them to return tomorrow at ten.

She was leaving the building for the day, waiting for Patrick to catch up with her. A skinny youth came barrelling down the steps, seemed to lose his balance, and grabbed hold of her jacket. There was a confused moment when she thought she was being attacked. She caught a momentary close-up of his face, all pockmarks and big nostrils and a bit of misaligned incisor, then she thought she felt his hand in her pocket. Pickpocketing right here on the courthouse steps! She stumbled backwards, the youth lost his balance and his weight threw her to the floor. He disentangled himself and muttered something that could have been 'Sorry', then he was off again.

She stood up, smoothing her skirt, shocked, then checked all her pockets. She didn't think he'd got anything. Card wallet safe, keys safe, purse safe. There was something unfamiliar in the hip pocket of her jacket though. She pulled it out. It was a scrap of paper with faint pencil marks on it. She couldn't read it in the bright sunlight, too much glare on the rattly paper. *Something something you don't even something.* She puzzled over it a moment. Why was it there? She tried to remember when she'd last had the jacket on. It was one she only used for weddings and yearly appraisals and suchlike.

'So. Can't tear yourself away, huh?' It was Patrick. 'You ready to go?'

'Did you see that?' she said.

'See what?'

She shook her head, didn't matter, and pushed the paper back into her pocket.

At home that evening she lay back in her bath and reached for the glass of Malibu-and-milk on the cane chair beside her. The glass was cold and heavy, the outside dewed with condensation. She brought it to her mouth and the first icy trickle played with her tongue, cool and sweet and exciting as a boy's mouth. I love Malibu, she thought. I love Malibu more than anything else. Malibu was for the night. Malibu was for pleasure. She drank Guinness when she was out, because Malibu seemed a bit girly and low-caste. But Malibu was what she truly loved.

Something something you don't even something.

Don't even what though? Who doesn't even something?
She reached for her jacket and found the scrap of paper
again. Thin porous recycled-looking paper. She was certain
she'd never seen it before today. It had absolutely no business
being in her jacket, none at all.

The script was all loops like fat little piggies and circles
over the i's and curly bits. GCSE General Studies
handwriting. *How can you*...Some word like jinge. Jinge
jingle jugle jueje. Juicy.

Then she saw it: juge. He meant judge.

*How can you judge me you don't even know anything
about it.*

She sat up straighter in the bath and looked, astonished and
fearful, at this message. It must have something to do with
that youth on the courthouse steps, the one who'd pushed her
over. He must have got it into her pocket when she thought
she was being pickpocketed. She laid the note carefully on the
cane chair and condensation from the glass trickled onto it
and made it wet.

It had no business being here, she thought, no business at
all.

PROCEDURAL STUFF

Straight down to business the next day. In fact the jurors were positively hustled into court as if a moment's further delay would be utterly calamitous. Elsa barely had time to say hello to Patrick.

The air suddenly became much cooler as they were led into the courtroom. Elsa felt like a backpacker, wearing lurid Lycra shorts and a 'The Pope Smokes Dope' T-shirt, suddenly walking into a foreign cathedral during a high mass. Everyone else in court was in sober black or at the very least professional dark grey. Many of the personnel were in gowns. Some even had wigs. She felt she was about to see some kind of heritage spectacle of the sort administered to tourists. *'Tis a year of wonders and portents, a year of terror and travail. For 'tis the plague year, 1665...*

Fourteen jurors had been called, twelve only were needed. The usher simply read out names from a pack of little cards she had until she had twelve, and the other two were hustled away, as if they had somehow failed and were not to be allowed to contaminate the successful jurors. Elsa didn't see them again.

The jury box, the place where the twelve had to sit, was

strangely cramped, as if it hadn't been designed with the requirements of twelve people in mind at all, but for some quite different purpose. There was no leg room, and since everyone was carrying their belongings with them, it was uncomfortably crowded. Everybody tried to shove their papers and bags and books under the ledge, but there really wasn't room. An usher came by with bundles of photocopied sheets which he laid out in front of them, like examination papers.

There were two ranks of six. Elsa was at the front, and found herself seated beside a great fat heap of a woman in a kind of green tent. Personal space was at something of a premium, so the largeness of this person was wholly unwelcome news. But Elsa smiled anyway, and the woman gave her a chirpy little smile back.

Another usher began to shuffle along the front rank of jurors holding a Bible and some laminated cards with the oath on them. Elsa recalled from the video that you could either swear or affirm. The difference was that you didn't have to drag God into it if you affirmed. Swear or affirm, she thought, swear or affirm; she was suddenly panicky, as the usher moved ever closer.

You had to stand up and hold the card, while touching the Bible. It was a lot to do suddenly, and Elsa was so tense that she dropped the card and the usher had to pick it up again. Her voice emerged, and though rather strained and perhaps half an octave higher than usual, it came out OK.

'I swear by Almighty God that I will faithfully try the defendant and give a true verdict according to the evidence.'

She sat down again, and felt the blood pounding in her ears. It really is exciting, she thought, it really *is*. Let me do it again!

The usher went on to the row behind her, leaning over the heads of the front row. She heard Patrick say 'affirm', and after he'd done it two others did too, both men, as if it were a new male fashion. 'Affirming' was a slightly grander affair than swearing, involving solemnly, sincerely and truly as well as faithfully, presumably to make up for the absence of God.

The swearing-in continued, leisurely and cadenced, the language exquisitely formal and orderly. This had been going on for hundreds of years, she thought, exactly this scene. She tried to think back to the last time she'd sworn anything, and couldn't. She had just taken an oath. It felt solemn and ancient and good. Her chest swelled with the grandeur of it.

Now she had a moment to look round her, she found that the surroundings were not immediately suggestive of ancient grandeur and so on. There was no panelling at all, for one thing. There was just a great deal of shiny pale wood, culminating in a big ugly throne-type affair at the far end, where the judge was. The judge was gazing into space, swivelling in his chair, and looking as if he was preoccupied with his teeth. Elsa caught a movement in a small gallery and glanced up. It took her a second to recognize who it was: the skinny youth who had knocked her down on the steps on her first day. And who, she had to assume, had been responsible for planting that note in her pocket.

She looked quickly away and tried not to manifest any unease at this, but uneasy she was. Who was he and what was he doing with that note? It couldn't be innocent, that was for sure. She risked another glance at him. He seemed perfectly at leisure, leaning with his arms crossed on the rail, smiling down at everyone. He caught her eye and made a slight gesture, the kind that people make in restaurants to call for the bill, a little doodling movement.

Elsa was horrified and wrenched her eyes away from him, they alighted on someone who was sitting behind a glass screen, somewhat like a cashier in a cinema. Shit, she recognized him too. He was the young man with the shaved head who'd made some kind of disgusting joke to her on her first morning, lepers and prostitutes or something.

He'd said it was his trial starting but she hadn't taken him seriously somehow. But here he was, the defendant in the dock, neatly suited, with a uniformed heavy sitting just behind him. He was waiting for her to see him, and gave her a randy wink. Then she watched in disbelief as he made the same little doodling gesture, and then pointed to the viewing gallery. Jesus Christ, what was he playing at? She dragged her eyes away from him and concentrated on pouring a glass of water instead. Surely defendants weren't supposed to be signalling things to jurors? Everyone could get into terrible trouble, couldn't they? She felt a sudden surge of panic. Shit!

Moments passed, though, and nothing terrible happened, no accusing voice or heavy hand on the shoulder. She looked circumspectly about her. Nothing alarming, no-one seemed to have noticed anything. Her heart bumped about but there was no danger.

You could be excused from a trial, she remembered someone telling her, if you were familiar with any of the parties to it. Although she also recalled someone saying that once you were sworn in, then that was that and you couldn't get out again. Maybe she should put up her hand and say something. I'll do it now, she thought, I'll just put my hand up right now and do it.

And then what? Go back to that bloody waiting room again? Or worse, she might even get sent back to work. At least something was happening now. And anyway she wanted to know what he'd done, the lad behind the glass screen. She had, she felt, an interest in the case.

A person Elsa had barely noticed, in gown but no wig, who was sitting on a kind of base camp below the summit of the judge's imposing birch-veneer tumulus, stood up and faced them. Elsa froze with irrational terror. He was going to accuse her, she knew it! *You!* he would yell. *You in the lattice-front top! Infamous!* But he didn't.

'Members of the jury, are you all sworn?' His voice was nasal and uninflected. He looked rather as if he had at some time worked behind the counter of a hardware shop. He didn't wait for any kind of answer, since he knew perfectly well that they were sworn, he could hardly have missed it. He was reading from a sheet, rocking slightly from side to side as he did so, the weight shifting from one foot to the other. 'The defendant, Mr B.J. Sweetman, stands indicted for that he on 22 June 1996 did assault Mr H.E. Hook, thereby occasioning him actual bodily harm, contrary to section 47 of the

Offences Against the Person Act 1861. On a second count, he stands indicted that on the same date he did, without lawful excuse, damage property belonging to Mr H.E. Hook, intending to damage such property or being reckless as to whether such property would be damaged, contrary to section 1 (i) of the Criminal Damage Act 1971. The defendant has pleaded not guilty on both counts. As it pleases Your Honour.'

With no particular warning the judge swivelled round to face them and began to speak.

PICTURES

From what she'd picked up from the opening statements the case was all about an assault that had happened last year in a flat over a charity shop in a faraway part of town that Elsa didn't think she'd ever been to. It was a part no one ever went to. The man who'd been assaulted was called Harry Hook. There had also been damage done to a computer and to something called an eighteenth-century brocade four-poster-bed pelmet. Hm. Didn't seem to promise all that much in the way of human drama, Elsa thought.

The case for the prosecution opened with a police witness, a young detective constable. He had sand-coloured hair that was rather long in the fringe, giving him a shy, enthusiastic look, as if he was going to talk to them about snowboarding or collecting Oasis memorabilia. Elsa expected him to be in a uniform but he wasn't; he was in a good suit, light brown, and a tie that he pulled at nervously. He looked about twelve, Elsa thought. Well, an advanced kind of twelve anyway. In the face, if not in the body. Elsa had seen him sitting towards the back of the court with a young uniformed female officer earlier and had taken him for a messenger or something.

He was the officer who had been called to Hook's charity shop on the night of the assault. He spoke in a rushed but very monotonous voice, so that Elsa quickly found that she wasn't listening to him at all but instead wondering whether or not he still lived with his mother, in which case who it was who had ironed his shirt, and did he pay any rent? She also found herself noting the way he played with his hands as he spoke, digging them in and out of his trouser pockets in a frankly distracting way. He had good wide shoulders, and the suit emphasized the leanness of him. He grinned boyishly; he even blushed at one point.

All the detective seemed to be there to do was to say what everyone already knew: that Hook had reported an assault, that the police had attended, and had found the scene in some disarray. No one else, except the plaintiff, had been present. It all seemed simple enough. But then the officer, whose name Elsa never did quite catch, described the injuries. Not from an expert point of view, he emphasized, just as an observer.

Bruising all over the face. Bleeding from wounds to the scalp, and from the nose and lip. Bruising to the shoulders and upper arms. Abrasions and bruises over the back and chest. And burns, such as might be caused by a lighted cigarette applied to the skin. The plaintiff had complained of pains in the chest and also in the back, and expressed the wish that he receive medical attention.

'And did the plaintiff accompany you to Brighton Police Station?'

'Yes, sir.'

'Was he attended by a Dr Cage?'

'Yes, sir.'

Elsa duly wrote it down, more to be seen taking an interest than anything. The fat woman peeked slyly at her as she did it.

'And on your advice were photographs taken of Mr Hook's injuries?'

'Yes, sir.'

'Under Dr Cage's supervision?'

'Yes, sir.'

The prosecution barrister, Mr Djabo, a handsome senatorial,

slightly raffish black man, went back to the table and picked up some sheets.

'And are these those photographs?'

The officer glanced at them and assented, and immediately Elsa felt everyone around her in the jury box stiffen. They wanted to see those pictures. Djabo waved the sheaf of photographs around.

'Your Honour, I am admitting these as Exhibit Number One. With Your Honour's permission I would like the jury to be allowed to examine them now.'

The defence barrister, Mr Parrot, half stood.

'Your Honour, having seen the photographs to which Mr Djabo refers, I do not think it would be of any benefit if the jury were allowed to see them. Mr Hook's injuries have already been fully rehearsed by Officer – '

'Mr Parrot, if you please.' The judge smiled at everyone, and the officer in the witness box blushed again. Elsa found that she was blushing too. The judge swivelled a little bit and then addressed himself to Djabo. Elsa noticed that the attention of the jurors, for perhaps the first time that day, was undivided. No fidgeting, no scratching. All eyes were on the judge. Was he going to let them see the pictures?

'Mr Djabo, how many of these photographs are there?'

'Eleven, Your Honour.'

'Yes. I wonder, is that perhaps rather too great a number for the ladies and gentlemen?' He beamed at the jury. 'We wouldn't want to wear them out now, would we, Mr Djabo? Do we need to see all eleven?'

Djabo chewed his lip for a moment. His eyes fastened on the wall behind the judge's head.

'Your Honour, Mr Hook was the victim of a sustained and very vicious assault. His injuries were spread all over his body – face, head, torso, arms, back – '

'Yes. Yes.' The judge smiled in an unblinking way at Djabo, rocking himself gently to and fro. He seemed magnificently at peace, as if he'd just hatched a scheme that would permanently solve all parking problems in the central Brighton area. 'Now, I understand that the doctor under

37

whose supervision these photographs were taken, Dr...'

'Cage.'

'Yes. I gather that you are not planning to call Dr Cage to give testimony on this matter.'

'That's so, Your Honour.'

'So the ladies and gentlemen will have no guidance as to what exactly these photographs may signify. The officer here has no status as an expert witness, you say.'

'Yes, that's so, Your Honour, but these photographs are really in my judgement self-explanatory in nature. They are not the kind of photographs that require expert elucidation...'

Ah, but then your judgement is only of secondary or peripheral interest around here, the judge seemed to say as he smiled and smiled. Your judgement is worth about the same as the shit on my shoes. Actually.

'Yes. I think, unless testimony is to be given as to the nature and interpretation of these photographs, I will err on the side of caution and suggest that the ladies and gentlemen not be shown all of the pictures.'

Djabo stood rooted to the spot, the sheaf still in his hand. Parrot caught Elsa's eye and shrugged an eyebrow, an entirely improper piece of communication that seemed to be saying, Unbelievable, isn't it, the cheap tricks the prosecution will stoop to? *Pictures*, yet! But, of course, you're above all that, aren't you.

Well, actually, I'm not certain that we are, Elsa thought. We want to see the pictures and we want to see every last one of them. Right now. If there wasn't going to be any sex, there could at least be a bit of violence. We have no shame. We are the jury. Show us the damn *pictures*.

The jury were allowed to see three of the eleven photographs. They passed them from one to the next in complete silence. The barristers, the judge, everyone was still and silent.

Picture one: a full-face shot of Hook, though he was barely recognizable. Both eyes closed, a trickle of blood from lip to chin, and crusted blood round the nose. Yellowing under the eyes: the bruises would take a while to come out fully, but these were clearly going to be beauties.

Picture two: it took Elsa a second or two to identify the body part. It was thigh, upper thigh, seen from behind. Dark shadows, three or four of them, two overlapping. What looked like whip marks or welts of some kind. The curve of the buttock was visible, and Elsa couldn't help but note the poor muscle tone, the wet cake-mix quality of the flesh, the folds and flaps and unbeguiling little crannies of middle-aged man's arse.

Picture three: the back. Many marks, some small and defined, others more diffuse. More welts and weals. And the marks that must have been the cigarette burns, on the neck, just below the hair-line: there was a blurred, dragging quality to them, even the suggestion of a shape, and Elsa thought, was someone trying to write something? An initial, perhaps? If so, then whatever it was, it wasn't a 'B'. Looked more like an H or an M or an N. M, she decided. M for what?

The boy detective was still in the witness box. He looked too young to be seeing pictures of people's arses, Elsa thought.

When all the jurors had seen all the pictures the usher came and put them back on the table in front of the judge's mountain. Elsa's attention strayed back to the pictures from time to time all that afternoon. She caught Sweetman's eye, and his eyebrows made their innocent puppy shape again. Well someone had done it, she thought. Someone had. The photographs proved it. She glanced back at him a moment later, and caught him throwing some derisive comment over his shoulder to the uniformed heavy behind him in the dock. He met Elsa's eye again, and this time, caught out, just winked. She tried to remember that he was presumed innocent.

NIGHT OF THE LIVING JURY

'Now, Mr Hook could you describe for us this pelmet and its various attachments, the pineapples and so on?'

It was 11.15, and Elsa was struggling. The problem was that none of it was actually very interesting.

'...pelmet?'

She jerked to attention, but she'd missed the beginning of the question. She glanced guiltily at the judge, who was as usual looking amused and unhurried, head down, writing away soberly. Why was he writing everything down, Elsa wondered, when there was a fat woman in a print dress at the front with a special typewriter thing doing exactly the same? Didn't he trust her?

Elsa watched her for a moment, watched the fat placid hands as they plumped up and down over the machine, her expression serene and untroubled by as much as the shadow of a thought. I wonder what kind of job that is, Elsa thought. I wonder if I might like a job like that. There would have to be some kind of special training, a course. She tried to imagine a classroom full of plump sensible women in print dresses, all with blubbery upper arms, all clumping away at their machines. It might be secretly thrilling, listening in on all these peculiar and arcane proceedings, listening to the lies and evasions, the pretended indignations, the real passions.

The plaintiff, the man who was the centre of the whole thing. Harry E. Hook. E for Edward. Elsa looked hard at him. He was forty-five or fifty, straggly, with messy greying hair that was thinning and badly out of condition. A nothing face, completely nothing. Nose, eyes and so on, but overall nothing. He was wearing a quite insanely inappropriate lavender and jade shell suit. He held onto the bar of the witness box and answered the questions in a rapid, pedantic voice, the kind of voice that Elsa associated with the building regulations people at the town hall.

In fact Elsa missed most of the direct on Hook, it just seemed to happen without her somehow. She found she was running 'Jerusalem' through her head.

She heard him say that it was Bryn who had come to the shop that afternoon, had demanded money which he claimed Hook owed him, and when Hook had refused, had violently assaulted him, smashed the place up, then run off. Djabo elicited his responses easily and fluently, and the rhythm was so good that Elsa felt herself nodding off a few times and had to jerk herself awake as choirs sang 'Till I have built/A pe-el-met/In England's green and pleasant...' She made herself listen. Listen, you bad, bad woman.

But it was over already. Now it was Parrot's turn with Hook. This might be better, she thought, as Parrot stood and swayed on his feet a few times, then smiled extravagantly at Hook, as if seeing him for the first time.

Immediately the atmosphere changed. All the nice sweet rhythm disappeared. Hook bristled, Parrot needled, it was like a prolonged family row.

'Now I want to turn to this initial meeting, between you and the defendant, Mr Sweetman. Please tell the court, in your own words, Mr Hook, how and when you first met Mr Sweetman.'

'I met Mr Sweetman last year, about a year ago, or a bit longer suppose.'

'Can you be specific, please?'

'May. Late May. Twenty-fifth, I think.'

'And how did you meet?'

'Well, he had some items he thought I might be interested in.'

'Items?'

'Yes, sir.'

'And would you tell the court exactly what these items were?'

'A drill.'

'What kind?'

'Black and Decker. Cordless.'

'Yes. I'm admitting that as Exhibit Number Two, Your Honour.' The usher crept forward and deposited a thick clear plastic refuse sack on the bench, and the jurors craned forward to see the drill and the bag. Parrot looked down at his notes for a moment. He stood as if in thought.

'And could you please tell the ladies and gentlemen where and how he had acquired this drill?'

'He'd bought it somewhere.'

'Where?'

'Car-boot sale. He said.'

'Yes. And I think you told the police that he couldn't remember the name or location of this sale, nor the exact date, nor the name of the person who sold it to him. You also told the police that he said he was given no receipt, that he paid in cash, that there was no guarantee.'

'Yes, sir.'

'Yes.' Again his head went down as he turned a page. He was blinking rapidly. He brought his head up and stared at the panelling behind the judge's head.

'And you accepted all this.'

'Yes, sir.'

'And you had no idea as to the provenance of this – '

'Your Honour...' Djabo intervened, and the judge nodded.

'Mr Parrot, I think we established in our discussions yesterday that how the defendant came to be in possession, or how the plaintiff thought the defendant might have come into possession, of these items was not a matter that we were going to detain ourselves with. Yes?'

'I am indebted to Your Honour.' Still blinking, Mr Parrot was frowning off at an angle, as if seeing something that displeased him mightily in the plaster behind His Honour's head, something that perhaps went right to the heart of the case.

'Can we now turn please to the events of 25 May of last year in more detail. Now you told the police that Mr Sweetman came to your shop at some time in the afternoon...'

'Yes, sir, three o'clock, I think.'

'And his intention, as he expressed it to you, was to offer for sale the drill and the other items...'

'The extension lead and the battery recharger.'

'Yes. You told the police: "He said he knew I bought and sold stuff and he wanted to make a few quid so he took me some things round."' Parrot's careful, deliberate voice made the statement sound absurd, pathetic.

'Yes, sir.'

'And these were the same items that he said he had bought at the car-boot sale?'

'Not all of them, no.'

'Not all?'

'No, he apparently already had the charger.'

Parrot blinked.

'Yes.'

He said nothing for almost a minute. Elsa gawped in frank and open disbelief at the insane tedium of this. So Ms Frith, she imagined someone saying, you bought the pineapple rings and the oven cleaner in Asda, you say? And you expect the court to believe that?

She made herself pay attention. She wrote something on her piece of paper: 'Cross-examination, Hook', then: 'the other items, already had them'.

'So, Mr Sweetman came to your shop, some time in the middle of the afternoon, and came inside. Would you please tell us what happened after that?'

'He showed me the things and I said I'd take the drill but I didn't want the other stuff.'

'And how much did you offer for the drill?'

'Twenty pounds.'

'And he accepted your offer?'

'Yes, sir.'

'Now.'

More profound scrutiny of the walls.

'And you paid him in cash, there and then?'

'Yes, sir.'

'And was there any record of this transaction, a receipt, anything of that sort?'

'No, sir.'

'No. Well, the ladies and gentlemen will draw their own inferences from that.' He glanced round at the jury, trying to suggest something, but Elsa couldn't begin to imagine what. In *Body Parts Everywhere!* there was a trial lawyer who was famous for his ability to convey things to the jury, subtle little shadings of meaning that would sway them without their even knowing it. Was this what Parrot was doing? Say it all again, she thought! Sway me with your subtlety again! I wasn't ready!

Draw inferences, Parrot had said. She looked around. Few if any of the jurors looked capable of drawing as much as a picture of their house. Some seemed barely able to draw breath. They looked like an out-take from a zombie movie, grey-faced, propped upright, covered with cobwebs and with insects crawling out of their eye sockets. Parrot continued nonetheless.

'Now, Mr Hook, you have a, er, an apartment over the shop. Is that right?'

'If you can call it that.'

'What would you call it?'

'Well, I'm staying there temporarily until my other accommodations are sorted out. I have a bed and a small electric stove and so on. It's purely temporary.'

'Quite so. Although you have in fact been living there since at least May of last year, is that right?'

'Yes.'

'And you spend some considerable time up there, is that not so?'

'Well, I'm living there, as I said, just for the moment.'

'Yes. And did Mr Sweetman come up to your apartment on the afternoon of 25 May, and on several other occasions?'

'No, sir.'

Ah, she thought, too quick. He's lying.

'And I understand that on some, if not all, of those occasions there was a certain, er, liberality, that you and Mr Sweetman enjoyed a glass of wine sometimes...'

'That's what he's saying...'

'And this is in fact what did happen.'

'No, sir.'

'No? So, according to you, this occasion in May was the first and last time you met Mr Sweetman?'

'I never said that.' The emphasis was on 'said'. Something hard and almost intimidating had come into the voice. It sounded coarse, urban, sarcastic, a voice that demanded things and enforced its demands. Bryn Sweetman licked his lips from behind the screen and Elsa looked quickly away from him.

'Please tell the court when else you saw Mr Sweetman after this first meeting, until the evening of 8 June...'

The judge sat forward.

'Mr Parrot, I hope you have no intention of introducing evidence relating to the alleged events of 8 June at this point. We still have no word on the status of the witness, Mr...'

'Hegler, Your Honour.'

'Mr Hegler. Yes. You know the situation regarding that as well as I do.'

'Your Honour.'

The judge sighed and sat forward and wrote something, quite slowly, with his beautiful pen. Elsa felt the urge to write something too: '8 June?!' The fat woman to her right took a sneaky look and wrote '8 June' also. Hook carried on.

'I met him a few times. I wouldn't know the dates. He just dropped round sometimes. A few times.'

'A few?'

'Yes, sir.'

'Half a dozen?'

45

'Something like that, probably, yes.'

'A dozen?'

'Your Honour...' Djabo was leaning forward on his books.

'No, not a dozen, half-dozen I said, maximum,' Hook said. Again the uncompromising edge in the voice. Parrot paused for a moment.

'I would like now to just touch on a few points that were raised when my colleague was questioning you a few moments ago. Now you are the director of a charity, BunkUp, is that correct?' Parrot speaking.

'Yes, sir.'

'And this is a charity that was set up by yourself to help address the problem of homelessness in Brighton, particularly among young male ex-offenders, is that right?'

'Yes, sir.'

'And the shop in question, the shop over which you have your, er, temporary, er, apartments, this is by way of being a method of raising funds for BunkUp's, er, activities?' Every word was scented with a whiff of disdain: 'apartments', 'activities', but most of all ' BunkUp'. Elsa even heard Patrick sniggering slightly the second time he said it.

'Yes, sir.'

'And this shop, it is in nature... Well, you call it "a craft and bric-à-brac shop". Yes?'

'Yes, sir.'

'Used goods of various kinds, household and electrical items, small pieces of furniture, that kind of thing?'

'Yes, sir.'

'Yes.' A lovely pause. 'Yes. It's a junk shop, isn't it, Mr Hook?'

Hook shifted about in the witness box.

'Call it what you like.'

'Yes. I think the ladies and gentlemen would probably call it a junk shop.'

Hook shrugged.

'Now in the course of your charitable work, which is, as I understand it, part-time in nature...'

'Yes. I'm an antiques dealer and valuer by trade.'

'As you wish. This charity work, by the way, has never been recognized by any official body, is that right?'

'I'm not registered if that's what you mean.'

'That is indeed what I mean. You are not a registered charity, nor have you ever been recognized by, for instance, Brighton Borough Council, by the police, by social services, by the probation authorities ...'

'That's right. But I soldier on.'

'You – soldier – on. Yes. Now, Mr Hook, you say that Mr Sweetman visited you after this first visit, with the drill and so on, about half a dozen times, is that right?'

'Yes.'

'In fact, he did some work for you, is that right?'

'Yes, sir.'

'Would you tell the ladies and gentlemen what that work consisted of?'

'I've got a workroom in the basement. He sanded down a table for me, stripped it down.'

'So that you could resell it.'

'Yes.'

'And this work took Mr Sweetman six separate visits, is that right?'

'About six.'

'So this must have been a particularly big table.'

'No.'

'No?' Parrot pretended surprise. 'Well, then, perhaps it was an unusually complex table, perhaps involving scrollwork, or, oh I don't know, delicate inlays or ...'

'It was a kitchen table, farmhouse-type table. Oak. 1950s or so. Quite nice.'

'And yet it took Mr Sweetman six visits to sand it down?'

'Yes, it did.'

'And on none of those occasions did Mr Sweetman visit you upstairs, in your, er, apartments?'

'He may have come up ...'

'Well, you state that he most definitely did come up on at least one occasion, the occasion on which you allege that he assaulted you.'

'Yes.'

'Had he come up prior to that?'

'I don't know. I can't remember.'

'Can't remember. Yes. Now earlier on, Mr Hook, when I asked you about your consumption of alcohol...'

'Your Honour...' Djabo was looking increasingly weary, and Elsa was starting to feel sorry for him. Parrot was on a roll.

'Your Honour,' said Parrot, 'if Mr Hook cannot remember whether or not Mr Sweetman visited him in his apartment, then I am just trying to explore how this loss of memory might be accounted for...'

The judge moved his tongue up under his lower lip, then nodded.

'In fact, Mr Hook, I have in front of me a record of an arrest made by the Brighton police in March of 1994.'

'Your Honour – '

'In which the name Harold Hook appears. You were apparently bound over to keep the peace by the magistrates, and one condition of your release was that you attend a group for people with alcohol-related problems, is that not so?'

'I haven't got an alcohol problem,' Hook said, and Parrot raised his eyebrows. Indeed?

'On that occasion, you committed a public affray, assaulted a WPC in the course of resisting arrest, to whom you referred as "you ugly gash", used foul and abusive language, and damaged property belonging to the doctor who was called to examine you, to whom you made threats of an indecent character. Is that not so? Is that not so, Mr Hook?'

No reply.

'"*I'm going to shove that fucking thing so far up your arse...*"'

'I haven't got an alcohol problem,' Hook said again.

Parrot gestured to the jury.

'Well, I'm sure the ladies and gentlemen will take their own position on that. I have nothing further, Your Honour.' He sat down, as if disgusted with the whole thing, and Djabo rose to see if he could salvage anything from this.

'Now, Mr Hook, in the course of your work, your charitable work I mean, you may perhaps have come across young men who are at a crisis point in their lives, is this so?'

'Certainly.'

'Many of these young men will have had histories of all kinds of transgressive behaviour, is that not so?'

'It is.'

Djabo was leading him by the hand again, and all was sweetness and accord.

'Transgressive behaviour that might include, for example, the sale of drugs...'

'Your Honour, really I must – '

'Mr Djabo, Mr Parrot is protesting,' said the judge, 'and in this instance I have to say that I am inclined to agree with him. In our conference yesterday, I thought we had agreed...'

'Your honour, I am just trying to map out my client's experience, the extent of his – '

'Yes. I really don't see how any of this comes out of Mr Hook's direct testimony.'

Djabo was ready though. 'Your Honour, Mr Hook stated earlier on – ' Djabo bent over his notes. 'He said, "Mr Sweetman claimed I owed him money." My questions are intended to address that point, Your Honour.'

'Yes. Yes.' The judge smiled and swivelled. 'Yes. So you say that your questions are in fact addressing a point that emerged out of Mr Hook's direct testimony?'

'Yes, Your Honour.'

'Mr Parrot?'

'Your Honour.' Parrot looked flustered. He was chewing his lip, and his disdainful calm had slipped away a little. He clearly hadn't thought of this. 'I mean, really. This is just...There could be a thousand reasons why Mr Sweetman might believe that Mr Hook owed him money. There had already been a direct financial transaction between them over the matter of the drill.'

'Mr Djabo?'

'I agree entirely, Your Honour, there could be a great many reasons and I am exploring what those reasons might be.'

'Well, I think the ladies and gentlemen have heard enough of that. Let's just move along, shall we?'

Elsa was again aware of a ripple of discontent. This was like the pictures again. The jury wanted to hear about the drugs. It was one up from pelmets, that was for sure.

'Mr Hook, I just have a few more questions and then I'm finished, and I'd like to thank you for your patience. First, a question that I should imagine is troubling quite a few of the ladies and gentlemen.'

Elsa glanced around her. Nope, nothing troubling no one back here, bub.

'Mr Hook, do you have any idea at all why Mr Sweetman attacked you?'

'I said already. He said I owed him money, he wanted money...'

'Yes, the ladies and gentlemen have heard all that, but I think what they're probably wondering is, why might he think that? Do you know?'

'No, I don't.'

'No? Apart from the business with the table, he hadn't offered you any other – services'

'Your Honour...'

'Yes. Please be careful, Mr Djabo.'

Djabo nodded his head and consulted his notes for a moment. Then: 'Are you familiar with the term "rent boy", Mr Hook?'

The question went off like a bomb, and Elsa could feel the ripples running all over the jury box. This was more like it! Sex and degradation rearing their ugly heads!

Parrot rose again.

'Your Honour, it is disgraceful that my client should be subjected to, should have to listen to – '

'I agree entirely, Mr Parrot. Ladies and gentlemen, Mr Djabo's last question was quite improper and you will disregard it. Unless you have anything further, Mr Djabo?'

'I have nothing more, Your Honour.' Nothing to add to the suggestion that the defendant is not only a liar and a violent scumbag, but also a drug dealer and prostitute.

'Then I would suggest we adjourn for a few minutes. If you wouldn't mind...' he said, and the jury were roughly awakened from their occult undead sleep and hustled off.

THE ENVY OF THE WORLD

'So what do you reckon?' Patrick murmured as the usher led them out of court and down a corridor. 'Guilty as sin or what?'

'What, Bryn?'

Patrick regarded her. 'No, I mean that so-called plaintiff. Did you see what he was wearing? Whatever happened to him it wasn't bad enough. Honestly, has anyone on earth ever gone to court wearing a purple and green shell suit before?'

'We need one of those law-book libraries like they have on *LA Law* where they have all the precedents,' Elsa said.

'I think the sentence would have to be a whole day in Poundstretcher.'

'Poundstretcher's too good for the likes of him. Q&S more like.'

'Well, I just wonder what he wears to funerals, that's all.'

The room they were taken to had 'Jury Deliberation Room' on the door. Like the jury box, it was much too small for its purpose. It was filled almost entirely with Formica tables which had been pushed together in the centre. There was barely enough clearance to pull out the chairs around the edges. There was a door leading off the room, which Elsa guessed must be to the toilet.

A man built like a boxer in a Nicole Farhi suit with a Nehru collar had very strong feelings about Patrick's suggestion that the photographs had been prejudicial to Bryn.

'What do you mean, prejudiced?' Nehru collar said. 'I'm not prejudiced against anyone.' Instant argument, his adrenalin only went one way, fight or fight, as if Patrick had been looking at his girlfriend, looking at *him* even. He had little tattooed blue dots on his knuckles, scumbag stigmata.

'I don't mean prejudiced,' Patrick said, 'I just mean that we're supposed to think less well of him after than we did before, that's all.'

'Yeah, who are we talking about?' said the youth with the I-like-*Baywatch* face. Thick kid. He looked dimly amused by it all.

Patrick gazed at him in some perplexity.

'The defendant,' he said. 'Sweetman.'

'Oh, yeah. Which one was he?' Thick kid said, and Patrick started to say something and then stopped. He looked astonished.

'That boy, the one who did it,' Nehru collar said.

'Allegedly,' Patrick said, and Nehru collar said right, whatever.

They were quiet again for a few moments. Elsa found herself looking at the woman opposite her, on the far side of the big Formica table. She was a small creature, well turned out in a nice if unseasonal wool suit that fitted really well on the hips and across the chest. Her hair and make-up were careful without being in the least flattering. About thirty. But what Elsa noticed most strongly was the look of fixed fury that was disfiguring her face, lips pressed into a bitter little bow tie, face sunk into a mask of disapproval and distaste. Pure seething fury. Elsa could smell it coming off her like perfume, Totally Pissed Off, the provocative new body spray from Impulse.

The woman caught Elsa's eye and sighed.

'So,' Nehru collar said, 'do you think we're going to get to see the rest of those pictures?'

'Why do you want to see them?' This was a quiet man who, so far, had barely looked up from his book, which had dragons on the cover. This was his maiden speech to the group. He addressed himself directly to Nehru collar, who now redeployed his rapid-reaction fight-fight reflex towards this new enemy.

'Why? Why? I'll tell you why. Because they're part of the *evidence* and I want to see *all* the evidence so I can make my *mind* up according to it. Isn't that what we're supposed to do?'

'Yeah, but what difference does it make about the pictures?' Dragons book had a slight giggle in his voice, as if the whole thing was some kind of dirty joke.

'Listen, we're the fucking *jury*, pardon me,' Nehru collar said, and left it at that. Dragons book just shook his head and looked away.

'I was just wondering ... '

This was a friendly-looking girl in Monkey boots, who was sitting next to a well-dressed older man who had stated earlier that he had on occasion worked *very* closely with the police, and that they wouldn't mount something like this unless they were pretty sure about it. 'It's just a resources thing,' he said.

'I don't suppose anyone knows what we do about lunch,' Monkey boots girl said. No one did. Conversations broke out and died down again randomly, meaninglessly, like brush fires, a mobile hubbub.

That barrister, he's quite a piece of work, isn't he?' The speaker was called either Graham or Tony, she couldn't remember which. He was sitting next to his analogue, as it were, who was either Tony or Graham. He didn't seem to be talking to anyone in particular.

'Which one?'

'The defence man, what's his name?'

'Jabber.'

'Ja-*boo*, isn't it?'

'Oh yeah, which one was he?' This was Thick kid, grinning.

'Phew, you know, it was all just...Well, it was a bit over *my* head, let me tell you. You know, all those different people and everything.'

He seemed to be addressing Nehru collar.

'And there was like this, this *judge* or something! Did you see that?'

Elsa waited for someone to explain to him but no one wanted to take him on. So she did.

'Yes, it *is* all a bit confusing, isn't it?' she said, using a voice she'd heard Claire use when talking to the general public on the phone. It had a sort of purring, stroking quality to it. 'Well, now. Let's see. Mr Djabo is the one who is representing the plaintiff, and so that makes him the prosecution barrister. The defence barrister is called Mr Parrot.'

'Parrot. That's who I mean,' said Graham-or-Tony. 'I couldn't think of the name. Parrot. He's a real piece of work.'

'No, but I mean, which side is he on? This Parrot, I mean.' Thick kid again.

'Side?' Elsa forgot her patient dinner-lady voice. 'Which side?'

'Yeah, is he on our side or the other side...'

'Sorry, sorry, maybe I'm misunderstanding something,' she said, 'but I didn't realize that we'd picked sides. Whose side are you on?'

'What do you mean?'

She blew air out of her cheeks, suddenly angrier than she knew how to deal with. She turned to appeal to Patrick, who was at the other end of the table, but he just raised hands: nothing to do with me. He was still grinning.

Thick kid appeared unperturbed by Elsa's fury and merely turned to Graham-or-Tony.

'D'you mean the one on our side?'

Graham-or-Tony looked helpless, and murmured something to the person beside him, who murmured something back, and they both fell silent again.

'You see,' Dragons book said, still the slight giggle in the voice, 'you see, we're not supposed to have sides yet. We're not supposed to have made our minds up yet. Until we hear all the evidence and that, you know.'

Thick kid looked bewildered, but subsided.

The room was quiet. Christ, Elsa thought, what was the point of any of this? We might as well just toss for it. Heads guilty, tails not guilty. And if it lands on its side ... Thick kid fidgeted for a bit, then muttered something to Monkey boots girl. She listened carefully.

'Oh, I see.' She smiled at him. She had a lovely, open smile, generous. 'No, Parrot, he's on our side.'

'Look, I'm sorry, I'm just not having this our-side their-side business ...' Elsa started to say, tremblingly, but Monkey boots smiled broadly at her.

'No, it's all right, he means which side of the room. Near to us or far from us.' She smiled and shrugged.

Drink, Elsa thought. Somebody get me a *drink*.

'Sorry, I don't know your name,' Elsa said, rounding on Thick kid and meeting him full in the eye. She gave him a big professional smile.

'Drew.'

Figures, Elsa thought. Stupid kid, stupid name.

'OK, Drew. Listen now. Ready?'

Drew nodded.

'OK. Here we go. Mr Djabo, prosecution, THE BLACK ONE. Yes? Mr Parrot, defence, THE WHITE ONE.' She became aware of Patrick laughing silently, his shoulders shaking as he watched her.

'OK?'

Thick kid shrugged, maybe. He didn't seem to feel that it could really be that simple. All those different people ... Elsa slumped back. She suddenly wanted to laugh. Here we are, she thought. The envy of the world. We the fucking jury.

They were called back in only to be dismissed for the day. They would reconvene at 10.15 tomorrow. Yippee! Bryn Sweetman made his innocent face as they filed out again, but she ignored him. He could be as innocent as he wanted, it wasn't going to make any difference here. You're with us now, she thought grimly. What had the judge said? The defendant is now given into your charge.

56

Downstairs again, she grabbed her jacket off the rack in the jury assembly room and made the hangers jangle. Patrick was holding the door for her. Outside she stopped and breathed in the air.

'Christ,' she said, and kicked a low wall. 'Sorry. I'm just so *tense.*' She took a few steps into the half-empty car park and made strangulated noises of exasperation. Patrick hiked his eyes and laughed at her.

'I know a good remedy for tension,' he said. 'I know just the thing actually.'

They were off the premises and half-way down the street when they heard rapid steps behind them.

'Hi.'

They both turned at once. It was Dragons book, smiling and bobbing his head: Elsa could think of nothing to say to him, and Patrick seemed to be in the same position. Dragons book himself didn't appear to feel the need to say anything anyway, and so they progressed three abreast in companionable silence.

'Well, we go this way,' Patrick said as they reached the main road.

'OK.' Dragons book went that way too, it seemed.

They'd passed two pubs and were outside a third before Patrick finally gave in.

'Actually we were thinking of having a drink,' he said, and Dragons book shrugged and said, 'Fine by me.'

Guinness. Ah, thank God. Elsa was as pleased to see it as she'd been in recent memory. I like my Guinness the way I like my men, she thought: thick and cold and sour.

'So,' Patrick said when they were all settled at a little corner table. 'So. Did he or didn't he? That's the question. That's the mystery. Did he truly wield the pelmet of terror?'

'I thought we weren't supposed to talk about it,' Elsa said, and Patrick pulled a face: oh, come off it now.

'I won't tell if you don't,' he said.

'Anyway,' Dragons book said, 'that's not the point. That's got nothing to do with it actually.'

'No?' Patrick had adopted a playful kind of voice, but Dragons book was quite serious.

'Nope. The options are not innocent or guilty. They're guilty or not guilty.'

'And that's not the same?'

'Uhuh. It doesn't matter if he's innocent or not. No one's innocent. No one's that innocent anyway. A courtroom is no place for innocence. All we're supposed to do is decide, Did they prove he did it or didn't they?'

'But you think he did?'

'Oh, sure.'

'Why?' Elsa said.

'Because he's there. You know, he got arrested, he got questioned, he got identified, he got charged. Police said there's a case, Criminal Prosecution Service said there's a case. For it to get this far he's either guilty or just incredibly unlucky. And unlucky equals guilty in my book. The two are the same. I mean, have you ever wondered why the words "accused" and "accursed" are so alike?'

'Erm . . . '

'And you will, of course, have noticed that the courthouse is situated on a line between two synagogues. No?'

'Er, well, no, actually . . . '

'Well, it is.'

'I see. Hm. It all falls into place. So your position is that even if he didn't do it, he should be punished in some sort of unspeakable cabbalistic way for being unlucky.'

'Unlucky like that, that's worse than guilty. That's accursed. You get an unlucky man on a ship, you know what you do? You throw him overboard. Wrapped in a sheet. Weighted.'

'Ah. I see.' Patrick blew a pocket of air into his upper lip and looked at Elsa, who looked straight back, straight-faced.

Dragons book shrugged, but wouldn't be drawn any further, though he was producing looks that suggested a whole world of convolution and secret codings, which he was wisely keeping to himself. He finished his beer and left, and Patrick leaned over Elsa and watched his back.

'I tell you what I think,' he whispered. 'I think *he* did it.'

'It's the judge I feel sorry for,' Elsa said. She and Patrick were on pint number three now. She felt slightly furtive about being here with him, but she was liking it anyway. She was surprised at how easy she found him. He didn't even seem to mind the snake eyes and the frosty face.

'Oh, yes. Which one was he now?'

'Don't. Christ. Do you know what, I was getting frightened of that woman, the one over the table from me. I thought she was going to run amok and start hacking people up. I'm sure she hates me. She keeps giving me hate looks.'

'She's probably in league with your fat woman. They're going to wait till you go into the toilet then come in and beat you with soap wrapped up in towels. Happens all the time on some juries, I understand.'

'And that cretinous boy just wants kicking down the stairs frankly. I mean, what is the point of him being there? Can you tell me?'

'Yeah, but did you hear what he said yesterday? When the other jury were in the assembly room with us while we were waiting? The usher came to call them back again and he stood up with them. Someone said, 'Er, actually I don't think you're on this jury, are you?" and he said, "Duh, dunno. I'm just following everyone else." Those were his exact words.'

'You're kidding.'

'I regret not. He actually said "duh". I thought that was just on cartoons. So not only does this person not know what day it is or who anyone is in court, or even, seemingly, the difference between a black person and a white person, but he doesn't seem wholly certain about what case he's on.'

'He could be on any case, it'd all be the same, wouldn't it?'

'Yup. Well, they're a scary bunch all right. I'm frightened of all of them actually. I think they're turning nasty.'

Elsa was starting to feel better. Guinness really is good for you, she thought.

'I thought you were going to start using rude words when you were doing that our-side their-side thing,' Patrick said. 'I thought you were going to stand up and start waving your arms about and making a dick of yourself.'

'God, I was so, I was just so...'

'Angry?'

'Yeah, but...'

'Filled with a smouldering sense of futility?'

'*God*, I tell you...'

'Nostrils flaring as the bitter stench of human stupidity rose up thick as tyre smoke, obscuring all...'

'It's not stupidity that's the problem exactly, though, is it? I mean, he could be thick and still care a little bit, couldn't he?'

'Ah, caring. Yes. Your speciality.'

'He hasn't got a prayer though, has he?'

'Who hasn't?'

'Bryn. Bryn bloody Sweetman.'

'Oh no. He's going down, as they say on the telly.'

'Just because some seedy bastard who runs some so-called charity – '

'Ah, now this charity interests me,' Patrick said. 'I mean, "BunkUp"?, Excuse me?'

'I didn't know you could just set up a charity like that.'

'It seems very narrowly specialized, also, doesn't it? Not just homelessness but youth homelessness, not just youth but young offender, and even then strictly the male variety only.'

'And what exactly is it that he's doing for them?'

'Well, to me it sounds suspiciously as if he's *caring* for them in a sort of not-recognized-by-social-services way.'

'Grubby little sod.'

'Grubby he is. But, Elsa, you saw the pictures. Didn't you? Someone did actually assault him. I mean, I'm sure he had it coming, and he gets his clothes out of the Suburban Hell Catalogue and all that, but it did happen.'

'I keep on thinking that too. But that doesn't mean it was Bryn Sweetman, does it?' Why am I trying to defend him, she thought.

'No, but then he is sort of convenient, wouldn't you say?'

She conceded that he was indeed convenient.

'And he does seem to have been on the premises quite a fair bit. And there would seem to be some quite genuine bad blood between them. And it really would be a strange mistake for Hook to make.'

Elsa sighed.

'Also,' Patrick said after a moment. 'I mean, I know it wasn't fair what Djabo said, about drugs and rent and all that. But, I mean, if Hook's playing round with ex-offenders, then what does that make our Mr Sweetman?'

Elsa pondered this.

'Yeah. Yeah.'

'Not that his previous record has any bearing whatsoever on this particular case...' Elsa curled her lip at him. He was being funny again. 'I mean, just because someone's done it once doesn't mean at all that they're going to do it again, now does it?'

'He could just be unlucky, like what's his name said.'

'The thing about unlucky,' Patrick said, 'is that the only people who ever claim they've got it really bad are the people who go out looking for it. So matey here somehow or other manages to find this alcoholic young-offender enthusiast, who is quite obviously unwholesome and weird. How does matey find him? Just unlucky? Things go wrong, and whatever the truth of it may be, he washes up in front of we the jury. We take one look at him and say, "Yup, he's our boy." We all seem to deserve each other somehow, don't we? Is that unlucky?'

'I don't know,' Elsa said. 'I just think we should hear the whole story.'

'Yeah, but from what his brief said he isn't going to testify himself. Remember? My client doesn't need to offer one word in his own defence? His brief's not going to risk putting him onto the stand by the sound of things. So we're not going to hear the whole story anyway.'

'Well. Guilty or not, he surely deserves better than this bloody jury?'

'Yeah. Like it's some kind of really, you know, *complicated* kind of a thing and not some brawl in a room over a shop.'

'Not a brawl.' She was thinking of the little cigarette burns on the neck, the scrawled attempt at cigarette-burn writing. Patrick eyed her up.

'And you care because?'

'Sorry?'

More eyeing.

'Look, this is just some kind of scumbag crap, toerag beats up weirdo in drunken rage. You know, this isn't O.J. Simpson. This is not interesting. But you, you seem interested. So I was just wondering why.'

Elsa raised her eyebrows.

'Why am I interested?'

'No, I mean why do you care? At all? I think just about everyone else on this jury thinks that the facts are speaking loud and clear for themselves, and that's pretty much that. But you seem to want more somehow.'

Patrick looked thoughtful suddenly and put his thumb to his nose for a second, and a big drop of bright blood splashed onto the white head of his Guinness. Elsa blinked in surprise.

'Shit. Shit, shit, shit,' Patrick said, and regarded it with dismayed fascination. He started rummaging in his pockets. 'Shit bastard fuck it to fuck, pardon me.'

Elsa was rummaging for tissues also; she had a fixed idea that there was at least one crumpled paper tissue in each of her pockets. It always seemed like that when you didn't want one, anyway. The inside breast pocker had a separate compartment and she thought she felt one in there.

But that wasn't what she found. She drew it out and saw that it was a half-sheet of that thin porous scrap paper they used at the courthouse. There was writing on it, blunt pencil, quite faint, difficult to read. She saw the word 'until' and pushed it back into her pocket. Patrick was looking expectantly at her, but she just shook her head. 'Sorry about this,' he said, and made a dash for the toilets, spilling a trail of bright splashes all the way.

Elsa contemplated the little pink indentation crater in the head of his Guinness, then looked up and around. The place was practically empty, just a few hunched figures. The man behind the bar was fiddling with the CD player.

Elsa drew the paper out again and smoothed it flat on the table.

I will be at the scented garden at st anns well I will wait until 8 oclock just in case you happen to give a fuck.

Same handwriting as the first note. She recalled the face in the viewing gallery, the lad who'd knocked her down, his hand in her pocket on the courthouse steps. Then she recalled the little squiggling, scribbling gesture Bryn had made from the dock. She, meanwhile, had left her jacket in a room where she knew the security was lax.

She really should tell someone, she thought, staring in dismay at this new note. What if Bryn was setting her up, what if he was trying to get the trial stopped by interfering with the jurors? But he'd just get into trouble if anyone found out about the notes. More trouble than he was already in. Was he likely to risk it?

She looked again at the paper. It was unsigned, unsurprisingly, and she speculated that the handwriting was probably not Bryn's but was more likely to be his friend in the viewing gallery's, so that if she went to the judge, Bryn could claim to know nothing about it. He might be able to pretend that it was a prosecution trick, again to stop the trial, although why that might be desirable she couldn't begin to imagine.

Shouldn't she go to the judge with it anyway? But what would be the point of that? If Elsa reported it, Bryn would only go to jail for longer, no one would gain anything.

No, the best thing was to just ignore it. The trial would be over in a day or two, Bryn would be sent down, and that would be that. Who really cared?

She checked her watch: 4.50. He could be there right now, waiting for her in the scented garden. Again she thought, but how can he be, isn't he in custody? Surely he can't just go wandering about on his own. What if he absconded? Didn't they have special places or something, remand, bail hostels, wasn't that it? She found that she was rather hazy on the details.

She was fingering the edges of the note when she felt Patrick's shadow over her. She jumped and made him jump too.

'All better,' he said, and flicked his eyebrows.

He sat again and looked at the Guinness.

'So what do you think?' he said. 'Do I drink my own blood?'

The note was still in front of her, in full view. Grey, grainy paper. Patrick was sure to recognize it as court paper. If he decided to take an interest. If she were to try to move it now it would almost certainly spark that interest off.

'Well, must just be my time of the month, I suppose,' Patrick said, and went to the bar, fishing in his pockets as he went.

If we have another pint, Elsa thought, that'll make it quarter past five, half past at the outside. St Ann's Well was a park, just a few streets down from the courthouse. She had walked past it that morning. No more than ten minutes away.

Not that she was even considering going there, naturally.

JUSTICE

St Ann's Well gardens. 5.35.

Behind the wall was a garden for the blind, chosen for its scents of lavender and jasmine and rosemary rather than its colour, so that the visually impaired of Hove could walk and stand and be ravished. A curiously sensuous civic gesture, as if the town hall had a department of joy, as if it didn't just accommodate its blind but loved them, wanted to seduce them with this rapturous gift of scents.

Early evening in the last week in August, with clouds massing to the south, great ragged streaks across the sky, a heavy mineral tint to everything, a weather front approaching, rain on the way. Suddenly you could smell the sea. Elsa held her bag closely and glanced around. She was trying not to look guilty, but guilty was what she felt. Furtive. And some kind of less definable churning going on, abdominal, low down. Law-breaking: it felt like indigestion. It felt exciting.

Bryn was waiting for her, smoking. She watched him as he stood, swaying in the sunlight. His shadow ducked about. He was bigger close up than he'd looked behind his screen, she thought, more fully grown. More capable. There was more of him, all over. Taller and heavier and more solid, clothes a size

65

bigger than she'd thought, more breadth in the back, more heft in the legs. And not just that, but he seemed to be animated in every part of his body; he didn't seem to be able to simply be at rest, but he was all twitching and shifting and little gestures. His voice was more or less what she remembered from her first encounter with him, displaced East End underclass whine with traces of ghetto-boy street talk, learned from *The Jerry Springer Show* probably. And this flicking, touching, hitching, as if whatever he had in his trousers was unruly.

And then there was his face. Cleft chin, full mouth, thick nose, green eyes, a slight turn to the left one. Creases down the cheeks, like a cartoon gangster. She didn't like to meet the eyes, they were unsettling, hot, seething, greedy. Horny. When he wasn't concentrating his lips fell apart slightly, giving him a dumb, doggy, avid look. Eager for it all.

'Didn't think you were coming,' he said, and grinned tightly. 'Didn't think you could be bothered to get off your arse out of that jury box actually, you looked so nice and comfy in there. All snug, sitting there tut-tutting about everything, getting a hard-on with those pictures.'

He regarded her, shook his head, spat sideways.

'OK, well tell me all about it then,' he said finally.

'What do you mean, me tell you? I don't know anything about you, do I?' Elsa said.

'Yeah, you got that right anyway. You don't know shit.'

She bristled. 'How can I know anything about it? The trial has only just started.'

'So how come suddenly it's what you think that matters round here? Eh? How come it's that all of a sudden? Considering, as you pointed out a moment ago, that the sum total of what you know about any of it is precisely shite?'

'How am I supposed to know – ' Elsa started to say, before she caught herself. 'Bryn, that's the whole point, isn't it? I have no interest in you personally, so I can be objective about it.'

'Ooooooh *objective*. You're going to be *objective*, are you? Tell me now, is that anything like being a tight-arsed know-nothing bitch?'

She stood up, trembling with sudden rage, then made herself sit again. She wasn't going to let him get away with that. She controlled her voice.

'No. Actually it isn't. What it means – '

'I know what it means. Just 'cos I'm thick doesn't mean I'm stupid. You know precisely shite about me or anything to do with what's been going on in this fucking so-called case, so you're the perfect person to ask about it. You and eleven other nodding fucking dogs. That's about it, isn't it?'

'Bryn, if I knew you they wouldn't let me be a juror.'

'So you admit you don't know anything about it?'

'Of course I do, how could I know – '

'So how can you judge me then?'

She sat back, exasperated with him. Was this what she'd come here for? Breaking the bloody law? Just to sit and listen to him complain about his bad luck? It wasn't as if she owed him anything.

'I can't.'

'So what are you doing on this jury then?'

'I was summonsed. Or whatever it's called. They make you do it.'

'Yeah, but what do you know, though, eh?'

'I told you, I don't know anything.'

He glanced about him, a habitual scanning. He was beset: court officials, police, social workers, key workers, probation officers, just witnesses. He knew more about the busy, watchful middle classes than she ever could.

'Yeah, well you said it,' he continued, 'you don't know anything. Well, at least you're honest anyway. Makes a change.' He spat again. Elsa intensely disapproved of spitting. For Bryn, on the other hand, it was clearly something akin to a second career, or at the very least an abiding and deeply felt interest. He probably took *Spitting Monthly*. A great delirious fluffy waft of hyacinth enveloped them for a moment, and Elsa saw his nostrils flare. Handsome boy, no sense in denying it. It was a factor, how could it not be? When was it not, ever?

'And you don't know anything about me,' she said.

'No, how could I?'

'But you think you do.'

'Well, now, I know what you're wearing, don't I? I know what you want me to know. When did you last wear that jacket? Wedding, was it? Little stain on the lapel. Cream or something. Had your hair done recently too, last week or so. Which could be a coincidence, I suppose, except they give you weeks' notice of this, don't they? So you had it done special. What's in that bag? Nothing. But you've got it anyway. See, I can see things too.'

'Want to look nice,' she said, defiant. 'What about you? Are you trying to tell me you wear a shirt and tie every day?'

'But I've got a motive. I'm on fucking trial, for fuck's sake. What's your motive? You haven't got one, nothing legitimate anyway. That makes you guilty. Or it makes you feel guilty anyway. Which is the same thing.'

Elsa said nothing for a moment. Then quietly, her voice shaking despite her efforts, 'It's none of your business what I wear.'

'It's...sorry, say again?' He cupped a hand to his ear, making a point. 'It's what exactly?'

'I said it's none – '

'Right. So let's see if I've got this straight. Everything I do is your business, even though you know shag-all about me, but nothing *you* do is *my* business. That sound about right?'

'Look,' she said, half standing again. 'Look. It's not my fault they put you on trial, it's not my fault I'm on the jury, it's not my fault your life is such a – '

'Such a?' He was enjoying her enormously, a big arrogant smile all over his face.'

'Well. As you say, I don't know you, do I?'

He stroked the grey stubble on his head. His legs were kicked out in a sprawling, fuck-off kind of way. Even his body language was obscene.

'So. Anyway, what's to be done about it?' he said ruminatively.

They sat in silence, Bryn's hand stirring on his leg, drawing patterns.

'You see, there is something we could do about it,' he said at last, staring straight ahead, his voice low. 'Actually.'

*

'What do you mean, know you?' she said, moving away slightly from him. 'How can I know you? I just met you.' God, she just couldn't believe him, the arrogance of him. She could feel her breasts pushing against her bra, she felt almost out of breath.

'That's what I'm saying. I'll show you. I'll show you everything.'

'Yes, but how can you possibly do that?' She laughed, suddenly, all the anger turning into ridicule. It was ridiculous. He was ridiculous. 'Know you! Anyway, that's what the trial's for,' she said, feeling proprietorial of the process, feeling her place inside it and his outside. Her power and his powerlessness. It felt good. 'That's why they have a trial, so that everyone can explain everything and then we can get to the bottom of it.'

'Oh, really? Oh, is that a fact? Well, I'm sorry to disappoint you, love, but you're never going to get to the bottom of anything that way. Not in there,' he said, pointing dismissively in the direction of the courthouse. 'No chance.'

'Why not?'

''Cos they're not going to let you. They don't want you to. They only want you to know what they want you to know. My brief says he doesn't want me to take the stand.'

'Why not?'

'Because he says I won't make a good impression. He says a jury won't like me.'

She said nothing for a moment. His brief, she thought, knew his business.

'Well, I'm sure he knows what he's doing.'

'What makes you think that? He let that black twat as good as accuse me of being rent. Didn't he? "Have you ever heard the term 'rent boy', Mr Hook?" And my fucking brief, who's so fucking brilliant at everything according to you, he lets him get away with it.'

'And you're not.'

'Pardon me?'

'You're not rent?' She was surprised by herself here, though her voice betrayed her, tense and tight and over-confident.

'Do I look like it?'

Elsa actually had no idea, but on balance, yes, possibly. It certainly wasn't too difficult to imagine someone being prepared to offer money for his services. How much, Elsa thought suddenly? I wonder how much.

'So you don't think he knows what he's doing?'

'How the fuck do I know? I only met him twice, and that was for about five minutes each time. I was assigned to him. All I'm saying is he's making me look bad.'

'Well, he must know what he's doing.'

'Why must he?'

'He looks like he does.'

'No, he doesn't. He doesn't look as good as the other one. Does he?'

'He looks fine.'

'How do you know? How many of them have you seen? And anyway there's only two of them in there and mine's not the best. Is he?'

'He looks all right.'

'He looks like shite.'

'So you don't like your brief. Fine. So the whole world's against you.'

'Yeah, actually it is, just at the moment.'

'Oh, right. Right.'

'If you had any idea what's going on with this case – '

'Really.'

'If you had any idea, at all, what the police are up to now with my mate, what they've been cooking up – '

'Really! The police as well, eh?'

'Look, you've got this little top on, you've got this hair-do... Where do you work? Some shop or something, is it?'

'Local government,' she muttered, feeling obscurely ashamed but also insulted that he should think it was a shop.

'So? OK, local government, whatever that is, but it's all on your side, isn't it?'

They were sitting now on a bench, cool and shaded and quiet. Sounds came from the nearby tennis courts, thwacks and bonks and shouts. There were a great many dogs also, doing what dogs do in parks. And her and Bryn, sitting side by side, in the scented garden.

The churning in the stomach started up again, a slow propeller. Also a kind of melting feeling. Christ, what was she thinking?

'Look,' she said, trying to take control. 'What is it you want to tell me?'

'Tell you?' he said. 'Tell you? They're telling you stuff in there, it's all shite. What's the good of me telling you more? You'll just think it's more shite, won't you?'

'Bryn, just give me the truth and I'll believe you.'

'No, you fucking won't.'

'Yes, I *will*.' Damnit! You arrogant little . . .

He rubbed his bristly head with his fists.

'You wouldn't know the truth from a kick in the cunt, love. Sorry to be the one to tell you, but.'

'No? Right then.' She stood up, arranged her bag. His eyes tracked her and his tongue protruded just a fraction of an inch or so. Assessing. She'd had enough. She wasn't going to stand here and be insulted by some little . . .

'Where you going?'

'Well, what's the point of any of this?' Elsa said. 'There's some truth out there apparently, but you won't say what it is and even if you did I'm too, too, I don't know, to believe it. So I'm just as bad as everyone else in your crap life, so why don't you just let me get on with putting you in jail? Just what were those notes about?'

'I just thought . . . I mean I just *thought*, look, get one of them, get them out of that fucking court, or zoo, or shithole, or whatever the fuck it's supposed to be, and just let them see. See what my fucking life's like. The whole thing. One juror, that's all I could manage, and they can go back and tell the others. Anyway it's all I can do.'

'And I was the one you picked.'

'Yeah.'

'Why?'

'No reason.'

'Must be some reason.'

'I liked your jacket.'

'Uhuh. And if I go to the judge, then you go to jail, for longer than you would have done anyway. Well, that's true, isn't it? Nobbling a juror? Got to be fairly major. ABH, that's only, what, two years, maximum? Why risk it?'

He threw off two or three coded gestures, a flick of the hand, a twist to the neck. She couldn't read them.

'Double or nothing,' he said finally, shaking his head and scrutinizing the paving slabs. Then he looked up, grinning. Licked his lips. 'Roll the dice. Know what I mean? Double or quits. Bastard police think they're *so* fucking clever. And by the way you won't find any fingerprint of mine on either of those notes. And anyway you're not going to any judge. Are you?'

Well, am I? she thought. Answer: no. She didn't even have to think about it, there was no way she was going to get Bryn into more trouble than he was in already. Plus, she'd have to explain why she hadn't done something about it earlier, and she didn't really feel up to it. With some surprise, she realized that it was already too late.

'No. I'm not. So what's next?'

'My side. You've had that lying twat's side already, haven't you? I done this, I done that. Well, there's my side as well.'

'He says you beat him up.'

'So? What if I did?'

Elsa took a second to find a response to this.

'What if you did? Bryn, that's what all this is about, isn't it? Whether you did or you didn't. So you know, it maybe does make a little bit of difference. Don't you think?'

'I'm not saying I did, I'm saying what if I did. Maybe he deserved it.'

'What do you mean? Is that what you're telling me?'

'What if I am?'

God. You are so bloody annoying, you little...

'Bryn, could you please make some kind of effort to talk straight once in a while. Is that what happened?'

He shrugged, staring down at the ground, his hand still stirring on his leg. He was still grinning.

'Maybe.'

'So you're guilty then.'

'You see, that's exactly, that's *exactly* what I mean. I tell you something, you go and say, well that's it then. Case closed, detective. He done it, so lock him up and just throw away the key, yeah?'

'What else am I supposed to think?'

'All right, listen.' He sat up straighter, adjusted his face, looked businesslike. 'Listen, right. I didn't smack him up. I was there but I didn't do it, and I can prove it to you. I can also prove I'm not rent. I never rented in my life. Some blokes do, that's up to them; some blokes don't, that's it. I don't. It's not what I'm about.'

'So you can prove to me you didn't beat him up? Really?'

'Yeah. I can show you.'

'Because, Bryn, that's something I'm going to need to know for sure. Yes? Because I'm not going anywhere with you if I'm not sure about that. Obviously. I have to be certain about that.'

'You think I'd beat you up. You think you're going to end up like those pictures, don't you.' He sprawled back on the bench, his eyes flickering over her, eating her up. 'You think I'd do that?'

'Bryn, how do I know?'

'Yeah, so your question really is, am I some kind of psycho or something? Right?'

Elsa met his eye for a moment, looked away again.

'No, my question really is, what are you like, really? My question is, can I trust you?'

'What do you want, a note from my mum or something?'

'Bryn – '

'OK. I know. Look. You took an oath, didn't you? I do solemnly swear and all. Yes?'

'Yes.'

'And everyone believed you, didn't they? The judge and everyone? They didn't start going, ah, but how do we know you'll keep your word, how do we know we can trust you? Did they? Eh?'

'No, but – '

'No. OK. Listen, I know this lad, right, he's got like A levels and degrees, everything, right? And he said, you know testify? The word? Yeah?'

'Yes...'

'He says, you know where it comes from? I mean the word, yeah?'

'Yes...'

'He says it's from ages ago, right? When people had to swear to tell the truth they'd swear like this.' He cupped his hand over his groin. 'You swear on your...you know. Yeah? Bollocks and that. Bit of a problem in your case, I can see that. But that's where it's from. Testify. Testicles. Yeah?'

'Yeeeees...'

'OK. Well, here we go.' He stood facing her and again cupped his hand over his crotch. Very serious face now. 'Right. I like solemnly swear, on my, like, bollocks and that, I didn't do Harry Hook. I never did him. I never did anyone. I wouldn't never do you. All right?'

Elsa struggled for a moment, then laughed aloud. She was imagining trying to explain this little scene to Claire. He couldn't be serious surely. He glared at her and sat down again, and she saw that he was actually *blushing*.

'Well, that's the best I can do. What more can I do?'

And it was this blushing that convinced her. You couldn't fake a thing like that. He was absolutely serious. She straightened her face.

'Sorry. All right. So. How is this going to happen, this showing? Surely they're not letting you just wander about while this is going on, are they?

'Pre-trial reports,' he said in a slightly affected voice, 'indicate insufficient warrant for custodial arrangements during trial. In other words, they couldn't get me put into one of their fucking bail hostels or anything like that. Not for want of trying though. I just have to sign in with the police every day, and of course I have to show up at court. Apart from that, it's business as usual, love.'

'Oh, I don't know about this, Bryn...'

'Listen. Tomorrow. Meet me. I'll sort out a message and that. We'll do it with your jacket again. My mate can sort it out. I can meet him in the toilets like before. Then I'll meet you, we'll go over it all. It'll only take a few hours. OK?'

'No. No. Bryn.'

She stood up. She shook her head.

'Look, I shouldn't have even come here today. I can't meet you. How can I? I'm whatever the word is. Empanelled. I could go to jail.'

'Oh, right, and I couldn't?'

You're going to jail anyway, she started to say, but bit it off.

'All right. OK. Tell me why I should,' she said. 'Give me a really, really good reason why I should meet you tomorrow.'

What she was expecting was for him to plead a little, give her his sob stories, how he never had a chance. She wasn't looking for too much in the way of explanation, but she did expect some kind of an appeal. To her better nature perhaps.

He stood up again. At first she thought he was hunting about for something in his trouser pocket, a lighter maybe, or doing a re-run of that testicles thing. Then she realized what he was really doing: he was in fact simply drawing attention to his cock, to its existence, its location. And then she realized that he had succeeded, and she looked away hastily, flustered, then back again, trying to keep her eyes decently above the belt.

'Justice,' he said, holding her eye, and winked. 'That's a really good reason. Isn't it?'

She had been expecting a plea; what she was being offered was some kind of a deal. But what? What exactly, she thought? Good God, what am I doing? Elsa Frith, local government worker, affianced of the lovely Liam, and now juror. And here she was, her heart bouncing around inside her bra and her mouth dry with fear, as she contemplated doing something that would, if discovered, not only lose her her whole place in the world, but also the good opinion of everyone she knew. And in return she got – what exactly? This was a whole heap of trouble.

So why did she feel so exhilarated?

'Bryn, what are you trying to do to me? Eh?'

He was still standing in front of her, now with his innocent face on.

'But that is a good reason, isn't it?' he said, wide-eyed.

'Oh, what, justice you mean? Oh yeah. Yeah, it's a great reason.'

MALIBU

When she got home there was a phone message from Liam, but she was in no mood for him. There was also a message from Bob Betjeman at work, an almost apologetic plea for information about the whereabouts of a file. If it was just him, he said, he wouldn't bother her about it until she got back, but she knew how it was, he said. She did indeed. She sighed and rang the office, but got the answering machine.

'Hello, Elsa Frith here, Bob. Wolf and Henderson, Lansdowne Avenue, common parts grant. All I could find out was that it had to go back to the managing agents, or rather someone they'd appointed to deal with the whole estate. He was called Trent or something, no, Tarrant, that was it. He had to get the freeholder to approve the schedule of works and she was in a mental home or something. So Claire would have had it but she couldn't have done anything to it, so I think it would have gone back to store. That's where I'd look anyway.'

She imagined her voice spooling out into the silent office as the setting sun flashed through the windows and the dust floated over the empty desks and the blank computer terminals, maybe a solitary cleaner having a sneaky look in the desk drawers. 'Well. That's it,' she finished lamely and hung up.

She'd visited Wolf and Henderson, the applicants, in their horrible dingy flat at an early stage of the application, and had been struck by their indignation, stupidity and seemingly wilful incomprehension of the mechanics of the grant application procedure, their inability even to fill in a form correctly.

Wolf, the ringleader, the brains behind the outfit, a striking girl with long black hair and an air of defiant disregard for the truth, had taken Elsa up the musty stairs, the thick maroon carpet curling and matting at the edges, and proudly shown her the pans under the drips, the ceiling paper blistered and brown with water penetration ancient and modern. One of the pans, Elsa had noted, still had crusted streaks and gobs of food, something red and glutinous round the rim and handle, which both of them seemed to notice at the same time. I'll see what I can do, Elsa had said. Leave it with me.

Elsa sat at the window and thought about Bryn. She sipped her Malibu as she dialled Claire's number. She felt the need to talk to someone sensible about it. But Claire would just have to do.

'Claire, listen,' she said. 'I'm thinking of doing something very unwise.'

'You're going to go and see *Riverdance*?'

'Worse than that.'

'I don't like the sound of this one bit. Tell me more, much more.'

Elsa explained about the trial, Bryn, the notes. Claire said nothing for a moment.

'Yes? And your question is?'

'What should I do, Claire? Should I meet him again?'

'Oh, obviously. Of course. In fact why don't you just marry him and have his children and go and live in Droitwich?'

'Droitwich? Claire – '

'Elsa, I don't believe you need me to tell you that you have to go to the judge immediately. You could get into trouble.

They have a name for this, and it's illegal. What are you *thinking* of?'

'Yeah, I know but – '

'But nothing. Christ, Elsa. Really. Get a grip now. This man, what's he called...'

'Bryn,' Elsa said miserably.

'He's trying to set you up. Or he's just retarded or something. If you don't tell someone right away then he's made you guilty of conspiracy to do whatever the word is. Accessory before the fact or some such bollocks. I can't believe you're even *thinking* about it...'

'Well, I am.' Blimey, she thought. I just said it so it must be true. What in God's name has got into me? 'Well, it's all right for you, Claire. Things happen to you. Nothing ever happens to me.'

'What exactly happens to me?'

Elsa shrugged down the phone.

'Things.'

'Elsa. Go and see *Riverdance* instead.'

Elsa said nothing for a moment, just swirled the Malibu round the glass.

'I know,' she said finally. 'I mean, I know it's not exactly a good idea...'

'But you want to do it anyway.'

Oh, yes, Elsa thought. Come to think of it, I really do.

'Well, the thing is, Claire, you see, I don't think he's getting much of a trial. I mean, his barrister's crap and you should see what these jurors are like. And he's just this kid really...'

'Hmmmmm?' A long, inquisitorial sound. Yes? And your point is?

'Claire,' she whispered, 'you should see what he looks like.'

'Ah. Ahah. Now we get to it. What does he look like?'

'He's like... Well, he's just this kid really, but he's got this...'

'Hm?'

'Oh, I don't know.'

'I see. Elsa. Now come on. What kind of reason is that?'

'Yeah, I know, but... I mean, I know...'

'And who's going to have to come and visit you in jail when it all goes wrong?'

'You'd better not. All the other prisoners will just think I'm a lesbian.'

'Yeah, but if Liam comes they'll think you're a loser.'

'Maybe I should get Ted Slaughter to come.'

'Excellent plan. Then they'll think you're the saddest twat on the planet and kill you.'

'So anyway. Just for the record, your advice about Bryn is: don't do it. Yes?'

'Correct. Resist him. Shun him, Elsa.'

'Whether he's guilty or not.'

'Oh yes. I just don't see what business it is of yours.'

'And no matter what he looks like?'

'Elsa, you sound like one of those demented women off that ad. You know the one? They're all there for their 11.30 appointment, but really they just want to drool all over some bloody window cleaner with his shirt off or something. Only you're willing to go the extra mile and go to jail for him. Elsa, try to be sensible. *Try*. Seriously now. Go to the judge. Promise?'

'All right, Claire. Look. I'll ring you again.'

'Elsa? I don't wholly like the sound of you. Are you sure you're all right?'

'Oh, yeah. It's just a bit of a trial. So to speak.'

She hung up and headed for the bath. She read Bryn's note again, then dropped it into the water, pulled it around with the cunningly contoured grip of a plastic razor, until it started to disintegrate. She took hold of the ooze and squeezed it through her fist, until it was just a grey, damp ball. She chucked it towards the wicker bin and it hit the side and clung there, like a snail on a fish tank.

11.30. She was half-way through Malibu-and-milk No. 5, the television was on, the open window bringing in cool damp air. She took her jacket into the kitchen and ran the hot tap, scrubbed at the little stain on the lapel with a cloth. She hung it on a hanger by the open window, sat down again. The

Malibu was thin and icy at the top, thicker and cloudier at the bottom. The ice clunked about in the glass as she circulated it with a finger. She licked the finger.

2.30. She was lying on her bed, looking at the ceiling. The gutters at the back were dripping, a miscellany of tiny quiet sounds, plopping and drumming against leaves and walls and sheds. The smell of wet soil came up. There were people talking softly at a window nearby, she could hear the alternating voices. The tinkle of a glass. She was dehydrated from the Malibu. She contemplated getting more.

4.00. She'd more or less given up trying to sleep, she would just lie here until daylight. It would be light in an hour or so anyway.

When she slept she dreamed of buildings, cavernous crowded buildings. She knew the way out, but it was complicated and involved climbing up ladders and squeezing through little cubbyholes. She turned to the person behind her and said, 'God, do you believe this building?' and he laughed.

8.00. She woke and looked at the ceiling. There was an hour before she had to get up. She allowed the dream nonsense to subside in her head. No Liam beside her, so she could sprawl about luxuriously and lie on her front and have all the pillows. She buried her head right into the gap between two of them, caressed herself absently and dozed. She could gauge the time to within five minutes. She woke and dozed and savoured the time as it slid past. Bryn came at her in a variety of guises, threatening, alluring. So he was in her head now. Poking around, having a look at things.

She decided she'd sound Patrick out. He wouldn't grass her up. And if he said the same as Claire she'd forget all about it. Be sensible like Claire said.

KITCHEN

Back in the jury deliberation room next morning, waiting. The fat woman's voice, quiet but insistent, was scratching the air.

'So they'll be there right now. He told me, you just go and have a good day, love, do your shopping or whatever...Barry, I said, I'm in court. Oh, what have you done now, he said. Anyway by the time you get back this evening you'll walk in and there'll be a whole new kitchen. Everything.'

Mrs Furious was smiling and listening as the fat sow woman talked. Elsa had been a few minutes later than everyone else and so had no idea how long this conversation had been going on. She was sitting with the rest of the jury, waiting to go into court. The stain on her jacket lapel was still just visible. The jacket itself was hanging on the rack in the jury assembly room downstairs. Elsa couldn't pretend even to herself that this was innocent on her part. She'd wait and see if there was a note waiting for her, then she'd decide what to do about it. Go to the judge or whatever.

'So I said, Barry, I don't want any mess now when I get back, and he said, Helen, all you're going to have to worry about when you get in this evening is who to call first to tell them about your *completely new kitchen*. Everything. Units, surfaces, appliances, I mean right down to utensils . . . '

Mrs Furious was soaking it all up. She was an entirely new person, Elsa thought, just look at her. She was smiling and nodding, loving it. She must be a sucker for stories with kitchens in them. Perhaps if Bryn was a kitchen fitter then he might stand more of a chance. Elsa smiled at Patrick, who looked grey and pouchy. She guessed he'd carried on last night after they'd parted. He shrugged, hello.

The room was warm and, apart from Helen's kitchen saga, silent. No sign of any court action yet.

Elsa tried to get Patrick's eye again, and when she succeeded, lifted her eyebrows and swung her gaze towards the toilet. He looked blank, and she did it again. He dragged the flesh of his face down and crossed his eyes. She shook her head, no, there, *in there*. She stood up and squeezed her way round the table. Graham and Tony sat side by side, staring solidly ahead, in different directions. They both looked miles away. One of them had on a rather strange retro seventies T-shirt, the kind of thing a media studies graduate might wear to Glastonbury. This seemed to have caused a bit of a breach in the relationship; it had driven a wedge between them, Elsa could tell at a glance. She trod on Thick kid's foot. She thought it make help wake him up a bit. He didn't seem to notice though.

She tried to signal to Patrick again as she reached the door, and managed a quick nod of the head: *in here, stupid*. There were two cubicles and a hand basin, so it was perfectly plausible that they might both be in there at the same time. There was no impropriety. Graham and Tony had gone in together yesterday.

She sat in one of the cubicles and left the door unlocked.

Patrick would tell her what she already knew, the same thing Claire had said, that she was mad to have gone to meet Bryn yesterday, that she could have been seen by anyone, she could end up on trial herself, she must on no account go any further with it. It was stupid and even dangerous. And what was the purpose anyway? She could imagine Patrick's voice, his incredulous expression, his look that said, oh really, you can do better than that.

The door swung open and she heard someone come to the hand basin, taps running. She poked her head out to see: Patrick.

They stood very close and whispered. He had his back to the door in case anyone else tried to come in, though it was unlikely since there were obviously two people here already and there was certainly no room for a third.

She told him the story so far, the scented garden and everything, and he did indeed give her a look that said, for God's sake, woman, are you mad?

'Have you been seen?' he said, pressing in urgently to her. 'Are you sure you weren't seen with him yesterday? How do you know?'

'No one saw,' she said. 'But look. He said he was going to get me a message today, where I could meet him.'

Patrick was regarding her closely with his disdainful look in place. This is a fascinating example of the human species, his look seemed to be saying, let's examine it a little more closely. Watch it wriggle.

'He says he's not guilty and he can prove it,' Patrick said. 'So why not prove it here? Seems like, you know, the obvious opportunity, what with the trial and all.'

'I don't know.'

'So. You're going to do what exactly?'

'He says he's got something to show me, about the trial, and it'll take a few hours.'

'Yes. What do they call this again? They've got some word for it.'

'Jury tampering?'

'No...'

'Nobbling?'

'No, there's some other word, but yes, nobbling, tampering, that's certainly the kind of thing, isn't it?'

'Yes, look, I know, but...'

'Hm?'

And in truth she didn't quite know what came next. Did she really intend to go on with it, see Bryn again, let him show her things, completely illicitly?

'Well, I'll tell you what I think,' Patrick said. 'I think you should be extremely careful. You shouldn't have told me, and you better not tell anyone else. If this is what you want to do, then just make sure you don't get caught. OK?' He studied her for a second. 'Tell you what else I think. I think you'd better be sure he's innocent before you go any further.'

'But that's what I'm supposed to be finding out.'

He shook his head.

'Uhuh. You better be certain now.'

'Why?'

'Think about it for a second. Let's say you allow that nice Mr Sweetman to, whatever, tamper with you, nobble with you, whatever it is he's offering. And let's say you don't really believe it. You find him guilty, like every other rational person would. He goes to jail, and what does he do? He says one of the jurors met him, offered to do him a deal if she got him off. He might even have arranged some form of corroboration. A little pal waiting about out of sight but within earshot perhaps? Or a tape recorder maybe? Not difficult to arrange. Which leaves you where exactly? Swimming in the sea of shit, I'd say. Not just that . . . '

'Patrick – '

' . . . not just that but even if you did believe his tale of woe, you better be sure you can actually get him off. No good just you saying it, judge will take a majority on something like this, he'll take ten to two, so you need to be able to swing two other people to make it nine to three, yes? And that's just for a retrial. Well, can you? I mean, can you do it right now? Because if you can't, then this really isn't such a good idea, is it? Because the result will be the same, whatever you say, Bryn will go down and he'll take you down with him. Take you darn wiv'im, I should say. So can you? Can you go back in there now and get two of those people to change their minds?'

Another silence. Elsa could hear the drone of Mrs Kitchen's voice.

'There's one other thing as well. Our Bryn has obviously set out to disrupt this trial. Why he wants to do that is his business, of course, though it doesn't exactly stink of not guilty, does it? But that's not the point. The point is, the penalty for something like this, the penalty for you, I mean, could be a lot. I wouldn't be at all surprised if it isn't the kind of thing they lock you up for. So even if he really is the most not guilty person ever to draw breath, and even if you do find out this great truth, and even if everybody is struck, as if by a bright light from on high, with Bryn Sweetman's essential lovely fluffy innocence, you could still end up going to jail, losing your job, trying to explain it to your *mum*. Yes? And my point really is, what do you care anyway? He did it or he didn't but actually what are any of these people to you?'

'Nothing,' Elsa muttered.

'Elsa,' he said. 'I'm not saying do it or don't do it, I'm saying think about it and be very careful in your thinking. He's a nasty piece of knitting this Bryn. You'd better be sure you and he are on the same side, because if you're not...So be careful. Then decide. You still want to do it after that, go ahead. Could be interesting.'

'We better go back out.'

'Oh, they'll just think we're shagging. Happens all the time on some juries.'

'You go first. I'll follow you.' She pushed him out, back into the easeful stupor of the deliberation room, and ran the taps in the hand basin.

'Oh, by the way,' said a voice behind her, and she jumped. Patrick again. 'I just remembered. The word is "suborned". Thought you might want to know.'

APPLE PIE

The jury were dismissed for the day at 12.30. The witness, Hegler, the one no one was allowed to talk about, had again failed to appear. A car had been sent to his address, no one there, no sign of him. He hadn't been seen for days seemingly.

Elsa sat in the jury box while the judge explained this and she refused to meet Bryn's eye, though it felt as if his eyes never left her. The judge was for once not smiling, clearly taking the dimmest of all possible views of this untidiness. Djabo protested about the disruption. Parrot sneered at the police for not doing their job.

Elsa looked on contemptuously. They all just seemed like a pack of children. Someone had taken their ball away. Bryn's friend in the public gallery wasn't there today, so there could be no note presumably. So the decision was made for her. She was relieved. Mostly. Disappointed, too, she couldn't pretend otherwise. It would have been exciting. It would have been *something*, anyway.

She went down to the jury assembly room and grabbed her jacket. She and Patrick wandered into town and washed up at the big old Co-op department store, meandering happily through bedlinens and haberdashery, everything scented with that faint nostalgic department store mustiness. There was a Tannoy, which emitted squawky garbled messages from time to time from little brown speakers high up near the suspended ceilings. The women staff members in complicated perms and cakey beige foundation who sat at desks and behind tills remained serene and unperturbed, coolly disregarding these sinister pronouncements. Through beds and cookwear, to the café.

Elsa was hunting about for change at the café cash desk when she felt an unexpected edge in the hip pocket of her jacket. Her fingers knew instantly what it was, and her heart turned over abruptly.

'Er, Patrick...'

They took their trays to a table and spread the note out.

2 oclock. Clock cafe, nr florral clock. Palmeira Sq.

'Well, well,' Patrick said. 'I don't suppose you have any way of knowing what time today this was put into your pocket?'

Elsa shook her head.

'I was just wondering,' Patrick said, and stopped. 'I mean, it occurs to me to wonder.'

'Wonder what?' Elsa said. She felt gritty and irritable from lack of sleep and this endless waiting around for things to happen. Grouchy. She was feeling pushed and pulled about by it all, and particularly by Bryn.

'Well. Bryn said yesterday that he'd get a note to you today, tell you where to meet, yes?'

'So?'

'But surely we should all be in court today, shouldn't we?'

'Yeah, but the witness didn't show.'

'Yes, El-sa, I know, but Bryn said that yesterday. He said he'd meet you today, *yesterday*. He knew the witness was going to be missing, yesterday.'

Elsa considered this.

'Well, he could have meant this evening after court.'

'Maybe. I'm just thinking aloud really, but he does seem very well prepared for these little eventualities, doesn't he? Paper and pencil, enough privacy to write a note and hand it to whoever, ready-made plan of action.'

Elsa thought: I didn't see his mate, funny face in the gallery. He must have already been and gone and done it before we got into court, while we were waiting about. So Bryn knew the witness hadn't shown up before we did, she thought.

'Yeah,' she said. 'I mean, I know what you're saying, Patrick.'

'You see, I think this witness might have fallen prey to the Bryn Sweetman charm offensive. You know what I mean? I imagine bruises in this season's colours, saffron, ochre, turquoise. Maybe a few whip marks, for frisson. Perhaps a few artfully placed cigarette burns? Perhaps as a kind of trade mark?'

Elsa looked at him. M, she thought. M. Not B.

'Really? Is that what you really think?'

He shrugged.

'How could he have done all that? He's been in custody, hasn't he?'

'Well, my guess is, not all the time.'

'I thought someone said something about a bail hostel?'

'Did they? You see, it's perfectly possible that he isn't in any kind of custody at all. I was talking to someone last night, a friend of mine. He says that they have to make a really good case to put someone in one of those places. Unless the accused is already known to the police, he'd have to be a risk to other parties in the trial, like witnesses, for instance, or he'd have to pose a risk of absconding. What keeps people out of remand or bail hostels or whatever is roots: fixed address, family, job. Being clean and sober helps. And then this is just ABH, actual not grievous, and the criminal damage is only window-dressing really. And I suppose it's even possible it's a first arrest. Just.'

'He doesn't look all that respectable,' Elsa said. 'He doesn't look fixed abode and all that, does he?'

'He looks clever enough to fix it, is what I think,' Patrick said. 'What would it take to fix up an address, or an employer's reference? I've lied more than that on every CV I've ever sent out. Not that it's got me far, but you know, it's not exactly difficult. If you're not an essentially truthful person.'

'What is it you do again?' She was sure he must have told her, but she couldn't bring it to mind.

'Astronaut. Male model. You know. That kind of thing.'

'Oh right. What was it you were saying, about not being an essentially truthful person?'

'I never said that. Well, all right I did. I lie a lot, actually,' he said, 'and I do it well. And I know how easy it is. I don't think our Bryn would have too much trouble lying his way out of getting himself put into some bail hostel. Anyway, even if he was in, do you know anything about the security at those places?'

'No.' She imagined something like a jail, sliding doors made out of chunky steel bars with chipped paint, two-inch-thick bolts, guards with lots of big nasty things on their belts. Electronic alarms and slab-faced sadists watching monitor screens in bullet-proof enclosures and reading *Practical Photographer*.

'Well, no, nor me actually. But this friend I was talking to, he said imagine a college hall of residence. Corridors and rooms, but the rooms aren't locked, only the front door's locked, and anyone with any experience at all of jail, or remand, or even just care, will know how to get out whenever they want.'

'He's fairly well informed then, this friend?' Elsa said, and Patrick smiled again, made a subtle eloquent gesture, shook his head. Made wide eyes.

'OK. OK. But that was in another land, and besides the wench is dead. OK?'

'What?' She couldn't quite understand what he was telling her. 'What did you say?'

Patrick motioned her away with a sweep of his hand, nothing.

'Well,' he said after a few minutes. 'Well. OK, I did something...ill-advised, let's say. This was more than twelve years ago, incidentally.'

'Before or after the male modelling?'

'Yes. Look, I've packed a lot in, OK? I like to move on.' Something had come into his voice, a new quality she hadn't heard before, a restlessness. He was scanning the café, his eyes following people as they came and went, sucking up the activity and motion.

'Patrick? Look, how old are you anyway?' she said. So far she'd been guessing he was a few years older than her, twenty-eight, maybe thirty, maybe a couple of years more, but she was starting to wonder. And in this light...

He shrugged.

'Thirty?'

'Thirty-five?'

'Done.'

'Not that it matters, I was just curious. Sorry. What was it you were telling me?'

'Oh, that. My fascinating past. So anyway. It was a little business involving computer memory chips. You know the things I mean? It goes like this: someone gets an in at a high-tech place, say a software house or a games publisher or somewhere that has a lot of hardware on site. Not difficult, you just sign on at an agency. A lot of the people in these places are agency staff or on short-term contracts, temporary, part-time, consultancy basis, freelance, whatever. People coming and going all the time. Of course you do need to be able to do the job as well. So you wait a few weeks, get a key and the security codes. Then someone else comes in at night, opens up the computers and does a little operation on them. Kind of like a lobotomy? Fairly crude surgery. Takes away their little memories. These things are tiny, expensive, untraceable and vastly in demand. Really good currency. Really good. Negotiable.'

'So which one were you in this little outfit?'

'I was keys and codes. Of course, what do you think? The sneaky end of things. But we were being watched. God knows how. I never found out. The case collapsed, thank God, but I was two weeks in a bail hostel before it did.'

'Why? Wouldn't you be the kind of good risk that they wouldn't bother with?'

'It's embarrassing,' he said. 'Actually.' He didn't speak for a further few minutes. 'You see, I was put in for my own protection. They managed to convince me someone was going to get at me, and I was shitting myself. I'm a hell of a guy, yes? It was OK. It was like a special hotel for incredibly thick people.' He shook his head a few times. 'Actually it was funny, in a way. Anyway. If I'd wanted to, I mean if I hadn't been soiling myself every night thinking someone was going to break *in*, I could have got out pretty much whenever I wanted to. I mean, these are not high-security installations.' More eloquent gestures, more eager scanning.

Elsa watched him closely.

'Patrick?'

'Yes, Elsa.'

'That's not your only criminal experience, is it?' and he gestured again, so that she didn't know where she was with him, not really. He was interesting though.

Time was ticking away. She went back to the counter and got more tea and some bloated-looking apple pie with a great chewy wodge of baker's cream on it, all wrapped up in a dish with cling film. The cream and the plastic interfaced in an unpleasantly intimate way, the cream losing its precise piped crenellations and reverting to a more primitive state, taking the shape of the plastic and smearing up insinuatingly into the folds and creases. Patrick made a big deal of looking at his watch. Five to one. He was having a great time. He kept rocking back in his seat and looking at Elsa with raised eyebrows until she said 'What?' and he'd shake his head.

'Floral clock? Where is that anyway?'

'Round the corner from the courthouse,' Elsa said. 'Just a few minutes away.'

'Convenient then. So from here it's, what, thirty minutes' walk? Ten minutes on a bus? Or you could be flash and get a taxi.'

'What makes you think I'm going to go?'

'Oh, I just know you are. El-sa.' He was mocking her, grinning at her, playing with her.

'OK, look. If I do go, do you want to – I mean, you could

maybe come too.'

'Yeah, I know. I'll be in a taxi behind. The driver'll be Costa Rican, and he'll keep saying "Santa Maria" and crossing himself when we take the corners. We pull up at the floral clock. Sorry, florral clock. Bryn, he'll pull a gun, but I'll have you covered. "I'll go. Drop it, you sorry motherfuck." I've got bedding plants and I *really* know how to get maximum visual impact out of them ...'

'Will you stop it, Patrick? All I mean is, you could just come and make sure – '

'Make sure what, Elsa? What are you imagining now?'

She was picturing a gang of men bundling her into the back of a car, with Bryn overseeing operations. After that she didn't know what she was thinking.

'Because, look, if you're frightened of him – '

'I'm not, Patrick, I never said – '

'If you are, Elsa, then you have no business doing this. Have you?'

'I just meant – Well, I just thought that I'd be happier if I knew someone knew where I was and was watching out for me. It has nothing to do with being scared. I'm not scared of Bryn.'

'No?'

'No.'

'And why is that?'

'Because I don't think he's guilty.'

'Because ...'

'Because.'

'Oh, I see. I had no idea you'd reached such an advanced point in your thinking. Clearly, you've subjected this to a pretty damn meticulous analysis.'

'Like in court?'

'They're doing their best.'

'No one's doing their best for Bryn.'

'Except you. Whose motive is so pure.'

She shrugged.

Will Mr Drecker or Mr Shoe undertake telemetry and withstand noise abatement under a bridge or a tall tower. Mr

Shoe, telemetry and noise abatement. Thank you, said the Tannoy, enigmatically.

'Listen,' he said. 'You know what I said before, about being a good liar?'

'Uhuh.'

'So I can tell when someone's lying, unless they're good. And you are crap-o-la. The worst.'

'Oh right. Great. Everyone I talk to these days knows something about me. Bryn knows I'm too, whatever it is, too blinkered or something to be able to see his – his – whatever it is, whatever he wants me to see. And you now, well, you just know all about everything I do.'

'Hardly. I just think you should be clear. I don't think you're being *clear*. Look, Bryn Sweetman is by any normal standards in a bit of a scrape. Yes? His orbit is unstable. Maybe he's got away with it all up to now, whatever scummy thing it is, but now he's in the tangy shit and he's panicking. This note business, Jesus, he must be desperate. He is also, incidentally, a very, how to say it now . . . '

Elsa watched him.

'A very fit young offender. No?'

Elsa pretended not to understand the question.

'Elsa?'

'If you say so,' she said, but she was blushing again.

'Oh right, you hadn't even noticed.'

'Noticed what?'

'Oh right. So if he looked like some weird old bastard in a shell suit, just for example, you'd be just as interested.'

'Yes, I would.'

'No, you wouldn't.'

'Patrick, I *would*.'

'You are a lying tart and you know it.'

'*Patrick* – '

'Look at you, you're blushing. You are the crappest liar in Western Europe. He's a fine firm spunky lad and you want him on his knees. Say it ain't so.'

She tried to look coldly at him.

'He is also extremely ready to use that in any way he can,'

Patrick went mercilessly on. 'He's energetic. He's using it on you. And you are happy for him to use it on you. Seemingly. Now that may make you many things, but what it doesn't make you is a tireless fighter for justice.'

'He's nineteen.'

'He's skilful. Elsa?' No response. 'You don't agree?'

She shook her head, not 'no', just not answering.

'Well,' Patrick said, and sat back, looked away from her. 'I think he's guilty. Which means I think he could be trouble. So yes, I'll come along too.'

'Thank you.'

'Don't mention it.'

There will be collusion and obloquy. There will be collusion and obloquy please. Thank you.

'OK, look,' she said, 'look, I might as well wait there as here. Let's go.'

He stood up.

'Wait. I'm going for a piss. Think. Then when I come back, if you still want to, we will.'

They decided on a bus, a little stunted old ladies' special. Elsa suddenly felt giddy, and reached for Patrick's hand. He looked at her enquiringly, but she shook her head, and let his hand go.

He rummaged about inside his wallet and produced a card: Philip Wetheral, bespoke web solutions, it said. Phone and fax and e-mail.

'Patrick? Why are you giving me someone else's business card?'

'My card.'

'Are you telling me that you don't use your own name, at work?'

'I believe I mentioned creative CV-making?'

'Anyway, this is your work number, isn't it?'

'Yeah?'

'So you're not at work, are you? You're on jury service.'

'Ah, but see, when you turn it over...'

Another number, a mobile number, in green biro.

She shook suddenly, imagining some circumstance in which she might need to ring this number; she pictured a rain-beaten phone box, desperate fingers made clumsy with fear trying to shove coins into the slot, then a face on the glass outside, grinning, bitten nails, hands forcing open the door, a rag shoved into her mouth. Oh no! It's Bible Bill! And what exactly does he think he's going to do with that staple gun...

'Right.' They stood on the other side of the floral clock while Elsa nerved herself up. Patrick was going to wait inside a kebab shop over the road, Elsa would come out and signal to him when she was sure she was safe. However she was going to know when *that* was.

'Why would anyone want a floral clock anyway?' he said, just to fill the time, pondering the big mound of earth with the clock in it and the ugly showy plants bedded in, on top and around. 7.45 it said, honest.

'Someone must have woken up thinking, I know! I know! We'll have a clock but it'll be in the *soil*. Yeah? And, and we'll put a shitload of plants all over it, and it'll never, ever tell the right time! In fact, it'll never even go at all! And someone else must have said, Ah, that's brilliant that is, Col. That'll put this place on the map all right. Let's go and dig a big hole right now.'

Elsa sighed. She wasn't in the mood for distraction. She was trying to concentrate on not feeling nervous.

'Well,' he said. 'You're sure you want to do this?'

She nodded tensely.

'OK. Be sensible.'

'Yes.'

'Be alert.'

'Yes, all right, Patrick...'

'Try not to be a complete dick. I'll be waiting. Ring me tonight.'

'Right,' she said. 'OK. See you in court tomorrow.'

She took a deep breath and pushed open the door of the Clock Café. There was no one at all in the place. It was too ugly for that. Decorated in a hurry in 1984, it had never recovered and was now quietly awaiting death. There was a vast illuminated picture of a mountain, which dominated one whole wall. The seats and tables were fixed; too narrow, too shiny, over-upholstered. There was much use of black-and-white-check Formica trim to things. Light came in only from the front, partly impeded by nets and fiddly little signs, partly obstructed by a big gloomy church nearby. The counter was stacked high with rock cakes and Penguin biscuits from the late eighties. A woman emerged from a dark, awful little area at the back and Elsa ordered coffee and a cheese sandwich, and took a seat by the window.

The sandwich when it came was exactly what she had ordered, almost ironically so. It was two pieces of sliced white bread with a piece of sliced processed cheese in between, and traces of a yellowish scrape of some sort on the bread. It would undoubtedly have met the legal minimum requirement for a cheese sandwich. It was, in its way, perfect. She didn't particularly want to eat it though. What it seemed to call for, in fact, was documentation: she wanted to photograph it.

She was a good half-hour early. She considered going out and coming back again, but felt unable to do so in case it threw Patrick into a panic. She looked out of the window and felt the counter woman's eyes on her. She didn't think the coffee was going to last a whole half-hour.

Bryn banged in ten minutes later.

'You right?' he said, and stood over her, shifting his weight, leaning towards the door.

'Don't you want a cup of tea or something?' Elsa said.

'What, *here*?'

She was aware of the woman's eyes following her as she stood. The ur-sandwich sat sadly on its plate, flat and grey and pristine.

'You right or what?' he said, hurrying her out, and she finished the coffee in one gulp.

'Coming. God, give me a minute, will you?'

**BOOK TWO
...INTO THE LABYRINTH**

Interview conducted by: Detective Inspector T.M. Waalgren
and Detective Sergeant M.M. Loamas.

With: Mr B.L. Sweetman, DOB: 5–2–1974.

Also present: n/a.

Interview number: 96–005183/ESPC/20–7–96; *Crime number*: 96–00518.

Interview held at: Interview room 5, Hove Police Station.

Date/time: Friday 26 July 1996, 10.35 a.m.

Pages 2–6 of 11.

DI Waalgren: *Of course, you know who we've got in the other room?*

B.L.S: *Give up. You tell me.*

DI Waalgren: *We've got your friend. Your little – pal. Mr Hegler.*

B.L.S: *Yeah, well, he'll just tell you the same as me. We was together, we never went nowhere near Harry's shop that day.*

DI Waalgreen: *Yes, we've heard all that. No, this is something different. Actually.*

(Long pause)

B.L.S: *Oh, yeah?*

DI Waalgren: *Yes. I think you probably know what I'm talking about.*

B.L.S: *Who me? No idea, mate.*

DI Waalgren: *No idea. Really. That's interesting. Do you know Mr Hegler well? Big pal of yours?*

B.L.S: *He's my mate.*

DI Waalgren: *Yes, we know about – about, er, that. Well, problem is, Mr Hegler has apparently been with us before. Possession with intent, class-B Amphetamines? I don't know if he ever mentioned that to you. Your mate.*

B.L.S: *Yeah.*

DI Waalgren: *Probation order, on that occasion. So if I were him, I wouldn't – yeah? I wouldn't be bringing myself to anyone's attention right now.*

B.L.S: *He's clean.*

DI Waalgren: *Oh, what, today you mean? Right now? Oh*

101

yes, we've had a good long look at him, and he is as you say clean. Today.

B.L.S: *You keep your fucking paws off my mate, you –*

DI Waalgren: *Please sit down, Mr Sweetman. Mr Sweetman! Thank you. Now as I understand it, a body search has been –*

B.L.S: *You keep your fucking dirty paws –*

DI Waalgren: *... has been conducted. Please try not to get agitated, Mr Sweetman –*

B.L.S: *You...*

DI Waalgren: *... an intimate...*

B.L.S: *You listen right, you so much as –*

DI Waalgren:*... an intimate body search. Nothing was found, on this occasion. On this occasion. But as you will be fully aware, Mr Sweetman, because of the terms of Mr Hegler's probation order, we will be finding it necessary to conduct further searches of Mr Hegler's, ah, person, from time to time... As often as we think necessary. To fulfil the terms of the probation order. Of course, if we feel that Mr Hegler is co-operating fully with us on this matter with Mr Hook... I'm sure you take my point here. His recollection of events may change. On some future occasion. We'll just have to wait and see.*

(Pause)

B.L.S: *Look. Look right. We weren't there. I told you. We was together.*

DI Waalgren: *Yes. Yes. Well. We'll see about that. In due course. Won't we! Oh, by the way, strictly routine, but as a known associate of Mr Hegler's, we will also be finding it necessary to conduct searches of your, er, person as well...*

DS Loamas: (coughing)...

DI Waalgren: *... as often as we think necessary. I take it you intend to co-operate fully... Mr Sweetman!*

BEING PISSED

'Patrick? Patrick, that you?' Elsa's voice was thick and stupid, because she was pissed. 'Patrick?'

'Hello? Elsa?'

'Patrick? Listen, Patrick? Is that you?'

'Elsa? Where are you? What time is it?' His voice was skewed and slightly indignant, because he was also drunk, though unlike her he had been asleep as recently as ten seconds ago. 'Are you all right? Where are you?'

So far the conversation had been made up entirely of questions, and Elsa sought to break the pattern.

'Listen. I'm in a phone box somewhere, up the other end of town, you know? Where no one ever goes? Anyway I thought I should ring you up, to – '

'Are you drunk?'

'Am I what? Patrick?'

'I said, are you drunk, because frankly I think you are.'

'Well, yes I am, actually. You see, what happened...'

Well, it was obvious what had happened, obvious to Patrick, obvious to Elsa. Bryn, who was twitching and cracking his considerable knuckles outside the phone box, it was obvious to him too.

She and Bryn had left the café, and Elsa had waved to Patrick: all clear! No gangs of beefy miscreants bundling her into the back of a car, no gag, no juicy spurting terror. Just Bryn, all cocky, and her.

They'd walked along for a bit, neither speaking. Bryn's cheeks were working, he appeared to be chewing something, but all it resulted in was spitting: the cheek movements were needed to assemble the gob, apparently. Elaborate, strenuous spitting. He also delivered himself of some wrenching hawking sounds, wet and deep and complex; Elsa could almost feel the tissues stretching and tearing inside his thorax. He didn't seem to have anything he wanted to tell or show, not right at the moment. He didn't want to communicate at all, he wasn't in the mood.

What he *was* in the mood for was a very serious kind of walking, all bollocks-too-big bandy swagger and loose arms and hands, all over the pavement, black urban terrorist stuff. He was wearing baggy jeans and Stussy top and knitted cap, big trainers. If there had been a mall in Brighton he would have been perfect, hanging round outside Snow 'n' Ski or Motto, with a posse, a little mini-gang of trainee young offenders learning the challenging behaviour, the lean-and-strut routines, how to look blank, how to menace without actually moving, how to spit, how to do that thing with your hand, that check-this-out flick of the cock. Only once did he falter, when a woman with a buggy forced him to break stride. It took him a few paces to get the rhythm back.

This went on for a few minutes, as they headed into the heaving centre of Brighton. Elsa suddenly thought to ask where they were going, and he shrugged.

'You tell me.'

'I thought we were going somewhere. I thought you were going to – '

'Yeah, yeah.' He was deeply preoccupied. He was not to be drawn into general conversation about where and what. This was high street cool; you didn't talk.

They reached Debenhams and she halted.

'Bryn?'

He turned to look at her.

'What?'

'Can we stop for a minute?'

'Why?'

'Because I want to know where we're going.' He gestured towards Burger King, Argos, wasps, and several thousand lost European teenage language students.

'Here. We're going here.'

'OK, look.' They were opposite a pub, perhaps inevitably; it would have been difficult not to have been. 'Look. Do you want to get a drink or something?' This was Elsa Frith, in the middle of a day. She almost never went into pubs in the day. It was tantamount to watching daytime television.

The pub was called *The Cock and Culprit*; it was one that she had passed many many thousands of times and never once even considered the possibility of entering. It looked cool and cavernous and empty and Elsa thought they might even have some Guinness in there somewhere.

Inside Bryn immediately sat at a small table and clearly expected Elsa to get the drinks. He dragged heavy iron-legged stools around until he had enough space to sprawl his legs out in the expansive way he favoured. Plenty of bollock room, his legs said. Don't fence me in, bitch, these are some *big* mothers.

'What are you having?' she said, and he shrugged, as if to state a preference might not be cool. She sighed.

'Bryn? I don't know what you want.'

He muttered something and she bent down to hear him better.

'Deaf or what? I said, Baileys black top.'

'What?'

'Bai-leys, blackcurrant top. Do you want me to spell it?'

Baileys? *Baileys?* But Baileys was just Malibu without the kick, why would he want that? And with blackcurrant? It would just be a sugary toothaching nightmare. It was the kind of thing Bible Bill might hanker after, actually, she thought.

Still. If that's what he wanted. She stood at the bar for a while, then went to look round the other side, where a girl in a sort of storm-tossed Jennifer Aniston hair-do dragged sleepy eyes to her and lifted one eyebrow about one eighth of one inch: yes?

The Guinness leaked from the tap, dank and mossy and smooth as a river stone. Jennifer Aniston looked regretfully away into the body of the pub, her head slightly tilted, her eyes shrouded with sorrow, her hand resting dispiritedly on the tap. Elsa caught the wonderful bright encouraging gleam of a Malibu bottle on a high shelf above the till, alongside bottles of more improbable liquids that surely only really came out at Christmas, if at all. Pimm's, Chartreuse, Archers. Would anyone ever stroll in here, saunter up to the bar, get the attention of this poor grieving creature with her heart-broken hair and say, Benedictine and Coke, love, and give us a bag of barbecue beef McCoys with it?

Bryn eyed her pint of Guinness as she came back to the table.
'What you drinking that for? You a lez or something?'
She managed to ignore him and applied herself to the glass.
He seemed to have his eye on someone, a moody figure sitting at the bar just over from their table, all fear-in-the-pool-room attitude. Elsa could make out only a shaved head and a thick forbidding leather jacket, plus one damaged ear. Quite what Bryn's interest was she couldn't discern. And there was someone else, deep in the dripping body of the pub, who seemed to be monitoring Bryn's movements. Again, she didn't know why. Except that she'd noticed that people just did look at him. She was doing it now. What must it be like, she wondered, to be the kind of person people watch?

'Patrick? So we were in the pub – '
'Elsa, you've said that already. Are you sure you're – '
'No, listen, right... What was I saying?'

Neither the Guinness nor the Baileys lasted long, and jilted Jennifer was soon dispensing again. Bryn just seemed to want to sit there, staring at the boards between his feet, which he shuffled occasionally, his profile describing various angles respective to the floor, the face working constantly, as if expressing some unending internal self-justification. Or perhaps he was just dislodging food particles.

Elsa hadn't eaten anything since the wartime apple pie with Patrick in the Co-op café. The Guinness was hitting her stomach hard. Also the residual tension of the day, of the situation with Bryn, seemed to be having an effect, loosening muscles and drying her mouth.

'So, Bryn,' she said, 'listen, I don't really know anything about you.'

He shrugged without lifting his eyes from the fascinating cracks in the floor.

'Yeah, so?'

'Where are you from?'

'Runcorn.'

'Runcorn? Where's that?'

He shrugged. 'You know. Near Liverpool. There's this big bridge and everything.'

So he came from somewhere where there was a bridge. Ah.

'Right, and what made you move down here?'

'Huh. Well. Yeah.'

'Or, you know, how old are you and are you married and have you got a job or anything? I don't remember any of that coming up in court.' It must have done though, surely? She can't have been listening.

'Uh?'

'Bryn, this really isn't going to work at all unless you tell me things.'

'Yeah, so what you want to know all that stuff for? Eh?'

'Well, it doesn't have to be that, it could be, it could be... Well, for instance – '

'Yeah, well, I'll tell you something, once this trial has fucking happened and finished, then I'm fucking off right out of here. I'm going to America.'

'Really?' She injected enthusiasm and interest into her voice, but he just looked briefly half-face at her, then went back to his study of shadow and floorboard.

'Yeah, I got a mate in Miami actually, he does this thing on the beach, he's a human juke box.'

'He's – sorry, he . . . '

Bryn shifted and sighed. He was increasingly listless. 'He gets inside this, this, it's like a box made out of hardboard or something, and on the front there are all these little holes and there's the name of a record beside them, right, and someone comes up and puts, they like push a finger into the hole, right, beside the name of the song, and then my mate, he sings it. Yeah?'

Elsa was at a loss. She was also appalled. It was such a stupid idea.

'Oh!' she said. 'That's interesting.'

'No, it isn't, it's a fucking heap of shite.'

'So . . . '

'So why do I want to do it?'

'Yes.'

'I don't.'

'But I thought – '

'Look, just forget it, will you?' He banged off to the toilets, watched by the shadow, the lurker in the back. The hunched leather jacket also turned one ear and a thick piece of rhino shoulder to take him in. You had to go up one step to the toilet and the door was stiff and noisy. In the infinite silent desolation of the pub it was like a Jean-Michel Jarre Millennial Extravaganza. Even Jennifer had a little disconsolate peek. Elsa felt very on her own suddenly, and dedicated herself to the Guinness. Fuck it, she thought, if he can have Baileys and black, I can have Malibu. Double. On the rocks. And if I happen to want a little lime twist as well, that's up to me, isn't it? She felt her shoulders stiffening defensively. Double Malibu, on ice, piece of lime. She practised saying it. She guessed there was no chance of getting milk to go with it in here, they'd never do it for you in pubs.

Bryn seemed happier when he returned. He exchanged a quick vibey glance with leather jacket, and slumped back into his seat. He drained off his Baileys and fiddled with the glass.

'Aren't you going to get one then?' she said, and he stared at her, completely wrong-footed for a moment.

'Yeah, all right.' He stood and she she told him what she wanted.

'Stopped being a lez, have you?'

She didn't reply, and he stood, right on top of her. She looked up at him.

'So? Give us the money then,' he said.

She let her eyes rest on him as he waited at the bar. He hooked one foot up onto the foot rail, and his arse suddenly came into focus. Everything he did seemed designed to display himself in some way or other, though possibly he couldn't help it. Leather jacket was mumbling to himself, and Bryn turned to look at him, caught his eye, winked, twitched his head. Leather jacket said something, Elsa couldn't hear what, some subsonic rumbling, and Bryn ducked in towards him and put one hand on the side of his head, tucked his head down, and whispered something. Elsa was sure there was going to be a fight but Leather jacket just wobbled his head – he was completely pissed, she realized – and moved his shoulders. He looked as if he was trying to stand up; his back tensed and his legs moved, he was ready to go. Then all was relaxation again; he gave up on the idea. Fuck it.

The Malibu was cool and overcast with icy patches. Bryn hadn't managed to get any lime out of Jennifer. Elsa suspected that he hadn't even asked. Half-way down the glass she realized that the loose feeling in her back and legs wasn't residual tension or any of that, but was the simple predictable effect of Guinness and then Malibu on a nearly empty stomach. She was on her way to being pissed. They hadn't even been here long, had they? Somewhere also was the knowledge that if she was just now starting to wonder whether or not she was pissed yet, then she most definitely was. Or was at least no longer quite sober, you might perhaps put it that way. She stood to go to the toilet, and had to nudge her stool back. She tried to do it naturally, soberly, and couldn't quite be certain she could remember how. It seemed to come out rather jerky. It would have to do.

When she came back Bryn was gone. Her eyes quickly found him, deep in the dark heart of the pub, standing by the shadow, the watcher. Oh, God, this looks like trouble, she thought, face off, and then she saw them exchange some kind of convolute jailbird handshake, an ordinary shake followed up with a fancy change of grip pivoting on the meat of the thumb and a sharp downward tug. Bryn's face was in the shadow's face. B-wing buddies.

He walked back and she was again struck by his gait. It was so much more than a way of moving his body around the world, it was a vehicle for all sorts of messages and slogans: don't fuck with me, fuck off, just fuck. He was back by her side and sprawling the legs again.

She was in the middle of thinking out what to say next when he was suddenly on his feet again, back to Leather jacket, more whispering. Leather jacket was too befuddled to really respond, beyond wobbling his head and moving his mouth around. He started to speak, but Bryn had gone again, back to Elsa.

'So. Where were we?' he said, and winked. Elsa realized that she had to ring Liam. It was now, unbelievebly, gone seven and he was due round at eight; they were supposed to be going to see a big-budget sci-fi film called *Native Breed*. There was a payphone on the other side of the bar.

'Li?'

'Yeah, I'm on my way, I just got a bit held up. Vicki lost all the presets on the telly – '

'No, Li, listen, er, listen. We're going to have to make it another night.'

Nothing back.

'Li?'

'Oh.'

'You don't mind, do you? It's just...' What? It's just what? Think now. 'I've kind of got held up myself actually. I'm...'

'Where are you calling from? It sounds like a pub.'

No good lying, he could 1471 the number.

'Yeah, I'm in this pub, it's er...'

She couldn't finish the sentence, and Liam couldn't come up with anything either. Thick fizzy silence down the phone.

'OK. Well, we'll make it another night then.'

'Yeah. Li?'

'Yeah?'

'Look, I'm sorry about this, it's just – '

'No, it's totally cool. Really.'

Totally cool, she was thinking as she came back to Bryn, totally cool. Where had he got that from? Chi, presumably. They were a pretty mixed bunch at chi: one of them had had a unique oneness experience recently. Which must have been a totally cool kind of a thing to have, she reflected, but what if one day Liam came back and said, hey, you're never going to believe this, but guess what I had at chi today? That's right, a unique oneness experience! Totally cool or *what*! On that day, she had long ago decided, she would tell him to fuck off for good and all. If he knew what was good for him he'd steer pretty damn clear of unique oneness experiences.

'Patrick? You know, I mean I'm not saying we didn't have a drink, because, you know, we did actually.'

'No kidding.'

'I thought, you know, it might make communication a bit easier because he's not actually the easiest person in the world to have a conversation with.'

'He's not?'

'Not really...'

'You again.' This was Bryn saying hello as she came back to the table. 'You back again, are you?.'

'So look. We having another one or what?'

'Go on then, twist me arm.'

She gave him a hard look.

'Against your religion, is it?'

'Eh? What you on about now?'

'Putting your hand in your pocket. Against your religion?'

'Don't get you...'

'Bryn. Are you going to buy me a drink or what?'

'What?' he said, and they both fell about a bit. They were much drunker than either of them realized.

'No, but really, I'm getting a bit low here.'

'Christ.' He stomped ill-naturedly to the bar and summoned Jennifer by shouting, 'Oi! Cunt-ache!'

'You see, the thing about Liam, I mean I really like him, I really really...'

'Yeah, well, that's just as well, isn't it, considering he's supposed to be your boyfriend.'

'You must meet him some time, I think you'd like him, I think you'd really really...'

'Yeah, well, I don't think so. No chance. He sounds like some kind of total sponkhead if you ask me.'

'Sponkhead? Liam?' She gave the matter serious thought for a moment. God, she thought, what if he is? 'Noooo. What, *Liam*? No.'

'Sorry to be the one to tell you, love, but he sounds a lot like one to me.'

'What, Liam? *Liam*? No!'

'Yeah, well, you obviously can't tell.'

'Yeah and you haven't even met him...'

'Don't need to.'

'You can just tell.'

'Yup.'

'Bryn, that isn't exactly very flattering to me, is it?'

'Yeah, well, that's not my problem, is it? There's only one thing to do about a sponkhead like that.'

'Which is...'

He smashed a fist into his palm. 'Just deck him.'

'Uhuh. Oh right. So I just deck Liam.'

'Yeah and then you say, OK, listen, sponkhead, fucking go and peddle it elsewhere, champ, because *I* don't fucking *need* it, right? You sad fuck.'

'Oh, that's what you'd do, is it?'

'Correct.'

'Bryn, this is my boyfriend you're talking about.'

'As I say, not my problem, love. Anyway, I reckon he's only got...' He made a gesture with his little finger pointing lewdly upwards. 'Yeah? Wrong, am I?'

This was choice wit, Bryn Sweetman style. She tried to look offended, but she couldn't keep it up and they were falling about again.

'No, but the thing about Liam...'

'Oh, will you fucking pack it *in* about Liam? Eh? I'm fucking up to here with him.'

'No, but you see the thing about Liam...'

He made his gesture and they fell about.

'Patrick?'

'Elsa, ask yourself the following questions. Are you being careful? Vigilant? Alert? Oh no. No, you're not. Try "pissed" You're being "pissed", aren't you?'

'Yeah, but Patrick? You see, what happened...'

She couldn't believe it was so late. She couldn't believe she was so pissed. Bryn was walking beside her and they were going back to his house. Was this going to be it, the showing? She didn't care too much though just at this moment, what she most wanted was to lie down. They seemed to have been walking for miles, right up the wrong end of town. They had fallen quiet, they were just jogging along together. The words 'ring Patrick' passed through her head from time to time, and she even articulated them a few times.

'Ring Patrick.'

'Yeah, you said.'

There weren't any phone boxes though. This was the land that time forgot. Off-licences and launderettes and video shops, that was about it. Bryn didn't seem to know what she meant by 'phone box'. Then she saw one, and aimed herself single-mindedly, if a little blurrily, at it. The door gave her some trouble. There was a wide range of services on offer on cards all over the information panel and on the scarred little ledge. Odd old-fashioned words you hardly ever saw any more, like 'mistress' and 'busty'.

'Patrick? That you?'

*

The door to Bryn's house crashed open and a bicycle fell down in front of them. He fumbled for the little push-button light switch and got tangled up in the bike frame and cursed. He grabbed hold of Elsa and they both fell, all legs and bicycle and noise. He grazed his shin and rubbed it.

'Well, I was going to try to be quiet,' he said, 'but you know.' His voice rang out up the dark stairwell and she shushed him.

They reached his door, which was on the ground floor towards the back, and he couldn't get his key in. 'Trouble with me,' he said, 'is that I'm a drunken bastard. Basically.'

He braced himself against the door and started giving it a good kicking, and Elsa coolly took the keys from his hot fist and opened the door.

More fumbling for the lights. You'd think I'd never been in here before he said, you'd think I should at least know where the cunt light switch is. You'd think that, wouldn't you?

The light came on and Elsa took everything in at once. At first she thought there was something wrong with the light, but then she realized it was just a quality attaching to everything in the room: it seemed to absorb more light than it reflected, it soaked it up into the thick spongy upholstery like treacle or salt water. Everything horrible, nothing nice, she thought. Horrible old crap everywhere.

For instance: a rectangular cushion, in shades of lime, beige and chocolate, rounded rectangular outlines of alternating colour in thick-and-thin lines, one corner torn revealing prosthetic-coloured foam rubber. This on top of a chair which is maroon and pink and flowery. (No good journey ever started out from this chair.) Big sideboard thing, too big for the room, drawers missing, bits sticking out of it, solid, scarred, club-footed. Huge, dirty-white wardrobe, sliding doors, grubby round the handles, which were curly-wurly and gold-coloured, attached with screws which were the wrong colour, and which were sticking out at odd angles. Take a look at the bed. And heaped up all round it clothes and bedclothes and bin bags. Assembled, woven, assimilated into it all were items of crockery with fag ash all over them and fag packets and ashtrays. Everything was an ashtray. The sink. Marble-effect Formica, peeling away to reveal...Look away.

'I'm supposed to be getting a better room after Christmas, when some cunt upstairs goes away or dies or whatever he's doing,' he said. 'Right at the top. So it's a bit quieter. There's something about sleeping on the ground floor. Don't you think?'

What she thought was that there was something about sleeping in an ashtray, but she managed not to say it.

The room was still warm from the day, with a fluffy, comfy smell of human and food and rubbish mixed up cosy together, sort of a *compote*. Light came in from the street, and Bryn stumbled over to pull the curtains. He started messing about with a Calor gas heater, trying to get it lit, but Elsa stopped him. He just didn't seem to know what he was doing.

'Ha hay!' Bryn said lewdly, and gave her his best narrow eyes, then slumped into the floral armchair wedged in by the fireplace and seemed to forget what he was supposed to be doing.

'Show you round in a minute,' he said. 'Get me breath.'

Elsa sat on the edge of the bed and watched him. His head was jerking forward periodically, then jerking back again as he dozed. She adjusted the bedding, trying not to examine any of it too closely but just even it out a bit so that it was possible to sit comfortably. Even her low standards were outraged. After about ten minutes she bundled some of it against the wall and sat against it, her legs stretched out on the bed, avoiding one very large stain in particular. She could still see the back of his neck and part of one ear.

'Yeah, well,' he said after about ten minutes.

She let half an hour go past, then she stood up unsteadily and put the light off, the room suddenly growing full of shadows from the streetlamps. Cars passed, and distorted beams and reflections crawled across the ceiling and down the walls. There were occasional voices as people walked past, brisk or excited or slurred. Many people were having intense arguments, more than you would expect in daylight.

For a time there were at least four voices at once, somewhere near by. The sounds rose and fell, sometimes overlapping. For a long time no one spoke and there were the sounds of shoes shuffling back and forth. Upstairs she heard a voice, ooooooh yeeeeeeah, it said, as if coming from the darkest part of the deepest dream. Heavy footsteps, doors. Water running. Then back. Oooooooh. Oooooooh *yeeeeeeeeeah*.

What in God's name am I doing here? she thought, as drunk battled with sober, and drunk won. Got to get home, got to get home *now*.

Then she passed out.

Some time that night she felt him fumbling his way into bed beside her, dragging at the ridiculous tangle of blankets and sheets and pillows. He was sneezing, reaching a cold elbow over her as he reached about for something, found it, and then he was blowing his nose, repeatedly, then an ugly honking sound as he tried to clear his sinuses. He wriggled about, bits of him flailing: at one point he had one foot and a bit of leg crossed over her ankle, then he twitched it away again. She lay awake for a few minutes. The house was now completely silent. He snorted occasionally and twisted about in his sleep.

OOOOOOH YEEEEEEAH

'Morning.' He was grinning over her with a cup of coffee, and she sat up in bed, trying to straighten out some of the chaos of bedding. She felt gritty and hot and bitten. Hung over. God, what was she playing at? She had court, didn't she? The memory of Guinness and Malibu briefly flooded her mouth and she swallowed repeatedly.

'What time is it?'

'Eight,' he said. 'Things to do.' He sat at the bottom of the bed and watched her wake up. She tried to drag her hair into some kind of order, but it was all over the place, delinquent, mocking her. Gorgeous, it said? Not today, baby...The room was flooded with light.

'You,' he said, 'look like shite.'

'Oh, well, great,' she said, and he laughed.

He rested his coffee on the bed, and stroked both hands over his stubbly head.

'You should get one of these,' he said. 'Bonehead. Then you never have to worry about having a bad hair day. Just run it under the hot tap couple of times a week, give it a shave every ten days or so, that's it.' His hands stroked the knobbles and contours, fingers exploring the scalp, digging into the flesh, then he rubbed vigorously with his palms and smiled.

'Plus it's very, very sexy,' he said, and stuck his lips out and squinted. 'Feels nice when you get it up under someone's bollocks. Rub it all over his nob and round his arse. Drive him mental. Particularly useful if he's taking a long time. Coming, I mean.'

'Well, I'll bear that in mind next time I'm in Toni & Guy for a restyle,' she said. 'I'll tell them that.'

'Anyway, what we've got to do, we've got to have a look round here 'cos I need to find Pest for a minute, then I need to go to my mate's because I've got clean clothes there, then I've got to see a man about a dog at about eleven.'

'Why are your clean clothes somewhere else?'

He leaned back and frowned at her.

'Well, look, they just are. Can't keep anything clean here, it all just gets...'

'...assimilated?'

'Well, I was going to say fucked. Same thing probably.'

'Anyway, how can you see someone at eleven? We're in court, aren't we?'

'Yeah, yeah, yeah. But you know, just in case it gets all fucked up again like yesterday...'

'Bryn, do you know something about this trial that I don't?'

'You what?'

'It's just, well, you seem to know, I mean you've made arrangements for later on, you know...'

'Just hedging my bets, love.'

He was up and moving around, sifting through a pile of assorted clothes. He was methodical, lifting and disentangling each'item, bringing it to his face and sniffing, then chucking it either onto the bed or back onto the floor. He seemed to have about thirty near-identical Fred Perry polo shirts. He was rhythmic too, and she watched him, the sure, quick, twitchy movements like a little machine dance or someone practising a golf-swing.

'Who's Pest?' Elsa said.

'Cunt upstairs,' he said, as he sniffed and sorted and swayed. 'He's upstairs. He's great. He's my mate. I'll take you up.'

Sniff, sway, chuck. In between some of the movements he threw in a little extra gesture, a flick or a twist or a nod, just for the hell of it or to fill up the rhythm.

'He's brilliant, he tells you things. He's always telling you things, which are mostly bollocks actually, as a matter of fact. He can never remember what he's said, so you'll go, oi, what about that girl that was supposed to be round? and he's, you know, what girl? He's my best mate in Brighton. He's my only mate actually.'

'I thought everyone was your mate.'

'Yeah, well, there's mates and mates. Pest's brilliant though. And he'll give you stuff. Although, when I first came here I thought he was a cunt. To start with.'

'Why?'

'Why? Because he used to throw his glue bags out the window and they landed on my ledge.'

'What do you mean, glue bags?'

'He's a glue boy. So you need these little, like, freezer bags, that's what you have, and then when you've had it you throw them out the window onto some bastard's ledge.'

'I don't understand. Why do you need the bags?'

'Look, I'll get him to show you, all right?' He was impatient. 'He can show you. Anyway he used to throw his bags out, and I didn't know what they were. Then I figured it out so I went up there and I was banging on the door like a bastard, but he wouldn't answer, so I just kicked it in, and he's sitting there going don't hurt me, don't hurt me. I never! So I said, any more of your little bags, champ, and I'll shove them up your skinny arse.' Arse came out 'airse'. 'Then he gets all brave and he's going, you and who's army? All that old chat. So we had this big row, and then he was all right. I still get bags, though, I think he just forgets. He gets all glued up and he can't think what he's doing. He's brilliant. He's falling about up there going, ooooooh yeeeeeeah, like he's having his arse fucked or something, but he isn't, he says he doesn't know why he does it. Ooooooooh yeeeeeeeeah.'

'I heard him last night,' Elsa said, and was surprised at the memory, the deep disturbing underwater moaning floating down through the silent house. It had sounded like the slowest most uninhibited sex, the kind of sound someone would make when they'd forgotten that anyone else could hear, that there was anyone else in the world, the sound right at the stretched aching heart of the thing. Ooooooh yeeeeeeah.

'Sounds like some stupid porn film,' Bryn said. 'Actually, he'd be brilliant for dubbing. He's better than a lot of them I've met. You wouldn't want to see him though.'

He finished his sorting.

'Listen, give us a couple of quid and I'll go and get something to eat. Yeah?' Elsa couldn't immediately think where her bag was, then saw a corner of it sticking out from behind some bedding. It was in the process of being assimilated apparently. She dug it out and handed over three pound coins. Bryn winked and swayed, looking at her for a moment, and she thought he was wanting more, but he was seemingly just looking at her. She felt herself start to blush under his scrutiny. His head swayed from side to side, though his eyes didn't leave her. He balanced the coins on the back of one hand and tossed them into his palm. Made a fist. Wink. Then he was gone.

He took her upstairs, and knocked on a door, and she heard a voice from inside the room say, 'Yeah?'

'This is Pest, I was telling you about.'

Bryn pushed the door open. Pest was smiling by the window, looking as if he'd just been caught out in something small but shaming. Bryn went over and grabbed hold of him, put an arm round his neck and rubbed his palm against Pest's head. Elsa stood in the open doorway, uncertain.

'My mate,' he said, and he and Pest stood together, Bryn's arm round his neck still, both bobbing and grinning at Elsa. 'My best mate.'

'I'm everyone's best mate,' Pest said and shrugged. Elsa smiled and said, 'Hello.'

Bryn released him and meandered round the room. Elsa couldn't remember why they had to see Pest; she wasn't certain in fact that Bryn had even specified a reason.

'Would you like to come in?' Pest said, shyly smiling, and Elsa came in. The room was much smaller than Bryn's and much tidier, with no smell. There seemed to be only one chair though so she sat in that, by the window. She found that she was looking at a stack of tubs of something, a neat array in front of the fireplace, and she leaned forward to see.

'Got your supplies then, I see,' Bryn said, and Pest nodded. 'Yeah.'

'How many you get?'

'Dozen.'

'They on offer?'

'No.'

'They give you a discount?'

'No, I just wanted them all at once. You know.' He sounded apologetic.

'Fucking Pest,' Bryn said, and twisted his arm up behind his back. 'Cunt, incha?'

Pest wriggled away and went to stand by Elsa, grinning at her. She picked up a tub and looked closely: it was called Thixofix. It was a yellow and grey tub, and the logo was a very pleasing one, raked a little forward, the slightly angular letters joined up with thick strokes to make it look like a kind of stylized handwriting, and the bar of the capital 't' stretched right across the whole word. Fastened to the top of the tub was a grey plastic thing that looked a little like a comb for a midget.

She realized what the tub actually contained.

'Oh!' She smiled at Pest, who was watching her anxiously, as if he feared that she would disapprove of something.

'It's a very good brand actually,' he said, and she nodded, oh, of course. 'And if you get the 600 mil. size then you get the spreader as well.'

'Yeah, and what do you want the fucking spreaders for? Eh?' Bryn demanded.

'Yeah, well, you get them anyway,' he muttered, and took the tub from Elsa's hand. He ran a finger over the logo, then carefully replaced the tub on the stack.

'He's got all of them going the same way,' Bryn said, and Elsa looked again and smiled politely, completely uncertain of what a good response might be to any of this.

'It's called facing them up,' Pest said. 'So they're all facing the same way, yeah? It makes them look nice.' He gave the tub a little nudge. 'I like them to look nice.'

'Tell her where you get them,' Bryn said, and Pest looked helpless for a second, as if Bryn was going to make him do something embarrassing. He looked at Elsa, and she realized that he hadn't asked her who she was or why she was there. He didn't seem to feel that any explanation for her presence in his neat room was needed.

'There's this shop down on Edward Street.'

'And what do they sell?' Bryn prompted him mercilessly.

'Used bread,' Pest said.

'Used fucking . . .'

'They do, it's second-hand bread. You go in, right, and there's Mighty White or whatever and you think, right, I'll have one of those and then when you get it home there are pieces missing. You can tell because of the gradient, you know, the way the shape goes . . .'

'I know,' Elsa said, and Bryn and Pest looked at each other. 'I mean, I know what a gradient is.'

'That's it,' Pest said. 'Because, you know how it's supposed to go, there shouldn't be one piece that's suddenly bigger than the last one, it should be a nice smooth curve, yeah, it must mean there are pieces missing. And also, you know the little sticky tag thing at the top, it's been taken off and put back again a bit twisted so it doesn't stick properly.'

Pest raised both eyebrows at Elsa, and she nodded, yes, uhuh. She was completely at a loss.

'They also sell this horrible lager called Boot and they sell toilet rolls and Glen Campbell CDs and Marching Bands and that, and they sell this plastic jewellery, rings and that with skulls on, supposed to look like silver and that.'

'What was that whisky you got at Christmas, what was it called?'

'Oh yeah. Glenauthentic.'

'It wasn't.'

'Yeah, it was. It had all these stags all over it, you know. And then they sell the glue of course. Just to look at it, though, you wouldn't know what kind of shop it was supposed to be because all they've got are these boxes of bags of crisps in the window. It's a bit of a funny place really.'

'They're nice though, aren't they?'

'Yeah, they're dead nice in there, they don't mind if you want to hang around a bit, if you've got nothing pressing on, you know.' Bryn was doing something behind Pest's back, Elsa couldn't see what exactly. She got the impression he was keeping Pest talking.

'Anyway, Pest now,' Bryn said, 'my friend here is called Elsa.'

'Elsa,' Pest said, and stretched his hand out. 'How do you do? I'm very pleased to meet you.'

'Anyway, show her what you need the freezer bags for.'

'What?'

'She wants to know. She wants to know about the freezer bags.'

'Why does she?' Pest said, looking in perplexity at Bryn, who abruptly stopped whatever it was he was doing and straightened up.

'Because she wants to. I said you'd show her.'

'Why, does she want some...'

'Glue?' Bryn finished the sentence, and turned an enquiring face to Elsa. 'She might do.'

Elsa started to say, oh no, really, no thanks, but Bryn shushed her with a finger to his mouth and gestured at Pest.

'You go ahead,' Bryn said, and smiled.

'You want some?' Pest asked Bryn and Bryn frowned furiously.

'No, cunt, no, I don't want any fucking glue. Do I look like I want any?'

'Yeah.'

'Well, I don't. Even I don't want any and you know what I'm like.'

'You did once.'

'Yeah, once, and it was shite. I've enjoyed myself more banging my head on a piece of concrete actually.'

'You've got to get used to it.'

'I don't want to get used to it, you stupid cunt. I've told you, the whole problem with you actually is that you're *too* fucking used to it. Aren't you?'

'Well,' Pest said, and stood slightly more stiffly, looking away from Elsa, 'we all have our little pleasures.'

'Yeah, well, knock yourself out. We'll see about my friend here.'

Pest looked from one to the other, then went away and took something from a drawer under the sink, a box of freezer bags.

He sat on the floor beside where Elsa was sitting and tore off a single bag.

'Well, what you do, you get your tub and you shake it up a bit. That's because it's thixotropic, which is why it's called Thixofix. Do you know what thixotropic means?'

Elsa said no, she didn't.

'Well, it means that it's a solid but it goes liquid when you shake it.'

'Yeah,' Bryn chipped in from out of sight, 'but you thought it was called Thixofix because it was thick and you could get a fix off it. Didn't you?'

Pest shrugged his eyes to the ceiling and didn't respond.

'Anyway. So you shake your tub.' He took one off the pile and readjusted the others so that there was no gap. He shook the tub in his hand, a casual expert movement, like a cocky waiter with a cocktail mixer. He was turning into Delia Smith, Elsa thought.

'Open your bag. Put tub in bag, open tub, using screwdriver if necessary, though you can usually just prise it ... off ... ' He faltered as he grappled with the lid.

'OK. Pour glue into bag. You can just do half, which is what I'm going to do now.'

'It being a bit early in the day for a whole tub,' Bryn said, and Pest again pointedly ignored him.

'Then, you close up bag and shake again.' He gripped the neck in his fist and shook it. 'This releases the juice in it and keeps it liquid. Now what you've got to do, you put the bag over your mouth and your nose. It's got to be over your nose as well or you won't get it. That's what he was getting wrong. So nose as well. Oh, before you do that, you've got to breathe like fuck. Hyperventilate. Do you know what that means?'

Elsa did.

'OK, so you breathe in out, in out, as hard as you can, like you were going to do a dive or something. Then put bag over mouth and nose, breathe into it first, blow it up so you get the air in, then you just breathe in as hard as you can. You don't worry if it hurts your lungs or anything, you just breathe it all in and hold it. Which he didn't do right anyway.'

'Christ, it's too much like hard work if you want to know what I think about it.'

'Yeah, which we don't, and that's it really, except you pass it on immediately, because if you hang onto it you'll probably just drop it and it'll get wasted, which is something else he didn't seem to be able to understand – '

'Yeah, yeah. Yap yap yap.'

Pest was squeezing the bag, palping it. Elsa was reminded of the technique of manually ventilating a patient with a ventilator.

He breathed hard for a few breaths, his face a mask of concentration, his eyeballs fixed on hers, and then he was into the bag. For a moment it swelled out like a balloon, then it collapsed as he inhaled, moulding itself to his jaw and cheeks and shrinking back onto itself, just the grey glue deposit at the bottom retaining its shape.

His eyes were bulging with the exertion, and he looked straight at her as he did it. He grabbed it off his face finally and gave it to her with a shaky hand.

He sat back on his elbows, and his head wobbled as he fought to maintain a level position.

'Fucked,' he said indistinctly, and his eyes closed.

Elsa watched, horrified, and wondered what she was supposed to do with the glue. She didn't want to be responsible for it losing its mousse, its éclat, whatever it was, but she didn't really know how to stop that from happening.

She held it disdainfully with dainty fingers on her lap and watched as Pest twitched and shook his head, as if he were trying to empty water out of his ears.

Bryn came up behind the chair and lifted the bag up to her face.

'Go on,' he said. 'You want to know everything. Have a go.'

'No, really I – '

'Have a go,' he said, ferocious now, trying to force it up to her face, but Elsa stood up and dropped it to the floor. Pest watched it fall with patient sorrow.

Bryn stood twitching for a moment. Pest smiled, resigned, and made an eloquent expression of regret.

'Come on, then,' Bryn said, 'that's it. Show's over.'

Elsa stood, still unable to take her eyes off Pest, who didn't seem to be able to see anything properly.

'You off?' he said from full fathom five, and Bryn pulled Elsa out of the room. As the door closed she could hear Pest's sound, his underwater porn-movie sound, ooooooh yeeeeeah, and Bryn hustled her down the stairs.

Back in his room, he slammed the door behind them and stood in front of her, his jaw working, his big veiny hands curling and uncurling rapidly.

'What's . . . '

He turned away and back faster than Elsa was ready for.

'What's the matter with you? Eh?'

Elsa said nothing, and Bryn paced a few steps away.

'I mean, what is the *matter* with you? Eh? I introduce you to my friends, I show you things, and what do you do?'

'Look,' Elsa said, 'look, I'm sorry if I've upset you but I never said I wanted any glue. Why did you want me to see that anyway?'

Bryn considered her for a moment. 'Background? Anyway I thought you wanted to understand things. How you going to understand anything if you don't try it? Eh?'

'OK, look, I just don't want any glue. That's it,' she said, and reached behind him for the door. He grabbed hold of her arm.

'I mean, how rude is that? Eh? I introduce you – '

126

'All right – '

'Is this what you're going to be like? Is it?'

'All right! I was rude to your friend. I'm sorry.'

'Yeah. Well.'

He twisted his face away and back again, he scowled like a cartoon baddy, he twitched and grimaced. Elsa watched him.

'Yeah, well, he's a cunt anyway.' He reached into his back pocket and drew something out: a five pound note. 'I got what I wanted anyway.'

'You mean you took that from him?'

'Yeah, well, he owes me. He was supposed to give it me on Friday and he didn't, so I've got every right.'

'You took money from him?' Elsa was appalled. Bryn bristled with righteousness, and put his innocent face on again.

'So?'

'Give it him back.'

'He owes me – '

'Bryn. Give it him back or that's it. I'll give you a fiver if you need it.'

Bryn nodded his head a few times, then shook, then nodded. He took out his lighter and flicked it on, held it under her nose for a second, winked.

'Actually,' he said, 'he owes me ten.'

Elsa held his eye for a minute then couldn't help herself and laughed out loud.

'OK. I'll shove it under his door later. All right?' he said.

'I'll be checking.'

'Yeah? What are you, the police?'

'The police are easy.'

'Ooooh, I'm scared.'

'You should be.'

He clasped his hands behind his back and leaned in close and sniffed her hair for a moment, then grabbed clumsily at her breast and she pulled away.

'You don't do that,' she said, 'you don't do that, ever, or I'm just going,' and he said, OK, fine, whatever. Fuck's sake. You said something about a tenner?

She wasn't going to have time to get home and then out again to court, she'd have to do as she was. She hated going without a proper wash and change, but there was nothing to be done. He said not to worry about it. She looked no worse than usual.

He said he'd come out with her and show her the bus stop. They'd arranged that he'd get a different bus. No point taking chances on being seen together. Outside it was hot already; the pavements smelled of parking and chips and bin bags. Pest waved goodbye from an upstairs window.

CONTINGENCY

'Just got to make a little call,' Bryn said. 'Won't take a minute.'

They turned into a side street and down some steps. He rang the bell and a woman of about thirty answered the door.

'He in?' Bryn said, and she let them in, smiling shyly at Elsa. It was a large basement flat, all in shades of mushroom and sand and nothing very much. Bryn headed for the kitchen.

'All right.'

There was a thin young man at the table. He nodded hello, and Bryn sat opposite him. Elsa perched on a tall stool by the fridge.

'This is Elsa,' Bryn said, and the young man smiled gravely at her. 'She's a friend of mine.'

'Elsa,' he said, and shook her hand. 'Luke. Really nice to meet you. Would you like a cup of tea or anything?' He had a gentle, slightly breathy voice, and very pronounced nostrils. Long wavy hair, tied back, and a little leather choker with a bead at the front. A studious, rather abstract face, as if he was pondering some new problem in quantum cosmology.

Elsa looked at Bryn, who said, 'Actually, no, mate, got to get away actually.'

Luke nodded, and opened up a soapstone dish that was

nestling under a jar which contained a fish slice, potato masher and a ladle with holes in. Inside the dish were some lumps of cannabis of various sizes, and Luke took them out and scrutinized each one in turn.

'Quarter, is it?' he said, and Bryn nodded.

'Right then.'

He opened a drawer and produced a steel ruler, a pencil and 2p.

'New system,' he said, and grinned at Bryn. 'I particularly like the idea that you can do the whole thing and not have a pair of scales knocking round. Just in case the police come calling. All you've got are common household implements.'

Elsa shifted on the stool.

'Yeah, but you've still got the, you know,' she said, and gestured at the dope. Bryn gave her a hostile look, but Luke just smiled. He had a very teacherly manner. You could imagine adolescent students getting crushes on him.

'That's so, certainly, Elsa, but you see the point is that to get a supply conviction they'd need evidence like scales or large amounts of cash or something. This way, it's all for my own personal use, however much there is. Not that they'd bother really.'

As he spoke he was laying the ruler on top of the pencil, balancing it. He reached for a joint that was smouldering in a large glass ashtray and inhaled deeply, his brow ridging with the exertion.

'This is excellent, by the way,' he said, as he exhaled. 'It's very nice.'

He turned on a ring on the cooker and put a steak knife into the flame. He held the lump of cannabis in the palm of his hand, squeezing and stroking it.

'The other reason I like this method,' he said, to no one in particular, 'is that it's intrinsically elegant. Economical. And it derives from first principles. It's like a bicycle, it's just a very clean piece of design. Efficient.' He dragged deep again, and passed it to Bryn. 'I don't know if you know this, but the bicycle is actually the most energy-efficient piece of machinery ever devised.'

Bryn said oh yeah, that's interesting, and shrugged eyebrows at Elsa when Luke wasn't watching. He made a gesture, yak yak yak, with his hand.

Luke's movements were getting slower and heavier. He'd clearly been smoking already, and was in a rather dreamy bovine mode. He reached behind him for the knife, and took a small wooden chopping board from behind the sink. The dope was placed dead centre, and he held the knife over it for a moment, looking, divining, dowsing possibly, for the exact place to cut. The knife descended, and a sliver was cut off, then a second, a third. The bits were all tidied up and wrapped and put back into the soapstone dish. Everything was taking a long time. Elsa sighed, and he turned and smiled at her.

'Nearly there,' he said, 'never fear.'

He held the lump again, allowed it to rest in the palm of his hand. Then he pulled a face, OK. He put the pencil on the surface, then laid the ruler on top. He nudged it backwards and forwards until it balanced.

'The tolerance on these things is incredible,' he said. 'It's just a steel rule, but the accuracy is awesome, really. Look at this.' He seemed to be speaking to Elsa, and she politely came forward and peered over his shoulder. 'See? The point of equilibrium is exactly 150 mil. I mean, exactly. You see?'

'Oh yeah,' Elsa said, trying to sound impressed, though actually she would have been surprised if it had been anywhere else. He was breathing heavily through his nose, and the nostrils were flaring in and out. The ruler seemed to be making him excited. 'I mean, it's for all reasonable purposes perfect, and it costs, what, two quid? Something like that. The power it gives you is just, just...' He seemed to have run out of superlatives. 'Computers, neural networks, biotechnology, *nano*technology, you know?' The contemplation of these troublesome matters seemed to be exhausting him. 'I mean, these are complex and oppressive, you know what I mean? But something like this, man, when the lights go out...'

The ruler was still and balanced finally. He fished in his pocket and produced the 2p piece.

'The final piece of the puzzle,' he said, and took another drag. He held the coin in one hand and the lump in the other. 'Watch,' he said, and Elsa dutifully leaned over him again. He placed the coin at one end and the lump at the other. The ruler fell heavily at the dope end. There was a definite click as it hit the Formica.

Luke stared at it. He sat back and fiddled with his hair, then smoked a bit more, screwing his eyes up. Bryn was tapping the surface top, drumming fast intricate patterns.

Luke came forward again and nudged the coin a little bit to the right. A bit more. The ruler was still lodged firmly on the Formica at the dope end. He pushed it in a fraction. 'Of course, it's a bit tricky to gauge the centre of gravity of an irregular mass like this. If it was a platonic solid of some kind then our job would be simpler. But, alas, we are on the sea of contingency.' He held up a hand as he spoke. 'All afloat,' he said, and made wiggling motions with his hand. He giggled, then blew air out of his superb nostrils. 'OK.'

He nudged the coin, nudged the dope, this way, that way. Nothing balanced with anything. The forces were disobedient today, the contingency unassailable.

'It's a very convenient coincidence,' he said as he shifted the weights about, 'or a very elegant piece of subversion, one or the other, that the government supplies ready-made quarter-ounce and eighth-ounce weights courtesy of the Royal Mint; 2p is a quarter, 1p is an eighth. And again, the tolerance is incredibly tight on these things.' Elsa watched as the coin and the lump were manipulated at either end of the wonderful steel ruler. One end went down, then the other.

He couldn't figure it out. He sat looking at it and smoking. Then Elsa saw him actually shift the point of equilibrium, the point the ruler was balanced on, the fulcrum, the justification for the whole rigmarole, he shifted it a millimetre to the right. A few final nudgings, and then suddenly, miraculously, the dope end swayed up, down, and then came to rest just clear of the Formica. He touched the coin and the thing was balanced.

He looked up proudly.

'I love to feel these tiny little forces, you know. I love to have them under my fingers like this. You know, with a lever long enough you could shift the earth.'

Bryn looked up at him.

'Is that it then?'

Luke gestured at the ruler.

'That's my deal. Seeing is believing.'

'But, Bryn, he was cheating.' They were marching away down the street now, Bryn still tapping rhythms against his legs.

'He wasn't cheating, he was just getting it right.'

'He wasn't getting it right, he was cheating. You could make anything balance with anything the way he was doing it. He'd already decided that that lump was it before he started any of that ruler stuff.'

'Yeah, but it balanced, you saw that.'

'He moved the fulcrum.'

'The what?'

'The fulcrum – '

'Bollocks to the fulcrum. I saw it, you saw it, that's that.'

Elsa was silent. She felt too hung over and weary to give him a proper row about it. They came to the bus stop and he danced about for a minute or two while they arranged where they would meet later, assuming that court got fucked up again. He would get the next bus, they came every ten minutes.

She needn't have worried about being late for court; she was in fact three-quarters of an hour early, and even when everyone was gathered in the jury assembly room there still seemed to be no immediate prospect of getting going. A harassed usher confided that there was a witness problem, the same witness problem as yesterday in fact. Still no sign of him. Hegler.

The fat woman, Helen, livened things up considerably by starting to cry. She had to be hustled out and comforted by Mrs Furious and Monkey boots. Monkey boots stayed in the toilet with her and Mrs Furious came back out to report.

'It's her kitchen, poor love,' Mrs Furious whispered to M4 Rapist. Elsa overheard the whole thing. The new kitchen, apparently, was not at all what she had been expecting.

'Of course it's not finished yet, so she's not getting the whole effect. But it's terribly modern, she says, poor thing. She thought she'd be getting the Harvest, but it's more like the Rationnell. You know? Birch veneer and granite composite? Poor love. Her John chose it all, he thought she'd like it. The knobs are called Transitiv. Can you imagine? And all she really wanted was oak or maybe beech and nice brass Chandler handles. It isn't what she was expecting at all. She's brought in one of the teaspoons.'

The offending object was passed round and tutted over. It looked enormous and chunky in burnished steel casing and green trim.

'She's ever so upset. She says she tried to make scrambled egg last night and just burst into tears.'

'Shame.'

'So anyway, she's going to have to wait until it's all done, but she thinks it's all going to have to be taken out and redone and God knows how long it's all going to take.'

'Is she all right?'

'She says she hardly slept a wink with the worry, poor soul...'

Elsa found Patrick and they adjourned to the smoking room.

'So. Elsya Blick. And what did you find out last night? Hm?'

He managed to fill his voice up with such a thick treacly cocktail of innuendo and disdain that she almost wanted to belt him one.

'Oh, yes, all right. Ha ha.'

'So you got pissed, you went back to his house – '

'How do you know?'

'How do I *know*? Because you told me about eight times Patrick! You see...'

'Oh, yes.'

'Forgotten, had we? *No, but listen, you see. Patrick! See, what happened was...*'

134

'Yes, all right, Patrick.'

'So did you find out anything at all?'

'Well...'

'Or did he *show* you anything?'

'Don't you start...'

'You mean he didn't *show* you anything?'

'No, but I tell you, there's something weird about this witness business.'

'Oh, no kidding.'

'And I'll tell you how I know. Because Bryn said he was meeting someone at eleven.'

'Yes, well, excuse me, but I seem to recall saying something along these lines yesterday – '

'...and that was without the benefit of some half-arsed Malibu-fuelled fact-finding session...'

'Patrick, do the words "smug" and "git" have any particular resonance for you?'

'Well, that's not very nice language, is it, Elsa?'

'Anyway, look, he seems to know there's going to be no business today. So I'm going to – '

'No, don't tell me, let me see now, you're going to meet him somewhere and get so pissed you can hardly stand, then ring people up all night...'

She allowed a short pause to take place in a dignified manner.

'No, I'm going to meet him later and we're going to have another go at it.'

'I see. Even though you now have it confirmed that he's in on this witness disappearance business.'

'That could mean anything – '

Patrick wasn't letting her off though.

'What I don't understand is why you went back home with him,' he said, and Elsa felt a little tickle of what it might be like to be Bryn, accused but innocent. If he *was* innocent. Patrick was demanding a clear and convincing explanation.

'Oh well,' she started, and then began again in a different, calmer, less pissed-off tone. 'Well, to start with I thought he was going to show me something, you know, to do with the case, like he said. But then we went to another pub, he said he was waiting for someone but they didn't come, and then we started doing this drinking game...'

'So you were what, humouring him, trying to put him at ease, that kind of thing?' Patrick gave her a look. She raised eyebrows at him. 'Or alternately you were perhaps simply pissed.'

'Simply pissed pretty much says it. So we were near his house by now, and I wanted the toilet and astll that. Iwas a bit the worse for wear, Patrick, since you must know. It'd been a long day.' She felt shifty and evasive. And she *was* innocent.

'Anyway, I think I must have just...'

'Passed out?'

'Nodded off.'

'If you prefer.'

'Anyway, I'm presuming him innocent. Like the judge said.' She was winding him up and she knew it. 'Isn't that what we're supposed to do?'

She left him and returned to the delights of Bible Bill. Serial ejaculator he might be but at least he didn't keep asking her a whole lot of stupid questions.

10.30. They were nice and snug in the jury box again. Poor Helen was squashed up against Elsa once more, and Elsa, despite trying with due diligence to feel sorry for her, was again on her guard against any sudden spasmodic movements. Helen sniffed and shifted about in a distracted manner, her head full of nothing but kitchens. She'd brought the teaspoon with her; she had it secreted on her lap and kept taking sneaky looks at it. Elsa looked at it too and had to agree, it was an unusually ugly item. If it was any indication of the look of the whole thing, then this must truly be a kitchen of quite alarming hideousness. Elsa tried to exchange sympathetic glances with her but Helen was shut off in her own world of consumer chagrin. Elsa saw her write the word Rationnell on her paper, then scribble over it violently.

The judge had yet to arrive, and the court personnel were in their familiar mode of hushed tedium. Parrot was looking even rattier, weasellier, more generically rodent-like. Djabo leaned exquisitely and chatted to an usher. All was boredom. The judge made his appearance and smiled as everyone stood up and sat down again.

Helen snuffled and twitched like a dog having a dream. The judge spoke quietly to the clerk, then looked expectantly at a suited figure at the back of the courtroom who came up to his throne and whispered. They all three conspired for a minute or two, then the judge sighed.

'Well. Ladies and gentlemen, I again must apologize for your inconvenience and thank you for your patience. I might almost say your endurance, given the circumstances in which we find ourselves. No further progress, alas, can be made in this matter today or, by the look of things, tomorrow either. So I am excusing you once more, and would ask you to return at 10.15 on Monday morning, when, we all fervently hope and pray, we might be able to resume. I hope you have a pleasant weekend.'

There was a stirring of annoyance in the jury box, and Elsa dared a little quick look at the dock: Bryn Sweetman, already turning to go, accompanied by his uniformed man. He was going to make his eleven o'clock anyway, by the look of things. But then she caught sight of his little pal in the viewing gallery who was recklessly leaning over the rail again and making his hand signal at her. He was also miming drinking. What was he on about? He had to stop before someone saw him though. Elsa, mystified, went back to the jury assembly room. She hadn't hung up her jacket so there couldn't be any note. Drinking. Drinking. He wanted to meet her in a pub?

She stood irresolute in the middle of the room, and suddenly the vending machine gave a mighty burp and rattle, and she thought, aha.

The note was stuck inside a plastic cup inside the opening, the maw, of the monstrous machine. She glanced about her and opened it.

no good today monday 11 same address

She hastily crumpled it up and stuffed it in her pocket. Outside the sun was shining and she had the whole long weekend ahead. Patrick was loitering about waiting for her and they headed off together in search of yeasty liquids.

WEEKEND

Saturday was largely taken up with alcohol and hangovers and confused periods of snoozing and waking and eating, mostly with Patrick. In between she kept up with Bible Bill, who was at this very moment up to no kind of good with an electric cattle-prod. Samuel: I and my kingdom are guiltless before the LORD. He was getting through quite a bit of seminal fluid, Elsa thought. Hope he's taking his zinc supplements.

Sitting in her flat that afternoon, she told Patrick many times that she really liked Liam, she really really...

'Not quite enough to answer his phone calls though?'

She stood up and banged drawers open until she found what she wanted, a photograph. She brought it over to Patrick and more or less threw it at him.

'Look.'

There were three people in the picture, a man in the middle with a woman on either side. The woman on the left was Elsa. All three were wearing woolly hats and scarves and looked cold and determinedly cheerful.

'So, this one in the middle...'

'Yep.' Elsa assented grimly. 'Oh, yes. That's him. That's my Liam.'

'Right. And this other woman?'

'It doesn't matter about her.'

'I'm just curious...'

'OK, she was called On, if you must know.'

'"On"?'

'Look, she was *Dutch*. We were all on a *ferry*.'

'Ah. Yes... Well. So this is Liam, huh? He looks...'

'He looks?'

'He looks – fine. Great. No, sorry, I hate to say this but actually he looks like a complete dildo.'

'I know.'

Patrick regarded her.

'I *know*, Patrick. You think I don't know that? What do you want me to do about it?'

'What do *you* want to do?'

'I want to go out and get pissed. I want to have a laugh. I want to not talk about...'

'T'ai chi?'

'Correct.'

'So ring him up. Tell him you're moving to Venezuela.'

'Oh, right. Right. I'll do that now, shall I?'

'Do it whenever you want. Don't leave it too late though. Because you know what you've got here, don't you?' He gestured to the photograph.

'What?'

'You've got a joke boyfriend.'

'Oh, sod it. Let's have a little drink...'

BODY PARTS, EVERYWHERE!

On the bus home on Sunday she caught sight of a newspaper sandwich board outside a shop and was astonished to see the headline PRINCESS DIANA DEAD. Good God, she thought, is there nothing that woman won't do to get her picture in the papers?

TRAGEDY

There was much Princess Diana talk in court on the Monday morning, and Elsa was astonished and a little dismayed to find that just about everyone else thought it was important; they even seemed to have feelings about it. Dragons book hinted darkly at sacrificial significance and ritual bloodletting. Graham and Tony, who had made up seemingly now Graham (or Tony) had come to his senses and found a sensible, non-tie-dyed T-shirt to wear, thought it was more likely to be some establishment coup thing. M4 Rapist thought it was a shame and that she'd been such a lovely person.

The judge was sombre.

'Ladies and gentlemen, in view of the tragic and appalling events of the weekend, of which I'm sure you are all fully aware, I would like to suggest that before we commence we observe one minute's silence in respect of the memory of Her Royal Highness Diana, Princess of Wales.'

Heads were bowed solemnly, and Elsa thought she even heard the odd sniffle. She caught Patrick out of the corner of her eye mouthing something to her: 'Which one was she?', and she had to stop herself laughing.

*

As for the case, there was nothing doing as usual. The jury were brought in, sent out; it was a bloody revolving door on this courthouse. Elsa was in plenty of time to meet Bryn at eleven.

MEN ARE FROM SLOUGH, WOMEN ARE FROM SWINDON

The address Bryn had given her was a street tucked away off Boundary Road, way out in darkest deepest Hove. She pushed the bell and was buzzed up. Bryn just nodded 'hello' then disappeared into the flat. Elsa found the living room, which smelled of Pledge and baby oil, and sat in a huge sluttish chair with grimy covers in front of a vast television and watched wall-to-wall coverage of Diana's death. Pictures of a tunnel, French police on motorbikes, flashing emergency lights. A torch swung up and for a moment dazzled the picture out, then slid away again. There were crowds of people overlooking the tunnel, and knots of uniformed personnel standing about.

Down the hall Bryn was getting changed. Whoever it was was due at eleven and it was now ten to. Bryn could be heard struggling with his clothes, losing his balance, knocking into things. He didn't seem to be particularly well co-ordinated, unless it was just a very cramped room, which was likely from the look of the other room Elsa had seen, a tiny rectangular 'spare' room with an oversized window and an odd mongrel assortment of furnishings, including a bed which was far too big and a clothes rail on wheels of the kind used in dry-cleaners' shops. There were a tiny television and video on a little metal trolley, again on wheels, as if whatever spare person used this spare room, for whatever purpose, put a particularly high premium on the ease and flexibility that only wheels under your furniture could provide. The TV was covered over, sealed almost, with a thin even layer of dust. An ashtray beside it had two cigarette ends and two matches, which had taken on the look of exhibits. Elsa picked one up and sniffed at it, as if she expected it to tell her something. Elsya Blick, on the case. The room was dry and dusty and warm. Elsa liked it. An answering machine clunked and beeped and whined every few minutes.

Bryn banged some part of himself into something, something which did not have wheels and which didn't give, and gave a high yell of annoyance and sudden pain. He seemed to be having quite a bit of trouble in there. She could hear wriggling and scuffling and bumping, followed by a short series of grunts. She wondered if she should offer to help, and then he was staggering out and back into the lounge. She twisted round to look at him.

He stood inside the door with his legs spread and arms behind his back, hands clasped, his head and neck unnaturally erect. He was wearing skinhead gear: bleached-out jeans, perfectly snug and tight round the substantial balls and cock, perfectly filled with smooth full arse and solid thighs; pale blue Fred Perry polo shirt, narrow red braces; 8-hole oxblood Doc Martens.

'You look...nice,' she said lamely, nodding and smiling and taking him in. He had tattoos all over both brawny arms; she couldn't make out what they were, one of them involved a chequerboard pattern. His skin was white, and his frame was tight and tough and exercised, solidly muscled. From what she could tell of his stomach, it looked as if you could bounce tennis balls off it. If you had a mind to, she thought, and found that she was blushing at the thought.

He stood motionless, his eyes trained on her in his psycho killer look, then he twisted his mouth to one side and started readjusting himself inside the jeans. There was too much of him, it wasn't sitting right, it was all bunched up to one side.

He patted and nudged and arranged until he was happy, then lifted his hands over his head and turned around to show her the back view. The back view was fine, she thought. The way the neck sat on the back, and the head on the neck, it was all fine. Strong, tight, not exaggerated, just right. There was another tattoo behind one ear.

Well,' she said, 'yeah, you look nice.'

'Not supposed to look nice,' he said, twisting his head round and demonstrating as he did so the braids and bundles of cartilage and muscle going up from collar bone to throat. It all looked fine, Elsa thought. 'I'm supposed to look hard.'

'Yeah, well, you do,' she said, embarrassed to discuss it any further.

'I'm supposed to look like the kind of bastard that takes you down an alley and twats you one in the bollocks 'cos he doesn't like your face.'

'Why?' she said.

'Why? Because that's what he wants.'

'Who?'

'Who? My eleven o'clock, that's who, who do you think?'

'Sorry, I don't ... ' But she did, of course. 'Rent'. She was about to say, I thought you said you didn't do this, but decided not to. She couldn't pretend to be surprised that he'd lied to her, though she was just a little surprised that he'd forgotten already. Christ, Bryn, she thought, it's no wonder your brief won't let you anywhere near the witness stand. I hope you're better at this than you seem to be.

'Yeah, OK, but he doesn't actually ... ' She stopped and turned back to the television, where a serious woman was talking to camera outside an official building.

'What? He doesn't actually what?'

'Your eleven o'clock. I mean, he doesn't want you to actually ... '

'What? Twat him in the bollocks?'

'Uhuh,' she said in a small voice, unable to look at him in her hot red embarrassment. It wasn't a conversation she was happy to have. She was waiting for the doorbell to take him away to whatever it was he was going to do. She didn't want to have to talk about it.

'Been known,' Bryn said, and gave himself a little extra hitch, more for confidence bolstering than for any improvement it might make in the line. 'Can't say it never happens. Depends how he's feeling, how I'm feeling. All sorts.'

'Anyway,' Elsa said, trying to sound unconcerned and purely and simply curious, though her voice was pitched slightly too high for that, 'surely, I mean, wouldn't it just be stupid if he said, go on, then, kick me in the – '

'Bollocks.'

'...yeah, and then you say, oh, all right then, that'll be ten quid or whatever it is.'

'Sixty quid,' Bryn said. 'Not ten. And no, it wouldn't be stupid, not if that's what he wanted.'

'But isn't the whole, I mean, isn't it a bit kind of...' What she wanted to say was 'pathetic' but that wasn't very polite. 'I mean, if it isn't really someone beating him up in an alley...I mean, if it's just you getting dressed up and pretending, you know, going "You ready now?", then what's the point?'

Bryn watched her sourly.

'You thick or what? Eh? Look, he doesn't really want his loose bits mashing, does he?' Bryn shifted his weight from side to side and waggled his head, keeping his eyes trained on her. 'Anyway, you can't just get that kind of thing to order, you know. And anyway, look, he's busy, he hasn't got time to go and get into trouble, and he doesn't want the aggro, all right, he just wants to come here, have a nice little whatever with me, sixty, that'll be champ, then we're finished, next week, yeah, shake the hand, everyone's happy.'

'You shake his hand?'

'Among other things.' Wink, nudge.

'And it's sixty pounds?'

'It is to him.'

She thought, that's five and a bit bottles of Malibu. That's quite a lot. Or four t'ai chi sessions. Two silk-and-linen tops from River Island and enough for a Beanburger afterwards.

'So, do you have, like, a menu?' she said, with no real thought in her head.

Bryn tapped his shaved forehead with a bent finger twice. 'Depends. This one it's sixty, unless he says he wants something in particular, which is twenty more, plus if he goes as much as a minute over the hour, then it's two. I've got another one coming at twelve.'

'What's that mean, something in particular?'

'Not telling,' he said. Another hitch, then a snort and a grin. A little giggle.

'What if he hurts you?' Elsa said suddenly, not realizing she was going to.

'What, him? Why would he hurt me?'

'What if he gets carried away?' She imagined restraints and wide fearful eyes, gagged mouth, a grim determined shoving motion, the eyes clamping shut suddenly, blood spurting.

'He's supposed to get carried away. As long as I don't get carried away . . . ' He stopped and blinked five times. 'Anyway, nobody's going to hurt anyone. It's not like that.' He regarded her. 'Look, if you really want to see this, I can probably arrange that.'

'Oh, no – '

'Only you seem so very interested – '

'Oh, no, no – '

'Elsa, look at me now.'

She twisted full round in the chair, and attempted a full no-thanks smile. He was lifting one eyebrow up and down, one hand in a pocket, the fingers working in there. He ducked down to her, whispered.

'Look. Tell me now. You want to see this? You want to watch?'

Elsa turned back to the television. A montage of clips, limousines swerving, people talking, a twisted piece of automotive wreckage. A computer graphic of a car bouncing around in a tunnel. Her pulse was loud in her ears, she felt an unwished-for lightness and wobbliness in the head which made it difficult for her to behave naturally. The doorbell went, a harsh synthetic bing-bong. She felt his breath on her neck for a long moment.

She waited until she heard the bedroom door close. When she was sure Bryn and his client were both busy and not likely to come out again any minute, she sneaked up and had a little eavesdrop. Nothing much to hear, except low conversation. She heard a laugh, not Bryn's, and the sounds people make moving about on a bed. Gradually there was less conversation and more bed noises. Some slurping and slipping. Cigarette lighters going. Little sounds like that.

Someone going 'uungh'. *Hold on a minute, champ, let me just, yeah, that's it, uungh.* Quite a lot of that.

The sounds were getting more rhythmic, when the bing-bong went again, and she jumped back from the door and scuttled for the front room. It was an undignified movement. She landed back in the armchair and was again assailed by pictures of people standing around central London looking uncertain about what to do as the TV crews scanned restlessly for an authoritative display of grief. The picture cut back to the studio and then out again, pictures of long black cars swerving up to some grand building, men in dark glasses, TV crews pushed out of the way. Flashlights, flowers, tears, confusion.

She heard Bryn answering the front door. He spoke briefly then she heard the bedroom door close again. The sound of someone coming down the hall. She stiffened.

Someone came into the room, and she somehow didn't dare to turn round or acknowledge him in any way. Neither did he seem inclined to speak, and instead just sidled by and sat on the settee and turned his face to the TV screen.

Elsa sneaked a look at him: he was possibly as old as fifty, slim, pleasant-looking, mousy-haired. He reminded her of Liam's father. He wore a look of perfect seriousness as the TV pictures rolled on, the low voices murmuring of momentousness, the faces caught in odd random moments of vacuity and confusion and unexpected turmoil.

He caught her eye and smiled, a slight, gentle smile. Elsa

149

smiled back and nodded. She still didn't feel able to speak. He was another punter presumably, and this was the waiting room. So who was she?

He gestured to the TV.

'Terrible.'

Elsa nodded, though she didn't actually give a damn. Oh, terrible, yes.

'I couldn't believe it when I first heard. Are you ...' he said, and gestured in the general direction of the bedroom, where the rhythmic thumping had started up again, accompanied now by an intermittent high-pitched sound, like an exclamation of surprise.

Elsa smiled apologetically.

'Sorry?'

'Are you ...'

'Oh, I see.' He meant waiting. 'Oh, no.'

'No, I thought, I mean, I didn't know he, you know, does women too.'

'Does women too' was spoken in a kind of mock cockney accent, and accompanied by a jokey little facial expression. Elsa laughed nervously.

'Well, I don't know actually. If he does or not. Women, I mean.'

'But you're not ...'

'No,' Elsa said with finality. 'No, I'm not. I'm just a friend, you know.'

'No, I thought it was mostly men.'

A picture of a black woman, head raised, sobbing hard. A picture of a woman and a man – she holding flowers, he fiddling with a NiCad battery pack – among a great seething sea of people with flowers, speaking to the camera. The woman broke off and turned through ninety degrees, put her hand to her face and began to weep with little restraint. Her boyfriend looked mostly just surprised, a little embarrassed, shaking his head. He moved as if to take the flowers from her and she turned back to the camera, tried to speak again, put her hands up and shook her head.

In the background a woman was praying silently, fervently,

and the camera found her and pulled the focus so that she now occupied the screen, an image that seemed to come directly from some catalogue of human attitudes that had gone out of fashion five hundred years ago. Her lips moved, her eyebrows lifted and fell, her eyes were screwed up tight. Joan of Arc looked like this, Elsa thought.

'He's very good, you know.'

This was the waiting punter. He spoke in a lowered voice accompanied by a slight, shifting, confiding lean.

The sounds from the bedroom were mounting, not just the thumping and surprised sounds, but a deep muffled grunting and occasional words: come on, fuck, shit, Jesus.

'Is he?'

'Oh, yes. Very good.'

Come on, come *on*, Christ, come on then, fucking. A new sound now, slapping, then the whole wall began vibrating as something, the client presumably, was banged against it, again, again, come on then.

'Yes. He really throws himself into it, you know.'

'Uhuh.'

'Very good at his job.'

'I like that in a man, don't you?' Elsa said, in some absurd effort at casual conversation.

'It can't be the easiest of jobs to be good at, I always think.'

'I've never tried it.'

'I must admit, I quite look forward to coming here.'

'Would you recommend him?' Elsa said.

'Oh, definitely, I would. Oh yes. Of course, it all depends on what you like. He's not what they call versatile. I booked him for my other half's birthday last year, but it didn't work, you know, they just didn't click.'

'What does that mean, versatile?' Elsa asked absently, just making chit-chat really.

'What, versatile? Well, it means, well, basically it means that he only, or that he doesn't, he *won't*, rather...' The man tailed off and Elsa didn't pursue it. The sounds had now simplified down to some kind of irreducible sexual minimum, a slow rhythmic thumping and a moan in response, louder and higher each time, also more prolonged. The man was practically singing. The language was deteriorating, cunt, cocksucker, fucking gag on this then. She thought of Pest and his oooooooh yeeeeeeah. He would have been a useful addition at this moment, she felt.

The man on Elsa's right glanced at his watch and she saw him suppress a yawn, his jaw clamping and trembling and his eyes watering slightly. He reached for a magazine on the table in front. *Hello!*. The television droned momentously on.

'And we can see again the pictures of the scene – in front of the famous Salpêtrière in Paris, where so much of last night's terrible, terrible events unfolded – and where a disbelieving world – learned for the first time, at around, er, four a.m. – the true, appalling seriousness – of what was taking place...' A low voice, speaking in fragmented phrases, attempting to summon up a gravity, an immensity of moment quite at odds with the rather boring pictures of a floodlit Paris building with police cars parked in front.

Oh, come *on*, will you?

'Should be finishing any time now,' the punter said, as much to himself as to Elsa, and they both watched quietly as the terrible, terrible events were rehashed one more time. It sounded like a particularly strenuous piece of dentistry was taking place in the bedroom. Bang bang bang, ooarh, fuck, *fuck*ing Christ. Then silence for a few seconds, low voices and, unexpectedly, a laugh, footsteps, doors opening, water splashing in the bathroom.

Bryn was back in the doorway, shifting from side to side. He was still in jeans and boots, the braces loose and dangling now. He passed his hands over his head a few times.

'Next,' he said, and winked at Elsa. The punter stood and stretched, getting himself ready and walked out.

'Fucking Thunder Mountain I am,' Bryn said, as the man passed behind him. 'Don't get a ride like me at fucking Disneyland.' He stood a few moments longer, his eyes vacantly on the television screen.

'They're not still going on about that, are they?' he said.

*

152

12.15. Everything seemed to be going swimmingly, at least as far as the noises from the bedroom were concerned. Meanwhile a nation grieved, live, on the television. People were standing about, leaving flowers, crying, hugging each other. Elsa looked on astonished. Who were they all? Oddly, they all seemed to know immediately what to do; it was as if they had been in secret mass rehearsal for months. Elsa imagined out-of-town warehouses full of people practising grieving. OK, everyone, now this time we're going for more of a 'they killed our angel' kind of a feel, and remember: you just couldn't *believe* it when you heard, and you can remember *exactly* what you were doing at the time. OK, on four now. Elsa settled in happily.

Suddenly Bryn was back in the room. He slumped down on the sofa and scratched absently. Looked at Elsa, looked away again.

'Has he gone then?' she said. It was only twenty past.

'Gone? Wish he fucking had. No, he's still in there.'

'Oh. So...'

'So why am I here and he's there?'

'Yeah.'

'Why do you think.'

She thought for a minute.

'Tea-break?'

'Oh, yeah, funny.'

'OK, you tell me.'

He wriggled a bit, then took hold of his crotch, shook it.

'You know?'

Elsa didn't.

'Fuck's sake, want me to draw you a picture? Eh?'

Moody silence for a second.

'Can't get this bastard to work. If you must know.'

'Oh. Oh, I see.'

'I doubt it, somehow.'

'Won't he mind, though, what's his name in there? I mean you leaving him alone?'

'Oh, he's all right, I've got him cuffed up, he's happy. I told him I was going to get him a nice surprise.' He gave himself

153

another tug. 'Which it would be, wouldn't it?'

He watched the television for a few moments. Prime Minister Tony Blair, looking like someone had just slapped him. He seemed startled and ever so slightly cross at the way things were turning out.

Bryn spoke again. 'You know. Well, you don't. But there's no fucking *blood* down there, yeah? It's just a piece of rope.' He stood and hitched it all about, sat down again. 'And, you know, since all he really wants to do is have a wank and suck me off, it's a bit of a problem. No obvious way of working round it really.'

Elsa didn't know how to help, beyond looking sympathetic. She and Liam had sex so rarely these days that it was never an issue. It was as though they were not boyfriend and girlfriend but comrades maybe, doughty fellow resistance fighters for whom sex would be a time-wasting luxury, and who had to lie silently together for the duration of some unspecified conflict. Even when they did try to have sex it often petered out to nothing much. Yield and roll back, as they said at chi. If I have no body, how can any harm befall me. Bryn sat on, handling himself morosely.

'It keeps feeling like it's going to, but then it stops again.' He stood again. 'Oh, well. Back to the fucking fray. Can't leave him parked there all day. Have to charge him more.' He lingered a moment in the doorway, eyes on the television, then bobbed out of sight. Elsa heard the bedroom door shut.

Ten minutes later, the noises had stopped and there was just some low rumbling conversation. Then Bryn was back again, hanging around in the doorway.

'Listen, all right. He says twenty extra if you watch. OK?'

Elsa turned her head to look at him. He couldn't be serious surely?

'Just watch. You don't have to do anything.'

She didn't know what to say.

'Come on, look, what can it hurt? Eh? It'll only be till he comes, then you can bugger off again. Ten minutes maximum. Twenty quid. Eh? Not bad for ten minutes.'

She shook her head, no, no way. Uhuh.

'Oh, right. Excellent.' He strode about a bit, then thumped a glass-fronted bookcase which was full of videos of fascinating, if specialized, content. 'Fucking excellent. Eh?' He stamped around the room, working himself up into a lather. Elsa ignored him, fixing her eyes on the television. He ducked back to her chair and stood behind her, then she felt his breath on her neck. 'This is like the fucking glue again, isn't it? Eh? Don't want to soil your fucking self. I thought you were trying to understand things. Fat lot you're going to understand sat there. Eh? Stuck up...'

She stood up.

'Yeah. All right.'

'Yeah?'

'Yeah, all right. I'll come and watch.' She was furious, defiant. He kept *doing* this.

'Right. Come on then.'

She grabbed hold of him outside the bedroom door for an urgent conference.

'But I'm not touching anything. OK?'

'No one's asking you, are they?'

'I'm just saying.'

The client was on the bed, hands cuffed behind his back so he couldn't really do anything except roll, sitting up against the headboard, mostly naked. He was pallid and worm-like in the soupy light, with fleshy flattened breasts and a stringy neck. There was a strong smell of body and baby oil. A video was playing on a large-screen television, college boys in jock-straps, flesh tones exaggerated and something not quite right about the colour separation, a third- or fourth-generation copy presumably. Oh yeah, that big cock feels real good in my ass. Elsa found she had to force herself to look away.

Bryn indicated the end of the bed, where Elsa was to sit. She hesitated, it was a bit closer than she'd imagined. The client's dick was well within arm's reach; the client's feet and, specifically, his weirdly shaped toes and crumbling ill-kept toenails right under her nose. Bryn seemed to have about three Superkings on the go plus a joint, and the smoke kept getting in his eyes. He got to work, straddling the immobilized client, groin in the face and working him off, and the client closed his eyes and groaned. Elsa felt supernumerary, insulted almost. What was the point of her being there if he wasn't even going to look at her? Then the client opened his eyes again, met her eye, and looked intensely serious. Elsa fixed her gaze just above his head, but his eyes didn't leave her.

'Hold on.' Bryn leaned over to one side and fumbled about for something on the bedside cabinet, a little brown bottle. He unscrewed it and applied it to the client's nostrils, first one then the other, blocking the spare opening each time with his thumb. Elsa became aware of a thin petrochemical kind of smell, pear drops with top notes of almonds and rotting fruit. The client sucked it in, and Elsa saw a change in his expression, from serious to perplexed, pained even, an appalled exaltation. He looked as if he might denounce something at any minute, abjure something, possibly even prophesy. Bryn screwed the top back on and replaced the bottle, then pulled himself out and hunkered in closer. He was feeling about for something else now, still with one fist round the client's dick.

'Wait a minute.'

Whatever it was he was looking for, it wasn't where he expected it to be. He was getting smoke in his eyes again.

'Hang on.' He fumbled about for the ashtray, then started feeling underneath the bed, the angle dragging the client slightly to the side. 'Oh, fuck's *sake*.'

He let go of the client, and the client expressed complaint, a pissed-off 'uungh' sound.

'Look, hold this a minute,' Bryn said, and Elsa took a moment to realize he was talking to her, and another to see what it was he was talking to her about. She looked to where he was indicating. 'Christ's sake, I only just got him up, he'll lose it again if I leave him,' he said.

Elsa stared at him in disbelief.

'Look, I can't do everything,' Bryn was saying, 'I've only got one fucking pair of hands, haven't I? Just *hold* this a minute, will you?'

Elsa thought of standing up and leaving. But Bryn was daring her again, and she wasn't going to give him the satisfaction of weirding her out.

She reached out her hand and closed it round the client's dick, and he grunted and started moving it up and down. I'll hold it, she thought, but no way am I going to do anything more than that.

It felt much like Liam's, though the shape was surprisingly different and the flesh on the shaft was thicker and there was more of it, more play on it. She swallowed and closed her eyes as the client jerked and writhed in her hand. Whatever was in that little brown bottle it seemed to be reaching the parts. Bryn was still rummaging about, when the client went into spasm and came. There didn't seem to be much of it, just a little blob of it around his navel, like an oyster. It was a rather provisional discharge. Elsa jerked her hand away, and Bryn looked at the client, then back at her.

'Chris, you don't fuck around, do you? Trying to put me out of a job are you, eh?'

Elsa left hurriedly. She'd got some on her hand and wrist and washed her hands with grim thoroughness, then went back to the front room. A nation cavorted in paroxysms of solemnity and the plastic-wrapped flowers and cutesy bears and streaky felt-tipped cards banked up in great obscene drifts. Ten minutes later she heard low voices and the front door slammed. Bryn wandered back into the room, fiddling with his teeth.

'And that,' he said, 'is how you make a hundred and forty quid in two hours. I hope you're taking notes.'

She was furious with him, he'd basically tricked her into that whole thing.

'So. What was all that about, eh, Bryn? More background?'

'Look, love. It's not like in court, where it's neat and tidy. I can't keep everything separate.' He gave her an appraising look. 'Anyway, I thought you did pretty well.'

She tried not to be pleased. She *had* done pretty well though. She hadn't stormed out or made a fool of herself or anything.

Bryn had challenged her, she had risen to the challenge. It felt good.

He sprawled out on the sofa and twitched for a while as the television clips rotated, a bit more each time and now in the process of being packaged into little themed bursts, introduced by expert journalists who were now all in black ties and thinking of the BAFTAs. In the studio a journalist asked another journalist whether or not this was the saddest event he had ever covered.

'Bryn?'

'What?'

'What does it mean, you not being versatile?'

'Means I don't take it up the arse, love. What did the leper say to the prostitute?'

She shrugged: don't know.

'Keep the tip.'

Bryn stroked his belly and was soon asleep. Elsa sat on, soaking in the grief. She glanced over at him, the absolute relaxation of him, no blocked chi there, he was all yield and heaviness. His hand was nestled into his crotch. He looked as happy as a human being could reasonably expect to be. The sun flooded the windows, and from far away came the occasional chirruping of someone else's answering machine.

Elsa woke to find him rummaging about again.

'Just got to leave him his money for the room now or I'll never hear the end of it.' He pushed two tenners under the lamp on the coffee table. 'Right. Half three now. Have to be at Glebe Villas by four. You right?'

Elsa was sleepy and hot. He was always having to be somewhere. She frowned up at him.

'Oh, and I put a call in and we can't do the you know what tonight, so it'll have to be tomorrow. There won't be any court, anyway, so it won't matter – '

'How do you know?'

'I just do. I just do know.'

'Bryn ... '

'Look, are you right or what? We've got to get a move on.'

'Why have you?'

'What, Glebe Villas?'

She nodded.

'Because I've got to pick up Imogen.'

'Who's Imogen?'

'You'll see. You'll love this.' He danced about over her. 'Come on, you right or what? Eh?'

VIOLIN

Imogen was waiting by the school railings with two other six-year-olds, in a maroon sweatshirt and grey skirt and trainers. She was swinging her violin case against her legs, banging it against her knees. The two other girls were both staring off in different directions. Imogen looked up as Bryn and Elsa turned the corner, looked at Bryn, looked at Elsa.

'Uhoh,' Bryn said out of the corner of his mouth as they approached. 'Not a happy bunny today. Mind you, she never is.'

Imogen tugged the sleeve of one of the girls, who stared at Bryn and Elsa. The third girl also turned, as if they were all three connected by secret wires, and three little pairs of eyes watched Elsa and Bryn as they approached. Elsa didn't know which one was Imogen and so smiled equally at all of them in turn. Not a hint of a smile in return.

'This is my nuisance here,' Bryn said, and tugged at Imogen's hair, and she brushed his hand away.

'Not a nuisance,' she said.

The two other little girls whispered and glanced at Elsa and Bryn, equally, in turn. Their violin cases touched conspiratorially, scandalously, at the nose.

Bryn reached for Imogen's hand, which was refused, and he shrugged at Elsa over her head and pulled a face, draging his mouth down at one side and raising his eyes. Uhoh, the face said. Elsa said hello, and Imogen said hello back, but only just, and she wouldn't look.

'Have you got your bag and everything?' Bryn said, and Imogen nodded her head very slowly three times. She had several bags in fact: violin case, music in a plastic carrier bag and her schoolbag which went over one shoulder. She was all straps and handles, and tugged and adjusted constantly. The maroon pullover was pulled down by the dragging of the schoolbag strap, and her skirt was up at the back a bit. Elsa wanted to straighten her out but had no authority.

'So. Nuisance,' Bryn said, and kicked the violin case a little, just to make it swing. Imogen transferred it with some difficulty to the other side and dragged at a strap.

She wasn't at all curious about Elsa, apparently, except that she wanted to take sly little peeks from time to time, just checking her out. All Elsa could see of her was the top of her head and a flash of maroon. Her hair was long and parted in the middle, pulled back with an Alice band. She had a wide, woeful sort of face, disfigured temporarily by a pouty stuck-out lower lip and a big theatrical scowl. Bryn imitated the face, lower lip out and twisted down, eyes hooded, brow ridged. He ducked down to show Imogen and she giggled and then put her own face back on. Bryn winked at Elsa.

'Trouble,' he said, and Imogen said, 'Not trouble.'

'So, aren't you going to talk to my friend?'

A long, slow shake of the head, a serious wide-eyed look taking over from the pout, then the pout again.

'Little cow.'

'Not a cow.'

'Are a cow.'

'Not.'

'OK, so what are you then?'

Nothing for a few steps. They were waiting to cross a main road, and Bryn again reached for a hand, though there were only fingers spare. He grabbed hold of the handle of the carrier bag and lifted it up until he could get a fingerhold. She didn't resist him, but she wasn't making it easy.

'Just hold my hand.'

'No.'

'Imogen, look, just hold my hand.'

'No. Your hand's rubbish.'

'My hand's what?'

'Rubbish.'

'Oh yeah?'

'Yeah.'

'Cow.'

'Rubbish.'

'You're rubbish.'

'You're rubbish.'

'*You're* rubbish.' The *you're* was getting a little longer each time.

'You are, you mean.' That seemed to settle it somehow, a knockout blow on the repartee front. The lights changed and they crossed, Imogen tugging Bryn ahead of her. The safety of the opposite pavement achieved, the hand was swiftly withdrawn and normal relations resumed. Imogen now wanted to walk slightly ahead. Bryn pulled faces behind her back and made chopping motions at the back of her neck. She was headed for the Wimpy.

'Oh, yeah,' Bryn said. 'We have to go to the Wimpy. She has to have the Knickerbocker Glory.' They fought their way down Boundary Road, which was a screaming chaos of fat proles in competing sportswear brands with top-of-the range buggies, late for their case conferences. Everyone was smoking Superkings, sucking on them with expressions of gravely disappointed connoisseurship, as if their highest expectations were not being met. The Care with Dignity surgical appliance shop exposed its shameless conveniences, while Campers' Paradise catered darkly for those still continent and mobile, retailing army surplus to weekend survivalists and Territorial Army fantasists.

They filed into Wimpy and Imogen dumped her bags on the floor and then tried to kick them all under the table. Bryn went to the counter to order, even though it was waitress service. He just couldn't sit and wait for anything.

'So,' Elsa said. 'How was violin?'

Imogen nodded, again the ultra slow motion, and the serious lip. Elsa was appalled to notice that her eyes were starting to fill up. Imogen was holding it all in, but she clearly wanted to cry, was going to cry any minute, the hot, desperate, stealthy crying of six years old. Elsa remembered it only imperfectly.

'Was it all right?' she tried, and attempted a big happy smile. 'Did you have fun?'

The lip started wobbling and the eyes were blinking. The wide, rather chubby cheeks were hot and flushed. Imogen was sitting very still, not fiddling with anything, just looking at the wall above the plastic laminated menus.

'I mean, did it go all right?'

Oh God, Elsa thought, as a big fat tear slid round the curve of the base of Imogen's eye and welled up, rolling out and down the soft, plump, downy cheek.

Elsa looked around rapidly. Bryn was shifting from side to side and leaning over the counter, saying something to the girl behind the milk-shake machine. She was staring at him and shaking her head. She looked faintly outraged. Whatever it was he was after, it just wasn't on the menu.

Imogen smeared her face with her sleeve, the material not absorbent enough to do anything except mess her face up with wetness and snot. Elsa considered taking her to the toilet and giving her a wash. No authority though. She offered a tissue from a metal dispenser, and Imogen took it but just held it. She was blinking like a maniac now, the lip completely out of control, the shoulders shaking, the hair shaking, the face wet and sticky, but all completely silent, not even a gulp or a snorting of tubes. Abject, smeary, snotty misery. Elsa was terrified she was going to cry herself.

Elsa reached out and patted the back of Imogen's neck, where the parting in the hair terminated in some loose fluffy strands.

'What's up?' she said quietly glancing at Bryn. 'Did something happen?' She knew what had happened, of course, or she thought she did. She tried to remember. Let's see now. Something had been expected or, worse, hoped for and hadn't happened; there had been a disappointment, there had been an injustice, someone had been favoured instead of her. Someone had *said* something. Nothing's ever quite as bad as it is when you're six, Elsa thought.

'Look. I used to play the violin. When I was at school.'

And recorder, and singing. Later clarinet. She had been fairly good, had gone as far as Grade V, failed the theory paper, given it all up, though she still couldn't pass by a piano without solemnly tapping out the theme to *EastEnders* and a piece called Menuetto.

Elsa watched her as her face flooded, swimming with fluids. The eyes were red and the nose was running. The maroon sweatshirt was smeared, not just on the sleeves where she'd been rubbing her face, but also down the front, slimy whitish smears. Her little belly stuck out underneath. Her ankles were white and fat. Not an attractive child. Was that the problem? *Had* someone said something?

'I was never very good at it. I bet you're good at it.'

Imogen nodded, slowly. She didn't look as if she was very good at anything.

'What can you play?'

Imogen started kicking her legs against the table legs.

'Study in G, Largo and Little Bird.' This delivered in a voice choked and broken with tragedy.

'I'd love to hear you.'

'Not doing it any more.'

'What do you mean?' Elsa said, panicked, as if Imogen's threatened defection from the straight and narrow of violin might be laid at her door somehow.

'Not going any more.'

'But why?' Elsa almost wailed, and was answered with a great long, detailed speech from Imogen, delivered with full accompaniment of sniffling and snorting and nasal noises of various kinds. Elsa couldn't understand all of it, and Imogen wouldn't look at her as she spoke, but just continued to kick the table legs.

'Violin,' 'Mr Allen' and 'Stella' came out several times. And then he but I had already only and then she but I *had* and Mr Allen but he didn't and I *had*, all week, and he *said*. Something about pizzicato, which Imogen delivered as 'pillicoco'. It wasn't fair! This last came out with passion and outrage. It wasn't FAIR! Elsa could only dimly remember this time, when you still shouted but it isn't FAIR and expected redress. Expected someone to make it fair. It was all rather a long time ago.

'Oh, darling,' she said, and again was horrified by how her own eyes were suddenly blurred and swimming, her own Eustachian tubes suddenly blocked and her own lips in free and full wobble modality. 'Oh, darling. God.' She grabbed the tissue back from Imogen and dabbed and rubbed. It was special non-absorbent paper seemingly.

Imogen watched with interest. Bryn came back from the counter, jingling change and winking. I got something in my eye, Elsa said, busy with the tissue, and Bryn and Imogen exchanged a look, pushed down lip and raised eyebrows: what's wrong with her?

Bryn sat beside Imogen, pushing her onto the other seat.

'So. Everybody happy?'

Imogen snuffled almost all the way through her Knickerbocker Glory. By the time she'd got to the runny raspberry stuff at the bottom she was all but finished, just the odd snort. She didn't speak while she was eating, just dipped the long spoon and licked, dipped and licked. There was a pleasing rhythm to the clicking of spoon against fluted glass. She was immensely serious; she clearly had an established way of doing this and it was not to be disrupted. She glanced up at Elsa a few times, to check if she was still crying. She wasn't. Elsa had tea. The tea-bag made a soggy squalid mess of the napkin. Bryn had coffee, black, no sugar. No one else came in while they were there, though people streamed past the window.

Imogen finished with the spoon and used her finger to clean up the glass. Bryn watched her with something like

165

indulgence, a look Elsa hadn't seen in him before. He was indulgent but he was fierce, too. Also completely ineffectual, exasperated, irritated by her. He would nag her about something and she'd sigh and cast her eyes up and he'd push her and she'd push him back, he'd call her a cow, so it went on. The conversation was mostly of the yes-you-will-no-I-won't-yes-you-did-no-I-*didn't* sort. Elsa couldn't contribute much. Once, in one of the tenser stand-offs, she tried something about school: what was Imogen's best subject? Imogen just stared at her, and after a moment Bryn did too. She stared back. Then they got back to bickering.

Only once was the rhythm disturbed: Bryn was complaining that he had to take time off to come and ferry her around every Monday, while her mum went off to see her fancy man in Ford Open, and Imogen, with a short preparatory look at Elsa, detonated what she clearly knew was the nuclear bomb.

'Er, time off what?' she said. The tone of voice wasn't her own, it was her mum's, and so was the question. That much was obvious to everyone.

'You know time off what,' Bryn said.

'No, I don't,' she said, brazen, and folded her arms, making a thick bundle against her chest. 'You tell me.'

'Don't start that,' Bryn said, and put his hands on his head. 'What have I told you?'

'Do you know what he does?' she said now to Elsa, her manner an arch, perfect parody of someone ten years her senior at least. 'Do you know what his job is?' This was said in an incredulous voice: wait till you hear this!'

Bryn was standing. The table and the chairs were fixed, all welded together, and it took him a little bit of dancing around to disentangle himself and reach over to grab her.

'He *touches* men's *willies* . . . '

Then she was up in the air, being hauled up and out of her seat in one clean movement, being dragged away between the tables. She was grinning back at Elsa as she was carted away to the toilets at the back of the Wimpy.

'What have I told you?' Bryn was shouting. 'Eh? How many times. Eh?'

Elsa caught the waitress looking over and smiled at her: everything fine here! The waitress came with her little pad, did they want anything else, and Elsa ordered one more of everything in her confusion, though this was almost certainly not the right procedure. Imogen surely wasn't supposed to have two Knickerbocker Glories.

Everything was on the table when Imogen and Bryn emerged from the toilets. Imogen was dragging him now, grinning all over her face, and he was saying, do you hear me, madam? Eh? Do you?

Imogen reached the table first, took in the new Knickerbocker Glory at once, looked in amazement and some suspicion at Elsa. A trap. Had to be.

'Go on, say it,' Bryn said, and Imogen giggled and squirmed off his hand, going boneless so her knees were dragging the floor.

'Go on,' Bryn said, and Imogen screamed and giggled. Bryn picked her up and held her straight in front of Elsa.

'Sorry for saying willies,' Imogen said, and then fell about in hysterics. Her fat white belly emerged from under her jumper and school blouse; she was all rucked up and hot and chaotic.

'What else?' Bryn demanded.

'Sorry for being rude.'

'And it's not going to happen any more, is it?'

She squealed, wriggled, it could have been 'no' she was saying, and Bryn let it go at that, with many stern looks.

She was quiet for a bit and Bryn tried to make conversation with Elsa.

'Dad?' Imogen said a few times, quietly then getting louder. 'Dad?'

'I'm talking.'

'Yeah, but, Dad ... '

'What?'

'Dad, where's Uncle Mark?'

He turned to face her and she held his eye for a moment.

'Don't start that.'

'Yeah, but where – '

'I'm telling you, don't start all that Uncle Mark stuff now.'

'Yeah, but...'

He raised eyebrows at her and tilted his face down. I'm not kidding, the face said, and she took him at his word, saving her energies for another assault later perhaps. She had a fine sense of strategy. She knew her enemy. She planned ahead.

'And if you think for one second you're having that,' he said, grabbing the long spoon and pointing to the Knickerbocker Glory, the thick bottle glass misted and beaded with condensation, and Imogen gave him a wide-eyed look and stuck three fingers into it.

UNFATHOMABLE THINGS

Bryn had to take Imogen somewhere, where someone else would keep her until her mum got back from Ford Open. She was to be passed from hand to hand, a little like an Olympic flame, only much much stickier, and perhaps slightly less emblematic in general.

She wouldn't say goodbye properly. Bryn again promised Elsa things for tomorrow. I'll show you it all tomorrow, he said. We'll have a what do you call it, reconstruction. You'll see. Promise. They arranged when and where and Elsa went home.

Four phone messages:

'Elsa? Liam. Listen, give us a call, yeah, OK, bye.' Very tight-lipped. He was all worked up about something, no doubt their cancelled date from last week, and the fact that she hadn't rung him today. She'd ring him later. Meanwhile he would brood as he practised his breathing, first the Buddhist then the Taoist. The brooding was inimical to any real result, chi-wise. It buggered up the yielding. Blocked the energy. She would be blamed.

'Hello, Patrick here. Any news? Do let me know.'

'Elsa? Elsa? Hello?' This was her dad. He believed that she was always in fact sitting right on top of the phone screening her calls and once she knew it was him she'd answer. 'Are you there, love? No? Give your old dad a call, nothing really. Wasn't it a shame about that Diana, she always seemed so nice. She came here to Warrington once, do you remember, I sent you the article. I couldn't believe it when they said she was dead. I thought it must be a mistake. OK. Well. Bye for now, love.' He sounded a bit drunk. He was also much at a loose end since her mum had died, had never remarried or even dated much, except for a brief and very unsatisfactory do with a divorcée named Bonny who kept 'taking him shopping', and he seemed now to have retreated into a state of numbed inaction. He was retired on health grounds and spent much of his time in front of the television with his breathing mask close to hand, and had to spend as much as ten hours a week in a sort of home oxygen tent. His voice got thicker and throatier all the time, and his accent was deepening as well. He was always worse in the summer. He hardly sounded like anyone she knew now, and she could remember only a small handful of events from her childhood with him. Her recollections all seemed to take place on crazy-golf courses or traffic islands. Sometimes both at the same time. Often he would be patiently pointing at something she couldn't see. No *there*, over *there*. She could never see it.

The last time she'd visited him he'd been bad and was practically housebound, *Racing Post* on his lap, checking the results on Teletext. He was endlessly interested in her progress in the world, proud of her, impressed with her career and her independence, worried about her being lonely. She was the only child, he wished there'd been others but there you are. He hadn't met Liam yet. She doubted that they'd make much sense of each other. She tried not to imagine in too much detail the conversation in which Liam outlined the theory and practice of t'ai chi ch'uan and its healing properties. She sighed. Next message. Ted Slaughter, team-leader.

'Yes, 2.15 on August the, let's see, um-de-dum, er, the' –

the sound of rustling about – 'er, no, actually it's September, isn't it? Monday anyway. Ted Slaughter for Elsa Frith. Now. I know Bob spoke to you the other day but I thought it might be better if I spoke to you myself, try to clear it up. Wolf and Henderson, CPG. Claire says she doesn't know how to get into your computer to look for it, but she says it all went down to store anyway. Can that be right? Why would it go to store? I thought Claire would have had it to agree the schedule of works with the surveyor, but she says she hasn't seen it yet. I've had the freeholder's agents on to me twice now wanting to know because they've had the tenants on to them. So. If you just leave a message or whatever. Sorry to bother you. Bye for now.'

For God's *sake*. Before she had time to think about it she was dialling the number and listening to the answer machine message, recorded by herself as it happened.

'Hello, Ted? Elsa. Yes, I explained all this to Bob. Wolf and Henderson, Lansdowne Avenue, CPG. Gone to store. Freeholder insane, managing agents imcompetent, solicitors impossible, tenants with a roof leaking. Someone's going to have to visit either freeholder or her agent. No further progress possible until managing agents given power to authorize schedule of works by freeholder, since estate solicitors refuse to act, even though it's their lease and it's a perfectly standard repairing covenant. So. Nothing I can do I'm afraid, Ted.'

She stopped and heard the tightness in her voice, the implacable listing of all these impossible parties to this endlessly protracted problem. All this just to get the bloody roof fixed. She took a breath. And no point badgering bloody Claire about it either, she wanted to say, it's only because she hates you like everyone else that she won't show you how to get into my computer, and why won't you listen to poor Bob Betjeman when he tells you things, you stupid, *stupid*, little man. The machine diligently recorded her furious breath and furious thoughts. 'Anyway. I have to go now, Ted,' she said, and hung up. Malibu. Right now.

*

Later.

'Patrick?' She was sitting in the front window with Norfolk Square below her, the trees blowzy and slow in the heat, stirring in the breeze coming off the sea. Seagulls called to each other endlessly from the chimney pots. Sometimes they carried on all through the night, the same thing over and over again. They just couldn't get it through to each other seemingly, whatever it was. Not the most intelligent of birds. Her hand was chilled from the ice in the glass. 10 p.m. She'd tried him twice before, left no message. This time he'd picked it up on the second ring.

'Patrick?' Now she had him, she wasn't sure what she wanted to say. Bryn's got a kid, she thought. Who's six. If the kid is six, then Bryn is not nineteen. More like twenty-three. Just a few years younger than me, as a matter of fact. He said he didn't do rent, but then he took me to watch him do it. He said he didn't know anything about that witness, what's his name, Hegler, but he quite obviously does. He says he didn't beat up Hook. But.

'You there? Elsa? Are you...'

'Yes, I'm fine.' Sigh. 'It's a lovely night.' She scratched one foot with the other, languorously, as she spoke. 'It's all summery. I can feel the wind.'

He paused for a moment, trying to get the measure of her over the phone. He heard her ice clunking.

'Er, Elsa, now I know you won't take this the wrong way but you haven't by any chance been – '

'Drinking? Well, you know. Only Malibu.'

'Oh, I see.'

'You know, Patrick, I've been thinking about this trial.'

'Hm?'

'You know. The trial?'

'Yes, Elsa.'

'Well, the thing is that Bryn probably did it, didn't he?'

'Yes, he probably did.'

'I mean, he says he didn't but then he says all kinds of things. If he didn't then who did?'

'No one.'

'But someone did, Patrick. There were those pictures.'

'Bryn possibly?'

'I suppose so.' She sighed massively, the cool moist air playing over her breasts and neck. She could hear the surf on the pebbles far away. 'He's got a little girl. Did they tell us that?'

'News to me. But if he's got child-care responsibilities then that'd explain why he's not in any kind of custody. That'd be enough right there.'

'He says he was married when he was eighteen for three months to this girl. Then she went off with someone else. The kid's six now. She's called Imogen. He sees her once a week.'

'Ah.'

'No, but Patrick, I mean he's a father, he's that little girl's *father*. You see? She kept calling him dad.'

'Yes?'

'I'm just saying. He shouldn't be going round beating people up if he's her dad. My dad wouldn't beat people up.'

'Dads do it too, you know.'

'I suppose they do. But why would he do it, Patrick? Why?'

'Probably just one of those unfathomable things. You know, the dark reaches of the human heart or whatever it is, or then again maybe he's just a violent little sod...'

'He doesn't seem all that unfathomable though, does he? He's quite fathomable actually.' She stumbled over 'fathomable' and had to have a few runs at it. 'It's a terrible world, Patrick. Why is it like this? Why is it so terrible? Why, Patrick? And now Princess Di and all that. My dad was all upset about it.'

'Elsa, snap out of it now. Try to stay focused for just a moment. I take it Bryn didn't come up with this proof he's supposed to be showing you?'

'No. Tomorrow. We're going to have a what do you call it?'

'Drink?'

'No, Patrick. You know. Like on *Crimewatch*. Where you have to wear a plastic mac and walk about by railway lines all night...'

'Reconstruction.'

'That's it. Oh, no court tomorrow, incidentally. We'll just be brought in and sent out again like today. It's a funny trial this, isn't it?'

'Hysterical.'

'Oh, did I tell you that he is, oh what do you call it now? Even though he said he wasn't.'

'What? I'm not with you.'

'You know, when you have to pay sixty quid...They have a word for it.'

'What?'

'Little short word. "Rent", that's it. He is.'

'Elsa, do I dare say that Bryn being a sex-industry worker isn't really that much of a surprise?'

'Nothing wrong with it though.'

'Isn't there? I wouldn't know.'

'I mean, he's got to make a living. He's got violin lessons to pay for.'

'Violin...'

She giggled. 'Patrick? You'll never guess what I did?'

'Give up.'

'Not telling.' She giggled again. Patrick sighed.

'So Hook's a punter then?'

'I don't know.' She spoke heavily, as if all the weariness in the world had suddenly got into her voice and was pulling it to the earth. 'It all seems very sad.' She thought of the client from earlier on, his serious expression and floppy breasts, his thick foreskin, like vinyl, his helpless meagre fluid. 'I mean, it just all seems very sad. To me.'

'Elsa? Try to focus now. Now, Elsa, if you really are thinking that he's guilty, do you also at the same time think it's a tremendously good idea to go and see this proof of his tomorrow?'

'Oh, *God*, Patrick.' She'd been on the verge of saying, I want a kid! I want a kid too!, though she didn't really. She'd drunk too much, she should just hang up now. 'God. You know?'

'OK, Elsa, now get some sleep, all right? And I'll see you tomorrow in court. OK? OK?'

'OK. Bye, Patrick. Patrick?'
'Yes, Elsa.'
'Nothing

She hung up and immediately dialled Liam, but got Vicki, the flatmate. Liam was out, Vicki didn't know when he'd be back. Elsa left a message for him to ring. She could never think of anything to say to Vicki, who vaguely troubled her whenever Elsa thought about her. She grew a great number of small plants in tiny pots which she watered with a teeny weeny watering can and was forever pulling her hair away from her face.

Elsa got undressed and lay on her bed in the dark little back bedroom and listened to the plumbing and felt randy and restless and alive.

SHAG THIS FOR A GAME OF SOLDIERS

Nothing in court the next morning, though they weren't sent home. Elsa nursed her hangover and drank milk and grapefruit juice for lunch. But then suddenly at 2 p.m. everything got under way. The jury were called in, the judge arrived and there was a more purposeful atmosphere in the courtroom. The briefs were again shuffling their papers and muttering to their solicitors, and there was a pair of uniformed police at the back. Even the stenographer looked slightly less blank than previously.

Bryn was fidgeting in the dock, returning some comment to the uniform behind him out of the corner of his mouth. He watched as Elsa and the other jurors filed in, and made a face: what will be will be, yeah?

The judge had a quick smiling conference with one of the police officers, and turned to the jury.

'Ladies and gentlemen, I am delighted to be able to tell you that our difficulties have been resolved and we are at last in the happy position of being able to complete our work here. I must again apologize for the inconvenience you have suffered with such good grace, and I thank you for your renewed attention now. I remind you that you are still under oath. Mr Djabo?'

Djabo stood, gown thrown off the shoulders, wig cheekily raked, his lovely manicured hands cool on his neat papers.

'Your Honour, I would like to call Mr Mark Hegler to the stand.'

Elsa risked a quick glance over at Bryn, who had frozen solid, and was now watching the door with undivided attention. One of the uniforms went out with an usher and then, a few moments later, Mark Hegler took the witness stand.

Elsa scrutinized him as he took his oath. He looked about the same age as Bryn, narrower and leaner, thinner in the face, with a choirboy haircut and a painfully new suit, very wide in the lapel and baggy in the leg. His voice was tight and brisk, heavily accented, and he shot his cuffs repeatedly as he spoke. He gave the card and Bible back to the usher and looked quickly round the court then fixed his gaze on the wall above Elsa's head, where his eyes stayed for most of his testimony. This is bad news, Elsa thought. Bryn was staring straight ahead now, jaw clamped. She saw him swallow heavily, saw the Adam's apple move down, then up.

'Mr Hegler.' Djabo gave his best smile. 'I'll keep this as brief as possible. Now you, I understand, have known the defendant, Mr Sweetman, for a period of about three years. Is that correct?'

'Sir.' This was delivered in a passable imitation of army style, a clipped uninflected bark.

'Would you say that you and he are good friends?'

'Sir.'

'And would you say that over those three years you have gained something of an insight into Mr Sweetman's character and nature?'

'Sorry?'

'You have come to know Mr Sweetman well?'

'Sir.'

'Now. I would like to draw your attention to the evening of 22 June of last year. Can you tell the ladies and gentlemen what you were doing on that evening?'

'Sir. Yeah, I was round Harry's shop.'

'Harry? Mr Hook?'

'Yeah. So I was doing something in the basement...'

'Can you tell us what exactly you were doing?'

'Yeah, he had this, like stuff, like boxes of old cloth and that, and I was supposed to sort it all out for him, you know, make sure there weren't no moths or anything, shake it all out and spray it with this stuff he's got, then he wanted it all boxing up again and putting away with these cedar balls he uses.'

'I see. So you were busily employed downstairs in the basement. And where was Mr Hook?'

'He'd gone up.'

'Up to his apartment?'

Apartment was clearly not the word Mark Hegler would have used.

'Sir.'

'All right.' Djabo paused and blinked a few times. 'All right. Now. Did someone – as far as you are aware, did anyone else come to Mr Hook's shop on that evening?'

'Sir.'

'And could you tell the ladies and gentlemen – '

Hegler was there already.

'Him.' He pointed half-heartedly to the dock where the ice statue of Bryn Sweetman sat.

'Would you please state his name?'

'Yeah. Bryn. Sweetman.'

'Thank you. Now, I'm wondering if you, or if *he*, or, I mean, were you surprised to see Mr Sweetman there on that evening?'

'Surprised? Why would I be surprised?'

'Well, that's really the nature of my question. So you were not surprised?'

'No, sir.'

'He had, perhaps, been there before?'

'What, Bryn? Yeah.'

'Do you know what his business on previous occasions had been?'

'Sir.'

'And would you mind telling the ladies...'

Mark Hegler shrugged and then giggled, and blushed, bright lobster red, but no words emerged. The judge leaned forward.

'Mr Hegler, do you understand Mr Djabo's question?'

'Sir.'

But still no answer. Elsa caught a quick look between Bryn and Hegler, freighted up with menace and entreaty and things too blocked and clotted to be named properly. The police meanwhile were sending Hegler control messages with their eyes, obviously aware that he could turn into a hostile witness at any second. The situation was all very precarious and cobbled together, Elsa realized.

Djabo tried again.

'Well, we have heard from Mr Hook that Mr Sweetman had been employed by him on half a dozen or so occasions.'

'Sir.'

'And Mr Hook has told us that Mr Sweetman was in fact employed by him to polish his table.'

Hegler snorted. 'Polish his what?'

'His table. A kitchen table.'

Hegler looked like he was trying not to laugh. 'Sir.'

'Well, is that not so?'

'If Harry says that then...' He shrugged.

'But that is not your recollection?'

'Well, it wasn't his table he was getting polished, was it?' Scattered giggles from various places. Elsa even thought she saw Bryn effortfully straightening his face.

'It was something else? Mr Hook is mistaken when he says it was a table?'

'Listen, right, he says he was getting his table polished, fair play to him. Totally. That's it. Yeah, right. Table. I remember now.'

'All right. Now. On this evening in June Mr Sweetman arrived at what time would you say?'

'Ten or so.'

'Quite late then?'

'Sir.'

'And was Mr Sweetman expected? Was he due to come and polish Mr Hook's table?'

'If you like. You could put it that way.'

'And what happened then?'

'Bryn goes up. They're up there half an hour or so. Then I hear all this banging and shouting. So I goes up.'

'Can you describe what you saw when you went up to the apartment?'

'Sir. Harry's all pissed up, he's staggering about, like knocking into things. He's like, he's got these marks all over him. He's out of it, totally. It's like he's looking for something. He's bleeding all over the place.'

'And what was Mr Sweetman doing?'

'Nothing. He's just standing there. He was off it as well.'

'Off it? You mean he'd taken something?'

'Sir.'

'Drugs? He was on drugs?'

'On drugs. Yeah.'

'And did Mr Hook say anything?'

'Well, he was shouting if that's what you mean. He's going, "I simply won't stand for it, I simply find it insupportable", all this.'

'And what did you understand by that?'

'Your Honour . . . ' Parrot's first words that morning. He was objecting to something, Elsa wasn't certain what exactly, but the judge agreed with it, whatever it was. Djabo was not his usual sure-footed self. Elsa guessed he'd only had a very short time with Hegler to prepare. The rhythm was off. 'Would you mind rephrasing your question, Mr Djabo?'

'I will go one better and withdraw it entirely, Your Honour. Mr Hegler, what did you see Mr Sweetman do next?'

'Well. He sees me, right. He goes, shag this for a game of soldiers, and he's off.'

'He ran away?'

'Sir.'

'And did either you or Mr Hook make any attempt to stop him?'

'No, sir. He was just out of there.'

'And what did you do next?'

'I stayed with Harry till he called the police and everything, then I left.'

'You left the scene as well?'

'Sir.'

'And could you tell the ladies and gentlemen why you didn't stay to offer your testimony at that time?' Djabo half-turned so that the jury could see more of his face.

'Sir. I thought they'd just think it was me that done it, and I kind of panicked.'

'But later you recollected yourself and offered, completely voluntarily, to co-operate with the police and come here today of your own free will to give us your eyewitness testimony.'

'Sir.' Elsa thought she detected a certain amount of nostril flaring on the part of the two uniformed police at 'voluntarily'.

'Thank you, Mr Hegler. Please stay where you are while my colleague asks you a few questions.' Djabo sat and looked mightily pleased with himself. Elsa sneaked a glance at the rest of the jury. In so far as they wore any identifiable expression it was one of yeah, so? We already knew Bryn was guilty. They might not like Hegler but they had no reason not to believe him. Bryn was dead and buried now unless Parrot could come up with something.

'Mr Hegler.' Parrot stood but didn't speak for a full minute. Elsa thought he was looking very pouchy. Grey nicotined hands shaky on the table. 'I won't keep you a moment longer than necessary. Now could you tell us what your occupation is, please?'

'Trainee computer operator.'

'And what exactly does that entail?'

'It's like you do this qualification, at college, and you do day release and that. NVQ and that.'

'Quite so. And do you have any other, er, profession as well?'

'Your Honour...' Djabo rose.

'Yes. Mr Parrot, I think Mr Hegler has answered your question already.'

'As Your Honour pleases. Now, Mr Hegler, you have told us that on the night of 22 June last year you were in the basement of Mr Hook's charity shop in Eastern Road, engaged in some business involving fabric or cloth or something of the kind? Yes?'

'Yes, sir.'

'And that you heard an altercation upstairs while Mr Sweetman was there with Mr Hook?'

'Sir.'

'And that you went up to investigate and found Mr Hook bleeding and marked. Yes?'

'Sir.'

'But how do you know?'

'Sir?'

'Well, I don't understand how you could see these marks. I mean, what was Mr Hook wearing?'

'Sorry?'

'I asked you what Mr Hook was wearing at this moment?'

'Your Honour...' Djabo had a weary eyebrow raised. 'Mr Hook's state of dress cannot be an issue here surely...'

'Your Honour, in his direct testimony Mr Hegler told the ladies and gentlemen that not only was Mr Hook bleeding when he went up, but that he was also marked. Marked I think was his word. So my question is intended to elucidate further the nature of these marks. Where on his body were they, Mr Hegler?'

'Your Honour, the ladies and gentlemen have on another occasion had a full recital of the injuries sustained by Mr Hook on this evening...'

'I'll allow it,' the judge said and swivelled back a little way. 'Would you like me to repeat the question, Mr Hegler?'

'No, sir. He was wearing his underpants, sir.'

'Just his underpants. Nothing else?'

'Yeah, he had something else on as well.'

'Indeed?'

'Yeah, he had a pair of cuffs on, didn't he?'

'Cuffs? Like shirt cuffs?'

'No, sir. Handcuffs.'

'Handcuffs?' Parrot sounded dazed. He just wasn't ready for any of this, he was asking questions he didn't know the answer to, he was floundering. He clearly thought he'd caught Hegler out, but instead he'd opened up something new and unexpected and wholly unwelcome. Whatever Bryn had told him about Hegler and his likely testimony, things had obviously changed now. All bets were off. Hegler was a prosecution witness and then some. 'Are you telling the ladies and gentlemen that when you went upstairs you found Mr Hook to be *handcuffed*?'

'Sir.'

'And yet he was not handcuffed when the police arrived. I recall no mention of that in the attending officer's report...' He made a show of searching about with his papers, then looked up expectantly.

'No, sir.'

'How are the ladies and gentlemen to understand this extraordinary state of affairs?'

'Yeah, I took them off him, didn't I?'

'You uncuffed Mr Hook before the police arrived at the scene?'

'Sir.'

'Why?'

''Cos he wanted me to. He wanted to get dressed. He was a bit embarrassed like.'

'And no mention of this was made either to the officers who attended the scene or at any later time?'

'No, sir.'

'Until this moment.'

'Sir.'

'And where are these handcuffs now?'

Hegler shrugged. 'Don't know, sir', and Elsa thought, I bet I do.

'Mr Hegler.' Parrot stopped dead. He looked as if he might cry. 'Mr Hegler, this really gets more extraordinary with every passing moment. We start off with an account of an assault on a man in a room over a junk shop and we end up, following your testimony, with the grotesque spectacle of this man, naked apart from his underwear and a pair of handcuffs, drunk, incoherent and bleeding, blundering around in an upstairs room knocking things over. His assailant, whom you now maintain was in some kind of drugged condition, simply arrives, assaults him, damages things, says, "Shag this for a game of soldiers", and runs off, while you meanwhile are placidly taking precautions against moth damage in the basement. And yet no one seems to have the remotest idea of why any of this should take place. Not even you, who describes himself as a good friend of the defendant's and a regular acquaintance of the plaintiff's, and who was on the scene at the time. Does this not all strike you as somewhat extraordinary?'

'Your Honour...'

'Yes. Yes. Mr Parrot, I know these are trying circumstances for you but we would be grateful if you would not invite the witness to speculate on matters that he has not himself seen, or to engage in characterizations of events...'

'Mr Hegler.' Parrot was staring down at the table top, his brows ridged. 'I would like to ask you a question that my colleague put earlier to the plaintiff, Mr Hook, which is simply this. Do you have any knowledge of why Mr Sweetman would go upstairs to Mr Hook's apartment on a balmy June evening, handcuff him, beat him, damage the pelmet and the computer, and then leave?'

'Do I know why? No, sir.'

'Can you think of any possible reason?'

'No, sir.'

'You say Mr Sweetman had taken drugs. But you are not a medical expert.'

'I've seen him like that before.'

'But that is still merely a speculation on your part.'

Hegler shrugged.

'Mr Hegler, I'm going to suggest to you that this is a complete and total fabrication from beginning to end.'

'No, sir.'

'I'm going to suggest that it was in fact you who went up to Mr Hook's apartment on that June evening, that it was you

184

who savagely beat him, stripped him, handcuffed him, damaged his property – '

'No, sir.'

'Then you ran off, and later concocted your story of Bryn Sweetman's visit – '

'No, sir.'

'Yes, sir. Mr Sweetman was never even there on that occasion, it was you and you alone who performed these dreadful actions – '

'No, sir.'

'...on a man who had been your benefactor and protector and erstwhile employer, after which you falsely accused your friend of three years' standing, my client, Mr Sweetman – '

'No, sir.'

'No? Well, I'm sure the ladies and gentlemen will have their own opinions about that.'

Oh yes, Elsa thought wearily. They'll think you're throwing round accusations you can't back up again. Bryn's had it. Parrot sat down again, slightly flushed, and Djabo waived his redirect. Mark Hegler looked uncertain for a moment, then stepped down and out of the courtroom. Closing statements. Elsa just sat patiently waiting to be released so she could join the hanging party in the deliberation room. Bryn stared straight ahead. Fucked. Shafted. Up the arse.

The judge turned to them and finally put down his pen.

'Ladies and gentlemen, you have now heard all the evidence. It is again my responsibility to explain to you the situation with regard to the law. In view of the delays also, I would like briefly to review the evidence we have heard.' Oh, do we have to? Elsa thought. He was consulting his own very detailed notes, and it was all pelmets again. This went on for hours, seemingly. Then he started in on all the presumed-innocent nonsense again, while Parrot and Djabo fiddled with their papers and Bryn sat stunned in the dock. By the time the judge finished it was too late to do anything more.

'In view of the lateness of the hour, I would suggest that we now adjourn for today and recommence tomorrow morning, so that you can begin your deliberations. You will elect a foreman who will speak to me on your behalf and any questions you may have can be conducted to me in written form by one of the ushers. You'll find a little buzzer on the wall in the deliberation room. I'm sorry to say though that once you are deliberating you will not be allowed to communicate with anyone except the ushers until you have reached your verdict. And I'd just like to thank you again for your attention.' He stood and left and it was over for the day.

Elsa was due to meet Bryn at ten that evening, though there didn't seem much point. It was hard to imagine what he could possibly show her now that would change her mind.

9.30. Elsa was dressed and ready to leave the house, standing jittery at the window, when the phone rang. She grabbed for it, feeling obscurely guilty, as if whoever was calling knew about what she was planning to do.

'Hello, Elsa?'

'Claire?'

'Elsa? Are you all right? You sound weird.'

'Claire. Listen. Quickly now. Just say, for instance, you were, oh, I don't know, on a jury maybe – '

'This is strictly hypothetical of course.'

'...and say you didn't think the defendant was getting a fair trial.'

'...yeeees...'

'And then, just suppose that the defendant said he could prove to you that he was innocent. Prove it, Claire. But it had to be just you, and it had to be out of court. Tonight.'

'Oh, yes. Uhuh.'

'And you had to decide in the next half-hour.'

'Oh, right. Yes. I see. Elsa, what in God's name have you done, you ridiculous woman? What have you got yourself into? Huh?'

'Claire, I might be able to get him off...'

'Just you.'

'Yes. Listen, I know how this sounds – '

'Elsa, you remember that time we were talking about those based-on-a-true-story American movies where the mom find

186

the inner strength that she didn't even know she had to kick out the child-abusing husband with the great body and all the guns, and take over the family car-breaking business?'

'Yes, Claire – '

'Becoming, in the process, a stronger, better person and a kind of role model to whole generations of American women?'

'*Claire* – '

'Elsa, you're turning into one of them. Aren't you? Hm? You're getting in touch with your power. Now aren't you? Admit it.'

'I wouldn't say power – '

'Oh, I would. You alone know the truth, you alone can save this poor boy, who incidentally, by your description of him, could be grateful in ways that most people can only dream of, only you have the power.'

'Well, I suppose that's true in a way but – '

'Elsa, I tell you what I think. Since you ask. I think you should go into the bathroom and stand in front of the mirror and say fifty times: I will *not* get in touch with my power. I will *not* be a role model to generations of ...'

'What is this power thing?'

'You know very well. I can hear it in your voice. You should hear yourself. And along with the power, are there any other symptoms? Exaltation? Feelings of impregnability or extraordinary capability? I don't know, Elsa, voices maybe?'

'Oh, God, Claire, I don't know what to do.'

'Yes, you do. Make yourself a nice quadruple Malibu on the rocks, put *Newsnight* on and stay in the house. Then go to court tomorrow and do whatever you're supposed to do there. Do *not* leave the house tonight. Elsa, are you listening to me?'

'Claire, look. I'll talk to you tomorrow.'

'Don't be crazy, Elsa. I mean it.'

'Yeah, yeah. Yap yap yap.'

'Elsa, if I have to come over there ...'

THE LAST CHANCE SALOON

10 p.m. Elsa was sitting upstairs at the Breach of Conditions waiting for Bryn. She was on Guinness, since it took longer to drink than Malibu and so dosage control was more accurate. She would keep a cool head. There were various club flyers lying around and she picked up a handful and scrutinized them minutely. She sipped the Guinness. Looked at the clock.

10.20. No sign. She would give him till half past then that was it. He'd probably done a runner anyway, after today's débâcle. Hegler had done quite a job on him.

10.30. She had two inches of Guinness in her glass. And when that was finished . . .

Then there he was. He sat beside her and grinned. 'Fucking Mark fucking Hegler,' he said, but refused to be drawn any further, beyond the observation that he was a cunt. He showed no sign of buying his own drink and Elsa again reached for her bag.

Last orders. Bryn was relaxed, so relaxed in fact that she began to wonder if he hadn't had something really quite relaxing before he came out. She imagined him and Pest making merry with the freezer bags. He kicked his legs out, leaned back, his head rolling slightly, eyes screwed up, and his hand rarely left his crotch. He was wearing an HL baseball cap and kept playing around with it, taking it off and reseating it, twisting it backwards, sideways, pulling idiot faces, tongue protruding. He was a laff riot. Elsa wasn't wholly in the mood, though, and he gave her a series of long interrogatory looks before saying, 'What? *What?* What have I done now? Eh?'

She thought, well, it's on my mind so I might as well say it.

'Bryn. You're a lying get, aren't you?'

'You what? What's that supposed to mean? Eh?'

'Look, it's becoming just a little bit obvious that you are in fact guilty as charged. It's becoming obvious even to me and I was the one who was giving you the benefit of the doubt. God knows why. You keep promising to show me your proof and you never do...'

'I know, pet. I'm trying, aren't I? You can't just arrange these things just like that, you know. But tonight is the night. Oh yes.'

'Oh yeah, well, it's sort of got to be, hasn't it really, considering that we have to what do you call it tomorrow. Deliberate. And anyway, look, even if you do manage to convince me, the most I can do is get you a hung jury. You do know that, don't you? So you're still going to have to have another trial, another jury... You going to do all this again? All this bloody notes nonsense?'

'I wouldn't mind a hung jury,' Bryn said, 'as long as it was *well* hung...'

'Oh, right. Right Yeah, you're hysterical...'

'What's the matter with you? Eh? You've gone all serious on me, haven't you?'

'Look, I just don't want you to go to jail. No, I mean, I don't want it to be me that has to send you to jail. But I'm going to have to, aren't I? I'm going to have to go in there tomorrow and say, well, it's kind of obvious, isn't it? Guilty. As charged. I mean, there really isn't much else I *can* say. I wanted to say not guilty. But how can I?'

'Why don't you?'

'Why don't I what?' She hadn't intended to say all that, about not wanting to send him to jail, not in that way anyway. But she didn't want him in jail, she realized, she wanted him out of jail. Here.

'Want me to go to jail. Why don't you? You think I'm guilty.'

'I just don't, I don't really believe in jail actually, not for this kind of thing anyway. I don't think it's a very conducive environment – '

'What are you like? Eh?' He rocked back and laughed right at her. 'Christ. Conducive what? Eh? It's not supposed to be *conducive*, is it? It's supposed to be a shitehole people like you send people like me to so we'll stop robbing them and that. In case you hadn't noticed, that's what it's there for, that's what they have the court and that for. I mean, I don't want to upset you or anything, love. I mean, I know how sensitive you are, you know, but you seem to be missing the point just a little bit – '

'Bryn. Look. I'm sure there are reasons, you must have your own...reasons...Look, I really don't care what's behind any of this. I mean, you were abused by your dad or your mum's boyfriend or whoever, you were put into care, your foster dad was an alcoholic, you ran away at sixteen, you started giving blow jobs in the backs of cars for a tenner, you got beaten up – '

'You what?'

'Whatever the details were in your particular case...'

She stopped. He was glaring at her with fixed icy eyes, cold, furious.

'Is that what you think? Eh? You really think that?' He was half standing, hunched over her. 'You honestly think I'd do anything for a fucking *tenner*?'

'I didn't mean, that was just an example – '

'Listen, love,' he said, and leaned in, twisting the baseball cap backwards so he could get right in close without the visor getting in the way. 'Listen. I don't care what you think.

190

mean you, the fucking jury and all that, think whatever you fucking like, 'cos I don't happen to a give a good fat shite actually, as it happens, but you start disrespecting me, and I'm telling you...'

His face was distorted with rage. He wasn't playing, and Elsa was startled by the sudden change.

'Or my family,' he added, more or less as an afterthought.

'Bryn? I didn't disrespect your family, I mean, I didn't mean – '

'Oh, yeah, like my dad's a fucking child abuser and my mum's a fucking boozer or something. Eh? I mean, where do you get that from? Eh? My dad's a holiday rep and my mum does telesales and packs hampers. All right? No fucking secret buggery, no abuse, no fostering, no care, she'd never stand for anything like that. No chance. She's done her best for me my whole life actually, and all right, she might not have any fucking money or work in the fucking government like some people, but that doesn't mean – '

'Sorry. I don't know why I said that.'

'Fucking *tenner*.'

'Bryn. I said I was sorry – '

'Tell you your trouble, love, you read the papers too much.'

'So, all right, so you tell me then. Why are you like this?'

'Oh, what do you want me to be like? Eh? I've got a big dick, I'm not scared of any cunt and I can look after myself, and I can earn a fuck of a good hourly rate, as I think you may have noticed. What do you get an hour, eh? In the government? What do you have to do for a fucking tenner, eh? And I'm good at it.'

'So what went wrong with Hook then?'

'What, him?' Bryn leaned back and exhaled slowly. 'Like I told you, that wasn't me.'

'Oh, right. Right. Fine. You show me now. Whatever it is you're going to show me.'

'What, now?'

'Yeah. Right now.' She was standing, getting her bag and jacket.

'What, can't I finish my drink?'

'Now I said.'

'You're the boss,' he said. 'Oh, listen, by the way, we're going to want some money actually. What cashpoint do you need?'

WORLD OF STUBBLE

11.15. Queueing to get into a club, some place on the seafront with a tiny little door. Elsa, naturally, has to pay the in, which is more than she'd thought. Bryn is mouthy with the bouncer, squaring up to him and then grabbing him round the neck. The bouncer is of phlegmatic temperament and knows him well in any case.

Inside it's dark and there has recently been a major dry-ice emission. The air is cold and thick and raw in the throat. He shoulders his way in and down some steps and then through, and then she realizes that she wants to put her bag and jacket into the cloakroom, so he drags her back again and there's more queueing. She can't understand the layout, but it's long and low and narrow, more like a tube carriage than anything, or rather two carriages stuck side by side, and there's some more space at the back. He shoves her up to the bar, where the drinks are ridiculously expensive. He takes the drink off her and finds them a place to stand.

'Right. Stay here. Don't go wandering off.' He winks, grins, and then before she can stop him there's a kiss that turns into a rather slobbery bite on the throat. Then he's off. Swagger, strut and lope. Make way for these mothers.

Elsa looks around, but can see only the backs of the people in front of her and a few shadows from the adjacent carriage, which is the dance floor, a narrow steaming smoky hellish place. From what she can see no one has any hair at all, this is World of Stubble. Her only other recent experience of clubs is Friday night hijinks with Claire, and she tends to favour the big mainstream places where there's leopard-skin bar stools and state-of-the-art air-conditioning and promotions for drinks no one really likes. All mainline drinks one fifty all night. Here it's more like trench warfare. Also it's almost all men, except for one of the bar staff, a girl with Heidi-type plaits and a bra top.

Elsa jumps backwards in shock as something slithers down what she calls her cleavage and wriggles down her belly. Water. She looks up and sees condensation running along a big thick pipe or duct. The walls are all corrugated steel, perhaps to emphasize the Somme Experience feel of things. The people in front are actually standing at the bar, but they are also simultaneously uncomfortably close to Elsa, right on top of her, and there's no way to get more room without ducking into one of the little cut-throughs to the dance floor. Two of the men in front have taken their shirts off and are moving rhythmically but not speaking. Elsa sips from the bottle. I wonder what they'd rush you for a Malibu and lime in a place like this, she thinks. The bottle is running with condensation as well; everything is simultaneously cold and dripping. One of the men in front is dripping too and she follows the course of a droplet on its journey from the wrestler's neck to the carefully exposed Calvin Klein underwear waistband. At one point he takes a half-step back and she feels his cool clammy flesh on her arm.

And Bryn meanwhile is doing what exactly? She doesn't know how long he's been gone but it's not long. Should she go and look for him? I'll give him to the end of the bottle, she thinks.

Then he's back. A score, he says. Twenty quid. She's beyond arguing now and digs it out and hands it over. He takes it from her in a slightly odd ferrety kind of way, hands kept low

Another wink and leer and he's gone again. Probably the last I'll ever see of him, she thinks. It's certainly the last I'll see of that twenty quid. And what happened to the twenty I was supposed to get for 'just watching' the other day? It'd come in quite handy at the moment. Costs seem to be mounting up. Whatever else Bryn might be, he definitely isn't cheap.

Suddenly he's back by her side and before she knows what he's doing he's pushing something small into her mouth, then he lifts his bottle to her lips and tips her head back and she swallows. And that's it. She feels it all slipping down her gullet.

'Bryn?'

He gives her his innocent of all wrongdoing look and she stares at him with absolute disbelief.

'Bryn? What did you just do?'

'Nothing. Listen, give it twenty minutes or so. You might feel a bit wonky for a minute. Then you'll be fine.'

'What did you just put in my mouth, Bryn?'

'Well, what in fuck do you think it was, eh? If you didn't want it you should have just said.'

'You didn't give me a chance to just say, did you?' She wants to shout at him but she's having to shout anyway to make herself heard over the frantic booming nonsense coming from the dance floor. The two shirtless ones in front are sweating more and more, moving with greater vigour. They look about incessantly, in different directions. Bryn winks and gestures at them and is gestured at back. She looks at her watch: 12.10. Her heart is pounding. What have I done? I can't take pills in clubs, I work in local government, for God's sake. What would Ted Slaughter have to say? The only people she knows of who've taken pills are the ones who died on the telly. Well, except for Liam, of course. And Vicki. And Claire, come to think of it, and oh well, all right, just about everyone she knew actually. They hadn't died. Elsa, though, she just never had had one somehow. In case she died. It had just seemed like a sensible precaution.

Bryn takes hold of her arm and leads her to the back, up some steps, into a little area where there are irregularly shaped tables jutting out of the dripping walls and stools that look like giant Coke cans. Night-light candles. Bryn sits and takes up his usual broken-boned sprawl and plays with the candle, pushing it around and moving his fingers over the flame as the bombs and tracer bullets scream out over the trenches and bunkers, no man's land. Elsa sits and surreptitiously checks her pulse and tries to resist the temptation to look at her watch every thirty seconds.

Bryn leans over and leers.

'Not dead yet then?'

12.30. She's actually thinking about something else when she becomes aware of a little buzzing fluttering sensation in her stomach. Interesting. She puts her head to one side to attend to it better, and notices that Bryn is no longer there. She sits up straighter to look round for him but he is nowhere in sight. She wants to tell him about the feeling in her stomach. Then it starts to climb and it is so interesting in fact that she has to put her head down on the table to monitor it properly. Blimey! Oh oh oh. And it had been such a tiny little pill as well, it surely couldn't be doing all this. She stands up and heads in the direction of the toilets. The women's is full of men and she has to wait for a cubicle, an anxious few minutes when she thinks she's going to lose her legs completely. She can't speak or meet anyone's eye. Finally she gets into the lock-up and sits down and puts her head in her hands.

Fuck.

Actually what she wants to do is lie down. Immediately. She sits on the floor with all the wet toilet paper and puts her head against the partition. The hygiene is quite lamentable when you get down to this level; there are all sorts of things down here on the floor, wet things mostly, and the pipe at the back has got a slow leak, it's crusted round the weld. Ah well. The lock doesn't appear to be fully engaged but she can't deal with that right now. She hears voices from outside. The people on the telly who died always seemed to die in toilets, she thinks. She'd always wondered why. She curls up.

*

And the voices are still there when she comes round, the light entering in short bursts. She's lying with her face on the floor, wet, not dead, and someone's tapping on the door. She looks at her watch: 12.32. Well, that can't be right for a start. It's still so early, and she's passed out and come round and cheated death already. It must be later surely: she could have gone to bed now and still been up in plenty of time to gain an hour on her flexi. So it couldn't really be 12.32.

But anyway, someone's tapping on the door and wanting to get in and she guesses she's pretty much finished cheating death here on the floor, in fact she feels full of vim and vigour and so on and gets up and smiles extravagantly at the person wanting to get in. Twenty or so, pony-tail, male. She allows her hand to travel over his waist as she passes, which is quite enjoyable. He's quite enjoyable all over in fact and she spends a few moments thinking what to say to him next before he's gone.

She returns to the table where she and Bryn had been a little time ago, but there are new people there now and her bottle seems to have gone. She needs a new one then, and she knows just what she wants. She's seen enough people with them and she wants one too: a bottle of water. Which, incredibly, costs as much as a real drink. Still. She compliments Heidi-plaits on her hair and even gets into a short discussion about hair care and the difficulties of maintaining good condition. The plaits, she feels, must be pretty high maintenance and Heidi confirms this, though you get used to it apparently.

Anyway. Now Elsa has to find Bryn. He's around somewhere, but she can't see him, so she has to push past a great number of people – well, men really, all of whom are bare to the waists and running, dripping with sweat. They all have to have her hand on their waists as she passes, and in fact some of them have to have hands on their shoulders and arses as well. One she even decides to give a little pinch to but he doesn't seem to notice. She traverses the whole length of the bar, right to the cigarette machine at the far end, but no sign. Has something changed about the lights? Seemingly.

Also she hates to say it but she's getting slightly interested in the way the corrugations on the walls and ceilings lie, she's interested in parralels. Not too interested, but more perhaps than she usually was. Or would be. In parralesl. Paralleals.

Parallels, rather. So. But no sign of Bryn. She checks her watch: 12.36. Can't be right. She finds a stool to sit on and gets talking to a man who has tattoos all over his forearms. He has some others as well, but she doesn't have time to see them. He's got a lovely neck, she thinks, and tells him so. Lovely neck. Lovely water. Very nice. She finds that she's thinking in little short bursts, and that it's quite strenuous, making her sweaty and hot. Very hot. She wants to take her top off, but of course you can't just yank your top off, not here in the club, though you could if you were a man, which just about everyone is. She wishes she had a bra top on like Heidi.

She's on her feet again. Blimey. She ends up at another little table and now she needs to put her head down for a moment, all very nice, the light coming in very nicely, all that, but it's definitely a head down opportunity, just for a moment. Someone is beside her and she puts her hand on his leg for support and just really for the simple pleasure of doing so. He's very nice, he doesn't seem to mind. I'll just put my hand on your leg for a minute, yeah, all right, love, no bother.

'You all right?'

'Yeah I'm altighht/alrifht/alright. Are you all right?'

'Yeah, I'm all right, it's not me I'm worried about really.'

'Oh. Well, I'm all right.'

Head down.

'What's your name?'

She tries to focus and smiles up at him. It's the same one again. 'Elsa.'

'Elsa? Listen, have you had a pill? Are you with anyone?'

She thinks.

'Well. I suppose so. Yeah. He's gone to . . .'

'Sweetheart? Listen. I think you maybe need a breath of air or something, yeah?'

'No, really, listen, you're very nice, what's your name again

'Alan.'

'Alan? Listen, I'm Elsa.'

'Yeah, I know, love. Are you with anyone?'

'Yeah, but, see, he had to go away and do. I mean, he had to find someone so he'll be back in a minute. What time is it?'

'Twenty to one.'

'No.'

'Yeah. It is.'

'Alan?'

'Yeah.'

'Listen, I really like you, and I'm having a really nice time.'

He laughs and pats her arm. 'Yeah, OK, look, just hold on a minute.' He turns away, and she gets hold of his leg again. Which she's taken quite a fancy to actually. He's discussing her with the people he's with.

'Elsa?' He's back again.

'Yeah?'

'We're going to get you outside. You want a bit of air. You've kind of passed out a bit.'

'No, no. No, really, I'm having a really nice time. You're nice. What's your name?'

'Alan. Look. Let's get you outside for a minute.'

'No, actually I've got to wait for, for, he was here a minute ago and he's just gone. What time is it? He just had to go and – '

'Elsa? Listen a minute – '

'Are you all right? I'm allrright. I'm havinbg a lovely time. I got interested in the, uopu know, the parra;lels. Parrarrls. Yopu know?

'Sorry...'

'Parrarrasal, I mean.'

'What?'

'Blaargh. Gargle. Ç✓ø†△∂!'

'Love? You're talking in code a bit.'

'Oh, sod it.'

She has now simply taken hold of him and is hugging him ightly, more or less for solidity, as he is gorgeously warm and olid, he feels very nice. He's got hold of her and he's trying to

make her stand up now but really she can't be doing with
and she lets herself go slack. She ends up with her head kin
of in his lap. And this is fine. I work in local government, sh
says to herself, I work in local government, everything
alkright. Aarihgt. *All right*, I mean.

12.45. She sits upright again and everything is fine. She wi
go and find Bryn and then they will go home. This is now th
only thing she wants to do. Go home. She carries the wat
happily, and people smile and pat her as she passes them. Sh
comes to a sudden halt for a moment, then she's off agaii
Sipping the water. She can only see a few feet ahead at an
one time so her progress is slightly erratic. She comes to or
of the cut-throughs to the dance floor and there he is, his hea
buried in someone's ear as he talks.

She sidles up to him and puts her hand round his wais
Bryn?

He looks at her and they are hugging suddenly. I lost yo
he says, I was looking for you. (Yeah, right.) Let's go home, sh
says, and he says, yeah, just give me a minute here. She res
her head against his lovely shoulder, lovely Bryn, as h
continues with whoever he's with, some big randy-lookir
beast. Elsa puts her hand on his waist. Then they're movin
Queueing for her coat and bag.

Out. Excellent!

200

GRISTLE

They arrive at Elsa's house, and she squeezes his arm on the steps up to the door, trying to tell him to be quiet. Her key slides beautifully in, effortlessly out. She leads the way up the three flights, noting the objects on the way, Scientology bollocks, stunted rubber plant, wicker basket, lumpy hand-made pottery thing, abandoned two-tiered bedside shelf in gold-coloured plastic, with the little fluted column between the two decks. Nice. She fingers it fondly as she passes.

1.05. The windows are open, bringing a low hum into the room, cool air stirring, air that brushes and strokes. She lies on her bed and Bryn paces about in the front room touching everything. She calls out to him every few minutes. Are you all right? I'm all right. Much jaw clamping and a great many little sips of the water.

He comes into the room.

'Listen, if we're going to do this we'd better get sorted.'

'Do what?'

'Reconstruction.'

'Oh right. I forgot. Yeah.'

'Yeah. You right?'

'What do you mean?'

'We'd better get going.'

'Oh yeah. Where?'

'The shop. Harry's shop? Remember?'

'Oh, we're going there?'

'Er, yes, love.'

'Oh.' She can barely speak her jaw is clamping so hard. She relaxes it every two seconds or so, until she is basically just chewing the cud, bovine style. Also she's getting flickering sensations, her eye movements have become jerky and discontinuous and the stereo vision is malfunctioning so that she gets each side separately in ultra-rapid alternation. Blimey! It's brilliant!

'What's wrong with your CD player?' he calls, and Elsa shouts back, 'It got Malibu in it. Bryn?'

'Yeah.'

'Just give me a minute. Listen, how long does all this go on?'

'Few hours. Four, five maybe. Depends what it is exactly.'

'It's lovely.'

'Yeah, well, that might just be why they call it ecstasy, love.'

He wanders back out again and she lies flat, playing with her vision. Checks her watch. God, it's so early. Everything going on, and it's so early. In the next room he's put the telly on, flicks channels. All is grief. The effect aimed at now is a species of lachrymose resignation. All-night vigils, little groups of prayerful faces illuminated by tiny candles, people camped out bizarrely in the night-time parks and public spaces of central London, children up way past their bedtime parents looking dignified and good and sorrowful for once instead of merely pissed off. The Barber Adagio is discovered and a nation is ravished. Pictures of a pretty blonde woman wearing a flak jacket with a kind of groin-protector attachment, smiling, grotesquely, as she touches maimed children, then wearing lamé and getting out of a limousine smiling the same disconnected smile in the glitter of camera flash.

People listen to radios and watch tiny tellies which are broadcasting accounts of themselves camped out listening to their radios and watching their tellies. There is absolutely nothing else happening anywhere on the surface of the planet, all the usual wars and papal visits and aircrashes have been cancelled. Bryn fidgets on the sofa and looks through the mail Elsa's left lying around, bank statements, pay slips, book club brochures, Racing Green clothes catalogues. He pokes about for change behind the cushions. He finishes off a bag of Kettle Chips.

1.15.

'Right. You set?'

He wants to get going. Elsa moves with extraordinary reluctance and gathers her things and mixes up some Malibu and milk. At the last minute she picks up the Malibu from the fridge. Just in case she fancies it later. He wants a taxi but she wants to walk. They walk, all the way through town, to where Harry Hook keeps his shop. Bryn is uproarious and there are a great many small incidents on the way, including a vigorous misunderstanding with someone about the intentions behind a piece of unauthorized physical contact on Bryn's part, and a good long staring match with a policeman in a patrol car, which ends in a stand-off as Bryn stops and gestures with both hands: come on, then. *Come on, then!* Also he is in and out of the late shops, ducking about, chatting up the staff, holding everything up at the till messing about with the crisps and the Pot Noodles.

It's raining now, streets glossy and smelling intoxicatingly of petrol and seagull shit and wet soil. Warm wet town, blowing about in the dark. He cadges three cigarettes and almost four pounds in cash, and somehow or other acquires a second baseball cap and a tape called *The Best Seventies Party Album ... Ever!*, both of which he gives away to a smiling homeless man who gives him a tract in return, something about The Council of Nine. *The Council of Nine are a ethnic race, That lays way out in the middle of space, The Nine guides us with their Energy Beams. And sends us messages from Unseen.*

This Bryn gives to Elsa. Elsa is just enjoying the lights. Sh keeps forgetting what she and Bryn are doing. She has no ide what the tract is about. She's talking about the lights.

It takes a surprisingly short time to get to where they'r going, which is a grey stretch of street full of unused churche and burnt-out shops with depressing Victorian bric maisonettes over them. Bryn stops in front of one of them. H has a key.

'Wait a minute,' Elsa says suddenly, 'he'll be here, won he?' The thought of meeting Harry Hook is appalling. Woul he still be wearing the shell suit? She peers in through th shop window, but it's just a grey blur and some smudg reflections from streetlights.

Inside she can dimly make out shapes, raised ledges covere with carpet which is composed seemingly solely of dus vacuum cleaners at drunken slipshod angles, a Workmate wit bits missing which will never hold a piece of two-by-four quit steady again, and which will tip you off and kill you when yo try to stand on it, a Bullworker (she is distracted momentaril by the glittering eyes of the smiling stud in the muscle vest o the faded box, who certainly didn't get the way he is by usir any Bullworker and has nothing but contempt for any poc seven-stone weakling who's fool enough to believe they car boxes of curtain material, boxes of books and crockery ar crumpled newsprint, boxes of objects of unspecified functio and not-so-recent manufacture. Something vaguely hal spherical and in two tones of brittle plastic, daffodil and sag But what *is* it? Frayed wires, plugs missing, casings cracked. It all hopeless, abandoned, obsolete. It's not even junk, it detritus, skip-food, landfill. What would an eighteenth-centur brocade pelmet and its hand-carved attachments be doing in place like this, she wonders. Mind you, they only had Hook word for it that that's what it was. By the look of everythir else here it was more likely to be some piece of crap.

'He's not here tonight,' Bryn says. 'Tonight he's elsewhere

'How do you know?'

'Because I know where he is, don't I? Because he's wit Mark fucking Hegler, isn't he?'

Bryn's got the door open now and there's another door going into the shop and a narrow flight of stairs. He leads the way; there's no light here. It smells of old carpet, old cat. Bin bags, of indeterminate age. Two, three weeks? Something like that. She follows Bryn's solid arse and shiny oxblood Docs up the stairs. Rainwater is drumming against the windows at the back.

The door at the top says STUDIO in stick-on gold letters, not quite perfectly aligned. Mr Hook's apartments.

Light comes in from the front, falling gently onto a bare mattress on a base, many badly fitted shelves and a truly surprising number of wine and whisky bottles, a real tippler's lair. Terrible long lonely minutes and hours, dead afternoons and then the awful slide into evening. The light gleams along the edges of a sink, splashes softly over a kettle and a hotplate, disports itself among ashtrays and table legs and shoes, finally coming coquettishly to rest on something gleaming bright and metallic by the bed.

Bryn strips off his T-shirt, undoes the top button of his jeans. No Calvin Klein waistband in evidence here. He spreads himself out on the mattress, one hand behind his head, the other working slowly at his crotch. Elsa is only temporarily at a loss.

'There are two keys. I've got one of them here, on my key ring. The other one is here. See? On the ledge by the ashtray. Turn clockwise to lock, anticlockwise to release. They're quite loose.' He shows her. 'There's a little catch here. See? Tiny little lever? Push it this way and they'll fasten tighter. That way stops them going any further in. All right?' He snaps one link on, then twists round away from her and brings both arms round the back. She takes him by the wrist and puts the other cuff on. Click. He rolls back face up and squints at her eyes, checking her pupils, smiles.

'OK. Reconstruction time.'

So this is what he says happened. I'm here, I'm on... something. I come up, I demand money. He says, don't you think we should discuss this a little, young man or whatever, and I just start twatting him one. Then I go berserk and smash up his fucking computer and his sodding pelmet. Shag this for a game of soldiers, off. That it?'

'Yes.'

'OK. I'm him. You're me. OK?'

'Yeah.'

'OK. Well. Go.' He tenses up and takes a deep breath, meets her eye and holds it. 'Ready. Go.'

'What do you mean?'

'I mean I want you to twat me one. Face and upper body mostly. We'll sort the cigarette burns out later.'

'Bryn, what exactly are you talking about?'

'You thick or what? Eh? I can't hardly stop you, can I? Come on.'

'Bryn – '

'Come *on*, I said.'

'How can I possibly do that? This is – '

'What's stopping you? As far as you're concerned I owe you money or something and you're off your head, and you're just this scumbag anyway, so, you know, just go for it.' He leans up, into a patch of light, his body all dewy deeps and hollows and bulgings, he nudges her arm with his stubble head. 'It's not exactly difficult, for fuck's sake. Come on then.'

She lifts her arm and pats him on the cheek. He regards her coolly.

'Uhuh. That it, is it?'

She does it again, takes hold of his ear, twists. Her arm falls back again.

'Oh, Bryn, look, this is just . . . '

'You can't, can you?'

'Of course not – '

'Why?'

'I just can't . . . '

'I'll tell you why not.'

'Fine. You tell me.'

He leans back against the wall again, falling back into shadow.

'You can't hit me because you're on a pill. You're on Th

206

Love Boat. You're on drugs. As Mark fucking Hegler would say.'

Elsa blinks and regards him, grinning up at her from the dark mattress, his shoulders and upper arms and throat bunched and beefy from the position he's in, his hot mocking eyes. God. God Almighty Bryn. She is full of a warm, undifferentiated feeling, like used bathwater, or soup. Like love.

'Well, it's true, isn't it? You could no more beat someone up right now than you could skin a cat. I'm right, aren't I?'

'Of course, I couldn't. I've never beaten anyone up ever, well, not since I was twelve, anyway. It wouldn't even occur to me to try...'

'OK. Hang on a minute.' He's wrestling himself up again, then he draws one leg back and kicks her hard on the shoulder. She rocks back, astonished, and he kicks out again, landing a good one on her hip.

'How about now?'

'Bryn, that'll, that's enough...'

He tips himself up further, swings up and headbutts her, hard enough to knock her off the bed and onto the floor. He's rocking back and forth, getting himself onto his feet, bracing himself against the wall. She backs into the room and he stands upright, wobbly, on the bouncy bed.

'You telling me you can't do it now?' There's some new quality in his voice, he's imitating someone. 'You telling me all that and you still can't get it up? Eh? That's what I'm paying for, is it, young man? I think maybe you need to think this one out again...'

'Bryn?'

'Incapacitated through recreational narcotic abuse, is that the story? You've got the audacity to ask for money for this – I was going to say cock-up but that seems inappropriate somehow, to come here and expect me to hand over good currency notes for some damp pizzle, some bit of limp gristle...' He's put on a sick sort of half-smile and cocked his head over to one side. 'Well, really, I find that completely insupportable, I must say I find that really pretty thick. Or rather, perhaps, not really quite thick enough...'

He's moving off the bed and stepping towards her now. Her

vision is flashing at her like crazy, the soupy love feeling is rising and falling, wave after wave. Bryn, wait...He's right on top of her, his body is cool and clammy and big. He spreads his legs, hands locked behind his back, thumbs pulling the material tight across his crotch. She runs her hand down him, over his throat and then his ribcage, then to his jeans, then on, under his bulge, the outline of his cock a raised meaty crescent running to the left, and squeezes. His voice is his own again now.

'I was on a pill. I was completely off my face, like you are now. I couldn't get hard, admitted, but there's no fucking way on earth I could have smacked him up one either. For exactly the same reason. No chance. As I think you'd have to agree. And that's the truth.'

'I see what you're getting at,' she says. 'But you don't seem to be having quite the same problem now...'

'That's 'cos I'm not on a pill now.'

'Yeah, but I am.'

'Yeah, I know, love.'

She manipulates him out and handles him. He's large and full and getting fuller. Blood is pulsing and pumping down there. Two handfuls long and a good bit extra, for bonus, for luxury. Far better quality than she's used to, much thicker material. She articulates the word 'girth' to herself That's what he's got. Heavy. Stiffening. All hers. He looks down, looks back up again, narrows his eyes, opens his mouth.

'You know this reconstruction...' he says.

'Oh, yeah.'

'We could maybe finish it off later...'

'Later, yeah...'

'Don't think of it as a dick, love. Try thinking of it as a Harley-Davidson.'

'Get that off a film, did you?'

'I get everything off films.'

'Harley-Davidson,' she says distantly. 'They call them "hogs" in America, don't they?'

'Wouldn't know, love. Just climb on top. Feel nice? Does it Eh? Not too hard, love. You're only borrowing it. You want to pull the skin back? Right back, that's it. I've got good balls oo, you know. Big. Hairy. None of your rubbish.'

'Oh, no, just this is fine, really...' Her voice is little and far
away.

'Course everything would be easier with these bastards off,'
he says.

'Hm?'

'The cuffs.'

'Oh, yeah,' and she agrees, but only in principle, and not
quite immediately.

Back on the bed now.

'No, honestly, I'm not kidding,' she says.

'Well, where did you put it?'

'I don't know.'

'You must know, you always have to know where you've
put the fucking key, that's kind of basic – '

'Look, I can hardly see straight to be perfectly frank, I'm
getting persistent double vision now...'

'Oh, brilliant. You've got the eye wobblies and you've lost
the sodding key.'

'I thought you had another one.'

'It's on my key ring.'

'Which is where?'

'How in fuck do *I* know?'

'Oh dear.' She has her head down, resting on his thighs now,
filling her vision, which is completely crazed, with his dick.
He's in no particular hurry, to be honest. He's wriggling up
again.

'Oh, wait.' She sees it, it's still in the lock.

'You got it?'

'No. I thought I saw it...'

'Elsa. Will you just try a bit harder please...'

'In a minute...Bryn?'

'*What*?'

'I just wanted you to know that I'm having a really *really*
nice time...'

'Oh, for fuck's sake...'

*

He's free again. She sits up and watches him. He's got Superking on the go now. His hand is moving slowly, working. I've got a lovely big fat cock here, he says, I've go this nice big fucking handful over here, I'm giving it a goo feel now. You want to come over here and get it, eh? You wan a bit? Eh? Yeah? Where do you want it? Eh?

He stops to find a condom, which takes considerably longe than she would have thought strictly necessary, though agai she's in no real hurry. He's bumping about down there. The he's back, slips inside her. He stays mostly still, keeping hi weight off her with his elbows, impassive, and she move against him. He's not completely hard but then again it's no really a problem just at the moment, there's enough to g round. Jesus, she thinks, I want to do just this for ever an ever, and after that I want to do it more. Lots more. I don ever want to do anything else. She leans up to kiss him, h tastes of honey and chips. *Jeeeesus Chriiist*. Now this is wha I call subornation . . .

She has all she wants, which is loads, tons, yards. Gallon: Then she has some more, just because it's there really. Sham to waste it. He starts to come, which sets her off again. O my God. Oh. Then he comes more or less at the same time a her, with considerable grunting, and pulls out. She watche him peel off the condom, which he holds up for a second an shakes, then puts it on the floor by the bed. There is a curiou but very familiar smell which troubles her for a moment. He lying in the dark and she wants to sit up and find a toilet. Sh clambers over him and finds herself looking at the condom She listens: he seems to be asleep already, heavy rhythmi breathing.

That smell now. She picks up the condom with som distaste and holds it in the light. The end is full of thic whitish fluid, which is of course quite within norma expectations. But the smell isn't. The smell is, frankly, a wrong. She finds her water bottle and takes a few sips. He eyes are more or less normal just at the moment. Still a bit c jaw but not too bad. She puts the water back down and, wit exaggerated squeamish distaste, pushes her index finger down into the condom, rolling it up the finger until she is paddling in the little squirmy reservoir at the bottom. She brings the finger out again. Brings it to her nose.

Puts it to her lips. And tastes. Oh, I know *that* taste. Now that is one taste I definitely do know.

Well. Either we are in the realm of the miraculous here, and Bryn is able to secrete cream liqueurs from his mighty unreliable prick, or else...

She sees the bottle of Malibu and milk by the side of the bed, the cap is off.

'Bryn!'

She shakes him awake and his reluctance is increasingly unbelievable.

'Bryn. Could I have a little word please...'

'Look, I just thought...'

'You can't tell the truth about anything, can you? I mean literally. It's like you are physically incapable of actually being straight about anything...'

'I just thought...' He's sheepish, but not that much. 'I mean, I just thought you'd enjoy it more if you thought, if it was realistic...I mean, I like to give satisfaction...' He's grinning again and then he reaches for the Malibu bottle and brings it over...

'Bryn, now – '

'And you did enjoy it. Didn't you? Eh? Or are you going to tell me now you didn't? I mean, that was what you were after all along. Wasn't it? I mean, you think I don't know when someone's looking at me? Eh? Or did I get it wrong?' He holds the bottle over her then slowly tilts, while she screams and tries to wriggle away, but he's holding her down. 'I'm going to sponk up on you again, watch out now, here it comes, here it comes...Ooooaargh...'

'Bryn, you dirty *get*...'

2.35. They're both at least half-dressed and decent again, though Elsa is still somewhat vague and her head remains on his thighs. He's stroking her hair as he speaks. She's made him promise to tell her the truth, and he's promised, and she's made him promise again. What more can either of them do in the circumstances?

'So I did Harry, probably about ten times over about two months. He loved it. Couldn't get enough of it.'

'After you came with the drill?'

'What fucking drill? Do you think I've got the time to fuck about with stolen Black and Deckers? That was all his own invention there. He just didn't want to admit he'd found me in *G-Scene* like anyone else.'

'What's that?'

'Gay mag. I've got an ad in there. Tom, 18, XVWE skin/bootboy, in/out, active only. Full unhurried service.'

'What's XYWE?'

'XVWE: extra very well endowed.'

'Is that true?'

'Well, what would you say?'

'I've had bigger.'

'No, you fucking haven't. And you haven't had better neither. I was the shag of your fucking life and you know it.'

'Well, maybe in some very restricted kind of *technical* sense... Anyway we'll come back to that. So Harry rings you up and you come round.'

'Right. He likes a bit of verbal and restraint and all that. Handcuffs, belts, all that old shite. Anything that involves a lot of fucking about with things instead of just getting on with it, basically. He'd seen it all on this video. Sad bastard.'

'What's verbal?'

'Oh, you know. Hold on. Er. Oh, you know, your mouth is my toilet, fucking crawl over here, cocksucker, and take my big dirty fist up your – '

'Right. Right. Uhuh.'

'...filthy gaping fuckhole...'

'*Bryn*. Snap out of it.'

'You know, it all sounds a bit stupid out of context. So I d him maybe five times or so. Something like that. Always cas up front, there's never any bother. The only problem is tha

212

sometimes he's so off his head he can't do anything. But he pays up all the same. Obviously. Anyway. 8 June.'

'Oh, God, yes, I remember all that from court...'

'Right. This is maybe the sixth time or so. He says, have you got a mate, and I say, all right, it'll be a hundred quid for both. He says fine. So I bring Mark fucking Hegler along, don't I? Harry's just watching really and tossing himself off. You wouldn't think to look at him but he's a big lad is Mark. Lovely body on him. Real fuck-monkey.'

'So you're being paid to have sex with Mark Hegler?'

'Which I'm doing anyway.'

'Are you?'

'Er, yes, love, since he's been my boyfriend for three years. Trouble with Mark is, he's a speed freak. He gets mental with it. So he starts kicking Harry round the room. Harry doesn't know whether to be into it or not to start, then he freaks out and I have to practically drag Mark off him. So we don't do it with three again after that, it's just Harry and me again, like before, just the usual. I have to do him for free once to keep him quiet. *And* we never got the hundred quid. Anyway.'

He reaches for the ashtray and mostly misses. Elsa has a sip of Malibu, then more water.

'Right. So 22 June. It's really hot and I can't be arsed to be honest, but I'm booked to see him. To polish his table.'

'Oh, yeah, what was all that about?'

'He needed a reason why I'd been there, didn't he? So he comes up with this table thing. That's what Mark was saying in court. It wasn't his table he was getting polished, it was his...'

'His...'

'Yes, love. You got it in one. Anyway. Me and Mark both come round, I've had a pill like I said and he's had a gram of speed in a can of Special Brew and then loads of little dabs. He never knows when to stop. I tell him to just stay downstairs.

'So I'm up here with Harry. He's been boozing all day of course. So I start him up but then, I don't know, I just get really *bored* suddenly, I think, ah fuck it, and I get up to leave. He's going, and where do you imagine you're off to, my young friend? 'Cos he's got this really annoying way of talking, it can really just piss you off. So I say, you want me to stay it's a hundred. He says, fine. He's already given me sixty, he'll go the cashpoint after for the forty. So we start again and we're getting somewhere, I suppose, but you know how sometimes you just can't be bothered? Yeah? Just cannot. Anyway, I'm not even really concentrating to be honest, and I'm on this pill and everything. So I start telling him what a sad fucking cunt he is, but he just wants to suck me off anyway. He keeps *drooling* all over me, I mean I'm really getting wet here, which is annoying, and he's saying what he wants to do, which is all talk, obviously.

'And it's just getting really boring. He can't get it up and neither can I, it's a bit of a state to be honest with you. The highest professional standards are not in operation here, yeah? We keep stopping and starting. He's got the poppers so far up his nose it's practically embedded in his brain actually – '

'What's that?'

'Poppers?' He reaches under the bed and comes up with a little brown bottle. 'Here.'

Elsa takes it from him and unscrews the cap. She passes it under her nose and recoils from the stink.

'No, love. Like this.' He takes the bottle and puts it under one of his nostrils then the other, as she'd seen him do with the client yesterday. Then one last one in the mouth. He passes it to her and she does the same, then says, 'God, Bryn, this is *horrible*,' and then she doesn't speak for a moment. It feels as if she's just run two hundred metres and then been punched in the stomach. In a paint factory.

'That's 'cos you're not a man. If you're a man it just grabs you by the dick and makes you want to come. For about sixty seconds.' He's giving himself a little rub and she waits for him to subside.

'Actually this could be just the stuff to get that stain off your jacket. Anyway. Where was I? So even with the popper and everything he's no use to anyone, I can't get him hard, can't get me hard, it's all bollocks. Short of hanging him or direct injection into the penis I'm out of ideas. And so h

214

starts, well, if you imagine I'm about to part with my hard-earned money for this, then I'm sorry to say you're labouring under a sad delusion, all this old twat. And really I just think, I mean I'm not really arguing, I just want to go, I cannot be arsed with it. But then he starts going on about my, you know...'

'Your...'

'Right. And he's being insulting. You know? Sneering. What exactly do you propose to do with that, young man, take my temperature? You know. He's a sarcastic little sod.'

'He hurt your feelings.'

'Yeah.'

'All this is because some old drunk hurt your *feelings*?'

'Yeah. Anyway I tell him to fuck off and I go downstairs. Mark's all wired up down there and he says, you should have made him pay you the forty, he's going on about it. Let's make him pay.

'So. We go back up again. Now Harry just thinks this is another threesome, and he's so off his head that he wants it even after what happened last time, he's forgotten or he just fancies it all again. I mean, he's a bit of a weird sod is Harry. Not exactly your usual customer. He gets funny ideas. So Mark makes him strip off and cuffs him. To the radiator. That's why the computer got bust, 'cos Harry's kicking round all over the place and he knocks the table, it just fell off. Then Mark blindfolds him. And Harry's into it actually, he's going, now we're getting somewhere. Your friend's got the right idea even if you haven't. All this. But I can see Mark getting crazy. I try to get him to go but he won't. He starts going to Harry, give us the money, you old cunt, and Harry's arguing. Young man, you certainly do seem to have a distorted sense of your own worth, all that. Then Mark says, you know the key to those handcuffs? Guess what? I just swallowed it. And Harry starts screaming at him, but he can't really do anything, he's just thrashing around and Mark's like laughing at him and kicking him to make him scream more. Then Mark says, see you then, and goes and slams the door.

'I follow him out, I'm trying to calm him down. He's

downstairs breaking things. He's getting all worked up, wha
he's going to do. Really up for it. I mean, that's why I won
work with him now, because quite honestly I sometime
think he's a little bit unstable. You know? In the head? We'1
down there for about half an hour and he has a load mo1
speed. Which is just what he needs, yeah right.

'So then he goes back up again. I can hear him through tl
door. He says he's going to take forty pounds' worth out
Harry's arse, then I can hear kicking and that and Harry
yelling and carrying on. But what Mark can't understand
that Harry's actually into it, he thinks it's like on the video
I go back in and Mark's got him by the neck and he's hittir
him with the printer cable off the computer, whipping hi
like on the arse. But Harry's into it, see, and this is drivir
Mark madder and madder. It's all a bit out of control.

'So then he gets this thing, it's some bit of wood, it's th
like carved pineapple off that fucking four-poster-bed thin
Then Mark's going, I'm going to shove this right up yo
fucking arse, all this. So then he's trying to shove it up ther
He can't get it in though. Because it's just not the right kir
of shape basically. You know, there are some things that ju
will not go up. Were not intended to go up. He gives it qui
a try though. Say that for him, he's a trier.

'Thing is, Harry's into it and he's not into it as well no
Yeah? I mean he's *trying* to be into it. But actually Mark's n
really skilful, he hasn't actually done a lot of this, he's got 1
style, you know? Then Mark gets his knob out and he's goin
I'm going to piss all over you, you old cunt, I'm going to pi
in your face, but Harry's into the idea of that as well. Ma
can't actually come up with anything Harry wouldn't be int
it's making him mental. And anyway Mark can't actually g
can he? You know how you can't go sometimes when som
one's watching? Actually no, you probably don't, do yo
thinking about it.

'So anyway Mark gets the knock finally and he says, rigl
let's see you be into this then, you old cunt, and he star
messing round with this cigarette. You want this, eh? Y
want this, do you? Where do you want it? Harry's definite

216

not into that, but Mark couldn't give a shite either way now, he's off on his own thing. I mean Mark's into it now. Only trying to write his fucking initials, isn't he? You know like some stupid brand? 'Cept he's not exactly skilled at writing. So anyway he's burning Harry with this cigarette and making him scream, and I've had enough and I just grab him and wrench him off, and he's kicking me now, and Harry kind of gets a bit more of a kicking as well, which he isn't into at all, he keeps complaining. He keeps going, my back, my back. Then Mark just buggers off.

'Anyway I let Harry out of the handcuffs and I leg it, before he can get the blindfold off. He's going, this time, young man, you've gone just a little bit too far, all this, and I just go ah sod off, you old cunt. So he hears me, my voice.

'Which is why he made the complaint about me and not Mark. He didn't know who was doing what to him, he thought it was all me. The last bit anyway. The last bit of kicking. And the cigarette bit.'

'Bryn, that is all so disgusting...'

'Yeah, well. I mean, you can maybe see why my brief wasn't over-anxious to put any of that in front of a jury, yeah? But Harry had it coming.'

'No, he didn't – '

'Yeah, he did, 'cos he was a twat. So what are you going to do? Eh? When he won't pay you? When he's being disrespectful? Not do anything?'

'You can't go round – '

'Oh, look, he's just some seedy cunt, right? It's not like he's your dad or your boyfriend or the pope or something, he's just this seedy little twat that wants his shag and then doesn't want to pay for it, right? And he's an annoying cunt as well, he thinks he's got a clever mouth on him. Well, what are you going to do? Eh? When he's giving you some big load of shag about something? Well, what do you have to say about that then, my young friend? You might care to reflect on it. All that. Well, the least of what he needs is what we give him, which was just a bit of a kicking no matter what he says it was. It wasn't anything, it was just a kicking, like he'd been begging for most of his miserable life if you ask me. If *we* hadn't done it for him then some other cunt would have and probably not as nice as we done him either. Anyway he was into it. Well, most of it. Well, I reckon he was anyway.'

'But you can't just go round – '

'Oh right, so what I should have done then, I should have gone down the police, yeah? I should have gone round the police and I should have stood at the counter and when Sergeant Give It Me For Free And The Drugs An' All Or You're Nicked Son comes to the desk I should have said, oh, sergeant, this bad man made me wank him off and then he didn't give me the money like he said, please are you going to make him?'

'What do you mean, Sergeant what you said?' Elsa says.

'Give It Me For Free?'

'Yeah, that.'

He looks at her, pulls his head back, retracts it like a warhead, hoods his eyes.

'I mean, has that happened? Actually? To you?' she says.

He pulls his head further back still.

'Yeah.'

'No, it hasn't.'

'Yeah, well, you're the fucking jury, you decide. Like it says on the telly: You The Jury. Yeah? And don't you love it?'

'Bryn. If you tell me that's what happened then I believe you. But I don't want some load of old tw...I mean I'm not just going to swallow any old boll... I mean...'

'I know, pet.' He puts his hands flat on his head. Surrender Unarmed. 'I'm telling you, aren't I?'

'So just tell me then.'

They're silent for a minute.

'We,' she says then. 'You said "we".'

'We what?'

'We just gave him what he deserved. "We" did. Not "he" did.'

'So?'

'So? Bryn there's a bit of a difference between we and he don't you think?'

'Slip of the tongue. As the chameleon said to the fly.'

'Right.' She gives him a fishy look and he returns it, raised eyebrows and downturned lip.

'And, you know, I'm not saying I wasn't there. Anyway. That's it. Hook calls the cops, says I did him and Mark was there too. Me and Mark, we say we were together somewhere, and we never went near him that day. Mark's my alibi. So Harry's got no witness, so it's just his word against me and Mark's and we're going to take our chances, 'cos I already know that Harry's got a bit of form. All Mark Hegler's got to do is stick to his story.

'Case is called. And suddenly Mark fucking Hegler isn't there any more. He's freaked out, he's off somewhere on a speed bender. So the cops are looking everywhere for him. He keeps ringing me up from phone boxes all night. I can't get any sense out of him. And then guess what he does?'

'Give up.'

'He only goes and gets himself arrested, doesn't he? Do you know what for? It's five o'clock in the morning, he's speeding off his head at some mate's house, he hears a noise outside so he goes out, there are these seagulls ripping open the bin bags. So of course he has to start kicking them, doesn't he, and just as he's spreading this bloody litter half-way down the street and screaming his stupid head off a cop car comes past and that's that. Then they match him up with the description Harry gave them and they put two and two together and they lean all over him to make him come to court, for the prosecution now. Took them a few days, hence the delays while he worked out his deal. 'Cos of course he would have about six tons of speed on him, wouldn't he? Soft cunt.'

There's just one thing bothering her.

'So look, why is Harry Hook with Hegler tonight?'

'Why do you think?'

'You say.'

'Because it's Mark fucking Hegler he wants now instead of me. He's got a taste for it, hasn't he? Which is the other reason why Hegler suddenly decides to turn up as prosecution fucking star witness at the last minute. They fucking deserve each other, those two.'

'You mean Harry's been seeing Mark Hegler?'

'Yep. Most of last year. He's got a real thing about him. An Mark's not exactly going to turn down the work, is he? That how I got this place clear tonight.'

She's starting to get tired now. The whole thing is wearyin her.

'Bryn, I don't really know that this makes you innocent.'

'No, but it makes me not guilty, 'cos I didn't do what h says I did. I never kicked him, I never burned him, I neve shoved a carved pineapple up his...'

'I don't recall that being on the charge sheet actually.'

'Well, would you want to admit to that?'

'But, Bryn, look. You were there. It was all your fault reall You put your price up half-way. And you as good as set Mar Hegler onto him. Didn't you? And you could have stopped it

'Yeah. Maybe. Maybe I didn't want to.'

'Because he hurt your feelings.'

He takes a deep drag on his Superking, twists his mouth t blow the smoke up and away from her. Long pause.

'Well. You can have enough of people. Know what I mean

'Bryn?'

'Yes, love?'

'I was just wondering...'

'Sounds like trouble.'

'Well, I'm not trying to start a row or anything, but sinc when does one pill cost twenty quid.'

DELIBERATIONS

10.10 a.m. Elsa's legs only barely carried her up the Hove courthouse building steps and through the security lock. Her bones had been hollowed out and filled with a thick liquid that lurched from side to side. Everything very heavy, many gravities. She was a few minutes late as she pushed into the jury assembly room where everyone was waiting for her before they were taken upstairs to begin 'deliberating'. She pushed change nonchalantly into the vending machine and leaned against it lankly while it hissed and rattled and shook. She'd come down from the ecstasy sure enough, but she was still buzzing somewhat, still slightly giddy and vertiginous, not really quite herself yet. Fidgety, tired, rather dreamy. Preoccupied, but with nothing that actually mattered. Distracted.

The usher arrived to escort them to the deliberation room, which was hot and airless, and she had to struggle to get out of her jacket, which was resisting her in ways she had never encountered before, plus she barely had the elbow room to complete the manoeuvre. All very taxing. She almost gave up half-way. Sod it.

Helen had Polaroids. A nuclear winter of a kitchen

installation, a blasted heath, a scorched earth, a killing field The overall effect was of plaster dust, through which could b discerned blocks and chunks and fragments of more plaster Here and there the bony ridge of a surface or a unit, like roc on the moon. Everything was in a kind of parched whited-ou veneer except for patches of zinc and green enamel. In on picture a stocky man in ruined terry-cloth shorts and a ho pink vest smiled chirpily, pointing to some exposed plumb ing. Barry the fitter, presumably. A big, untrustworthy sol trader's face, smeared with streaks of plaster grime.

There was a little cabal gathered round to see the pictur M4 Rapist, Mrs Furious and the man who'd worked closel with the police on several occasions. Graham was groomin Tony, picking bits of something out of his hair. Nehru colla was drawing nooses. Patrick made a face at Elsa.

She went straight into the toilet and waited for him to follov

'So what's the verdict?' he said, and she shrugged. Sh fingered the little pebble soaps.

'Not guilty.'

'Yeah?'

'Yeah. Well, kind of not guilty. More or less. After a fashior You know. He's not guilty enough.' It was actually hurtin her to speak, her jaw had stiffened up from all the clamping

'You're quite sure?'

'Yeah. Oh yeah. He didn't do it. He couldn't have done i Really.'

'You look terrible.'

'Yeah, well I was up late.'

'Did you have fun?'

She gave him a sly smile. 'Yes, Patrick. I did actually.'

'More fun than, say, a six-day bike race?'

'Pack it in.'

'So you had fun, and now Bryn Sweetman is not guilty. N guilty enough anyway.'

'Yes.'

'Only the last time we spoke, if I recall correctly, you wei of the opposite opinion . . .'

'Yeah ... '

'But one night with the defendant and – '

'Oh, what do you care? I mean, who are any of these people to you anyway, yes? Look. It's not guilty. OK? I know.'

'Because he told you.'

'Yes. He proved it to me.'

'And the possibility that he might be lying like a rug never crossed your – '

'Patrick. I'm in no mood for argument. Just take my word on this please. There's doubt, there's enough doubt. If there's enough doubt for me then there is for you too.'

He folded his arms and rocked back, squinting at her.

'Well, Elsa. You're not quite the same woman I recall from a few days ago. Now you're quite sure about this?'

'Yes.'

'OK.'

'Yes?'

'Not guilty it is. Now all we need is one more. One other juror.'

'How though?'

'One of the O.J. Simpson jurors said after the trial that she knew he was innocent all along because if he'd done it he would have told his mama. That's the level we need to be working on. We'll think of something.'

'Are you sure about the judge taking ten to two?'

'No, but I think it's likely. He'll probably give us a few hours to try to be unanimous, then he'll go for a majority. I think.'

'But wouldn't he take nine to three?'

'Nope. Nine to three is hung.'

'Well hung.'

'What?'

'Nothing. So we need someone else.'

They ran through the possibilities. Reached a short list of four. A short short list of two. And finally there was just one.

They went back out. The man in the decent dark suit was speaking.

' ... on occasion worked *extremely* closely with the police... '

223

Well, how close is it possible to get, Elsa wondered irritably. She imagined him in a tiny crowded room with policemen all round, elbows and knees everywhere and coffee spilling out of plastic cups as they jostled him.

He was foreman, of course, he had it all stitched up. He took an open vote: ten guilty, and two not guilty. Surprised muttering.

'Right. Well, it might perhaps be of value if the two not guiltys were to share their thoughts with us...'

Elsa just shrugged.

'Not guilty. That's it.'

'But you can't say why?'

'No.' She couldn't be bothered arguing. The pill had used up about two weeks' worth of good humour last night, she had none left now. Anyway, what could she say?

Patrick made a little speech about presuming innocence and corroboration and margins of doubt, a very good speech but of absolutely no use to anyone.

Graham or Tony piped up.

'Well, I just think, at the end of the day' – he was making short firm chopping motions as he spoke – 'you've just got to take the evidence as a whole and come down on one side or the other, and that's it.' M4 Rapist sighed softly. Elsa sat back. She was so tired.

'Shall we review the evidence?'

10.45. Dear God.

'Not guilty.'

'I mean, no one's trying to put you on the spot but...'

'Not guilty. That's it.'

'Because...'

'Because.'

She didn't care what anyone thought any more. She caught M4 Rapist and Mrs Furious whispering and glancing at her. They were all silent for a few moments.

'Well. We appear to be stuck, don't we? Shall we talk about it some more?'

'We could have another vote.'

224

'All right. Let's make it secret this time.'

11.15. Ten guilty and two not guilty.

'I know,' Patrick said. 'Why don't some of you guiltys try to persuade us not guiltys. Give us your reasoning. Fill us in on your thinking.' The foreman glared at him and Patrick looked sweetly back. 'I mean, I'm open to persuasion. We're not in any hurry, are we?'

11.50. Elsa was miles away, she was back in the room with Bryn, lying on his thighs as her vision sparkled, breathing on his Harley-Davidson...A strange little memory capsule. Was that really me?

'Well. We've made no real progress now for...' The foreman looked at his fancy watch. 'Almost two hours. Perhaps we should inform the judge? Shall I press the buzzer?' No one seemed to care much. 'Yes?'

Nehru collar grunted an affirmative and the buzzer was pressed and a note passed to the usher. They sat on. It was getting hotter. Muttered comments were made. Elsa looked out at the big tree.

'Ladies and gentlemen, would your foreman please stand? Now, I understand that you have not yet managed to reach a unanimous verdict and can see no real prospect of doing so. Is that correct? Just say yes or no please.'

'Yes.'

Djabo looked up, surprised, astonished even, and scanned their faces for clues. Bryn sat in the dock, stroking his head. Parrot turned and muttered to his solicitor.

The judge swivelled and smiled. Beamed at all of them, as if they were his favourite relatives, and he their favourite indulgent uncle.

'I am minded to suggest that you return to your room and continue to deliberate. You will in any case be taking your lunch in a few minutes. Things might take on a different complexion after lunch. It's always possible.'

*

The usher took their orders for sandwiches and Diet Coke. Dragons book requested a banana and an unsweetened organic yoghurt and everyone looked at him. There was a list of what everyone had ordered and how much money they'd given, but it looked rather chaotic and Mrs Furious, who'd handed over a twenty-pound note, was clearly anxious about getting her change.

12.30. The table was covered with wrappers and cans and napkins. M4 Rapist was busy taking requests for tea and coffee, and Nehru collar was helping.

'Maybe we should have the seance now,' Patrick said, but no one was laughing.

Elsa was watching, waiting. The plan was to wait until their chosen candidate went into the toilet, then she and Patrick would go in as well and arm twisting would commence. She didn't know how much longer the judge was likely to give them. She gnawed her nails. Patrick was flicking a pen up and down.

Then their target moved.

'No, listen,' Patrick was whispering urgently, as Elsa blocked the door from the inside. 'The law says we have to presume him innocent. You do understand, don't you?'

'Yeah.'

'So therefore we must *find* him innocent.'

'What about the evidence and that?'

'Doesn't make any difference. At all. We have to presume him innocent, which means we have to presume that all the evidence against him is false. That's what presuming innocence *means*.'

'Be'ave ... You're having a laugh, aren't you?'

'It's perfectly true,' Elsa said and smiled. 'That's the law.'

'Go 'way ... I mean, what would be the point of it all? The trial and that?'

'Well, that's not for us to say, is it, we must just obey the law. You heard the judge.' Patrick was trying to be very serious but he wasn't really quite managing. Their victim wa perfectly affable but he wasn't having it.

'And like what about everyone else? How come they don't think the same?'

'That's between them and their consciences,' Patrick said gravely. 'And God,' he added, just for good measure.

'Nah...'

No go. Patrick glanced over to Elsa: any ideas?

'Wasn't it a shame,' she began tentatively, 'about poor Princess Diana?

'Oh, yeah,' the candidate said. 'I just couldn't believe it when they said. I was...'

'Yes. And she was always, you know, I mean she always took the side of the underdog, didn't she?'

'Oh, yeah.' He was shaking his head sadly. Elsa even thought she saw his eyes misting over.

'Poor poor Diana,' Elsa went on, feeling her way. 'She was so pretty, wasn't she? And she really understood about life, didn't she?' She paused and looked thoughtful, then said in a low, reverential voice, 'You know, I wonder what she'd have done if she'd been on this jury?'

Patrick gave her a secret finger-and-thumb-circle sign. This was better. Elsa went on.

'I think she would have wanted us to just forgive, you know, give him a second chance, she wouldn't want him to go to some awful, awful jail...'

'Well, she believed in what was right,' their candidate said dreamily. 'Yeah. She'd never do nothing she didn't think was right.'

'Well...' Elsa said, 'well, I think she might...' but she'd lost it now, she could tell.

'So if she thought he was guilty, she'd say guilty, 'cos that would be the right thing.'

Elsa sighed and looked at Patrick. Blew it. Over to you.

'All right,' he said, and leaned in closer, aggressively close. Nice cop, nasty cop. 'Look. Look. It's possible that he's not guilty. Yes?'

'Yeah, well, anything's possible, innit?'

'But that's my point. If it's possible then it's not impossible.

Yes? And if it's not impossible then there's a doubt. So yo[u]
can't be sure. And the judge said, he said several times, yo[u]
must be sure. But you're not sure, are you? Because there's
possibility...'

'Yeah, not much of a possibility...'

'Ah, but how much do we need? How much possibility[?]
How much doubt?' He'd turned briefly into St Augustine, an[d]
Descartes and Kant could not be far behind, but their victi[m]
was smiling and shrugging and saying, nah...They ju[st]
weren't playing him, right. They weren't getting to that O.[J.]
Simpson juror level.

She glanced at Patrick. It wasn't working. The judge wa[s]
bound to call them in soon. Plus they couldn't stay holed u[p]
in this toilet for very much longer, it was getting ridiculou[s.]
She heard the words 'work surfaces' from outside. Bryn wa[s]
going to jail. Any minute now.

And then she saw the way...

'Wait a minute,' she said. 'Wait just a minute now. You se[e]
I think you've got it all mixed up. I think you're mi[s]
interpreting the significance of the defence's redirect on th[e]
plaintiff...' Patrick stared at her in astonishment. What wa[s]
she talking about? She pulled a piece of paper from her pock[et]
and pretended to study it. She put on her most judicial ton[e.]
'Now. The plaintiff, when asked by defence counsel...' an[d]
their poor victim looked at her with gently perplexed bro[w]
and said, 'Oh yeah, sorry, now, which one was he again?'

They emerged four minutes later, four long minutes of swift[ly]
improvised but ruthlessly complete misinformation abo[ut]
the white one, the black one, the defence, the prosecutio[n,]
the near to us and the far from us, until poor Thick kid wa[s]
so uncertain he would have indicted the stenographer. The[y]
all emerged, Thick kid looking sheepish and thorough[ly]
confused, scratching his head. He smiled apologetically rour[d]
at the ring of expectant faces.

'Changed me vote,' he said. 'I had it all the wrong wa[y]
round, didn't I? *Not* guilty, innit. That's what I meant.'

The foreman glared evil death first at Elsa and then [a]

Patrick, who gave him the most innocent of all possible smiles back.

'Perhaps you might like to press your little buzzer again...'

HORNY

Elsa and Patrick lingered in the sunshine outside the courthouse for a few minutes, both reluctant to just say, well, see you then. She had his phone number and he had hers, but would either phone ever ring? They watched Dragons book shuffling away, calling goodbye over his shoulder, and a few moments later Parrot emerged, squinting in the sudden light, and loped off, head down, surprisingly bald without the wig.

'Well,' Patrick said.

'You know what you were saing,' Elsa said. 'About CVs?'

'Umm...'

'Well. I was wondering. About CVs, I mean.'

'Ah.'

She was silent again. She played with a cigarette end with the toe of one of the cream courts.

'Wondering...?' He looked at her, she shrugged. Looked away over his shoulder. Wouldn't say what was on her mind

'Tell you what I think,' he said. 'CVs are just part of the package. I think we need to think about totally rebranding you. Reniching. Relaunching.'

'Which would involve...'

'Well, I hate to have to say it straight out like this, but you know those little tops?'

'You mean...' She indicated the mushroom silk at her breast.

He nodded. 'I'm afraid they may have to go. I just don't think they're saying anything useful about you. You know. Who is Elsa Frith? What does she *mean*? What is her unique selling point? I mean, OK, there's the joke name and everything, but what else?'

'Look, Patrick, I just want help with my CV, I don't need any fashion advice, thank you...'

'It's all the same package. And then, of course, there's the vexed issue of the crap boyfriend.'

'I've got eight of these tops.'

'Then let there be a great conflagration. The smoke will rise to heaven. Then we'll think about the CV.'

'OK, look.' She snapped to attention, looked at him, looked away. 'Just have to go and make a phone call first.'

'Anyone in particular?'

'No, no.' She fidgeted, wouldn't meet his eye. 'Just someone.'

'Ah. I see.'

'Yeah. Yeah, got to tell him something.'

'Anything in particular?'

'Just something.'

'I see. So if I've got this straight, Elsa, you've got to ring someone, just anyone really, and say something to him. That about right?'

'Yeah. That's about the size of it.'

'Right. Right.'

'Then we could maybe go and think about, you know, CVs.'

'I know just the place.'

'OK. Wait here a minute.'

'Er...'

Patrick tapped her on the shoulder and she looked: Bryn and Mark Hegler deep in disputation as they came through the doors and down the steps, Bryn gesturing violently with one hand while the other was moving inside his trouser pocket. His jacket flew back in the wind. Hegler was shaking his head, and then turned briefly to the left and spat, brilliantly, virtuosically.

Elsa ducked away and tried to shrink down behind a concrete tub full of ugly, spiky shrubbery. But Bryn had spotted her and when she looked back he was leering and winking as he passed, free of it all again, for the time being at least, lewd and cocky and irresistible and horny as fuck as he cupped a big handful of himself and squeezed, ooooooh yeeeeeah; and Patrick raised his eyebrows as Elsa turned back to him, flushed, and wondered if she was finally in touch with her own power enough to ring Liam and tell him to just bugger *off*.